THE DEVIL AND HER SON

THE DEVIL AND HER SON

MARGERY ALLINGHAM
writing as
MAXWELL MARCH

OPEN ROAD
INTEGRATED MEDIA
NEW YORK

ISBN: 978-1-5040-9233-3

This edition published in 2024 by Open Road Integrated Media, Inc.
180 Maiden Lane
New York, NY 10038
www.openroadmedia.com

THE DEVIL AND HER SON

1

THE LONG SHADOW

I t began with the girl.

As she sat looking down at the white breakfast table in that cold boardinghouse dining room, the gloom only broken by the warmth of her hair and the deep cream of her skin, she did not know that the hour was approaching when the thing that was to happen would swoop down upon her and those others, to envelop and crush her beneath its heavy shadow.

She did not know then, even, of the three impressions which were to remain vivid and terrifying in her memory until the day she died: the sight of the clean line of a man's throat and jaw, brown against white linen; the feel of an old-fashioned ring, paralyzingly tight, on the third finger of her left hand; and, curiously, the smell of wet leaves rotting cleanly in the long grass.

At the moment she was thinking rather shyly of a little love affair, so frail and tender a plant that she did not dream of the long tenuous roots it was to put out, which were to creep out blindly to bind her still more helplessly beneath the shadow.

Nor did she dream then of that other love which was to come.

"You're early, Miss Coleridge."

3

There was a hint of reproof rather than reproach in Miss Campbell-Smith's voice as she paused for a moment before the small table in the darkest corner of the oppressive room to look down at the girl who sat waiting for her breakfast.

"I'm surprised. You were out rather late last night, weren't you?"

Miss Campbell-Smith had not kept a good middle-class boardinghouse for twenty-three years without learning the gentle art of criticism by inference, and now her little round red face, which should have been so kindly and was nothing of the sort, was like a spiteful pink parrot's, the beak opened to bite.

Mary Coleridge stirred and looked down her small delicately modelled nose with that peculiar mixture of embarrassment and disapproval which secretly infuriated the boardinghouse keeper, making her feel somehow a little vulgar in her own house.

"I don't think I was very late. I went to the Marble Arch Pavilion to see a film."

"With Mr Muir?" Miss Campbell-Smith's tone was insinuating.

Mary raised her round grey eyes with the perfect brows, which no plucking had made smooth and narrow.

"Certainly with Mr Muir."

Miss Campbell-Smith choked down her exasperation, bit off the sentence which was on the tip of her tongue, and, turning her back upon the girl, strode off down the gloomy room amid the cheerless little tables. Her woollen cardigan poked at the back, and her flat heels and stout black stockings made her into a figure which would have been negligible or pathetic had it not been for a certain dominance in her movement and the magnificent stiffness of her carriage.

In the doorway to the kitchen she paused and beckoned the untidy, weary individual who combined the duties of waiter, hall porter and boots to the select boarding establishment of Merton House.

"Stephen," said Miss Campbell-Smith loudly, "Miss Coleridge is evidently hungry, since she is down before the first bell. You may serve her."

Mary Coleridge did not hear the thrust. She was lost in her own thoughts, her eyes fixed upon the scene which she could just glimpse through the window on the opposite side of the room. It was an autumn picture. The leaves on the few trees in the Crescent were yellow, and every now and again a great flock of them swirled high into the air as the wind caught them, to flutter down to the grey pavements, moist in the mild damp morning.

Mary was a pretty girl. Even old Stephen observed it with a flicker of satisfaction defeated even before it was born, as he floundered towards her, slopping milk and coffee over the enamelled tray in his unsteady hands. She was tall and slender, with the limberness of youth. Her skin was fine and cream coloured, and her face oval and calmly beautiful under hair as warm and bright as the autumn leaves in the Crescent.

Although scarcely more than twenty-two, she possessed already that indefinable poise and grace of manner which is so impressive if it is natural and so impossible if it is not, and which can best be described as an innocent dignity. It was this quality in Mary which Miss Campbell-Smith never forgave.

Yet old Stephen did not find her stand-offish. In his opinion Miss Coleridge was a lady and a nice young lady too. She smiled when he apologized for the horrible mess of milk and coffee upon the tray, and he brightened considerably.

"See a good picture last night, miss?" he ventured.

"Oh, lovely, Stephen," she said. "Absolutely lovely."

She spoke so vehemently that she surprised herself, and the colour came into her face. The old man smiled.

"It makes a difference 'oo you're with, don't it?" he said so naïvely that the words carried no offence.

Mary Coleridge hesitated, and her round eyes were young and very bright.

"I—perhaps it does," she admitted, and looked down at her plate so hurriedly that Stephen had no need to glance towards the door.

"Mornin', Mr Muir," he said over his shoulder as he pulled out the chair opposite to the girl. "Nice to see you down early. I'll bring your breakfast along in a jiffy."

He shuffled off, and Peter Muir sat down. He was a squarely built, sturdy young man with yellow hair and bright-blue eyes. Older than the girl in front of him by six or seven years, he yet possessed an incorrigible boyishness, ingenuous and attractive. Most of the ladies at Merton House had looked upon him with interest during the seven months of his stay, but, although always irreproachably polite, he had shown no inclination to become better acquainted with any of them save Mary, and when she had shyly assented to a request that he might share her table he had seemed pleased and slightly relieved.

They were both lonely young people, and Mary had looked forward to her mealtime conversations. She talked about herself and thought little of it that Peter Muir, so entertaining upon general subjects, never referred to his private affairs.

It was understood at Merton House that he worked very hard in the City all day and spent the evenings studying in his room. Certainly he hardly ever went out, but much headway in friendship may be made across a white tablecloth, and Mary had come to regard Peter as her one human companion in the long dreary business of making a living in a London which had not been introduced.

The evening before he had asked her to come and see a film with him, and she had been surprised to find how excited she was about the little adventure. They had come home together in

6

a taxi, and in the darkened hall, while old Stephen found their keys from his cubbyhole office, he had held her hand for a moment and whispered something. It had all been very innocent and childish and quite absurdly delightful.

At the moment they were alone in the dismal dining room. None of the other boarders was down, and Stephen was in the kitchen. The girl glanced shyly across the table and stiffened. Peter Muir was looking at her steadily. There was no smile upon his lips. His face was pale and his eyes troubled. He seemed uncharacteristically ill at ease. She smiled at him.

"Did you dream about the French Revolution?" she said lightly, referring to the film they had seen. "I did."

"No," he said so quietly that she looked away from him, her heart contracting. It was coming, then.

He leant across the table, and instinctively she prepared herself to listen to that most exhilarating experience of all, the first proposal.

"Do you remember in the hall last night I told you I had something to tell you?" he began abruptly.

She nodded, her cheeks burning.

"Well, here it is." He spoke with unconscious brutality because of his unhappiness. "I'm leaving here today."

She stared at him, waiting for laughter to come into his eyes as he reassured her, but they remained grave and somehow pained.

"Leaving?" she echoed, fighting against the chill which crept over her, making her breathless. "For good?"

Stephen arrived with Peter's breakfast, and the young man sat looking at her while the waiter set his food before him and lumbered off again.

"I don't know," he said at last. "I shall be gone for three months anyway. It's—it's my holiday."

"Three months' holiday?" said Mary, her surprise momentarily chasing all other considerations out of her mind.

Peter Muir did not meet her eyes.

"Yes. I take three months holiday every year," he said gravely.

Mary was struggling with herself. To her horror she found she was panic-stricken and perilously near tears. She had been so sure that he was in love with her and had been so very near love herself, and now this idiotically dramatic farewell completely demoralized her, and she felt her composure slipping away. The man began to talk hurriedly, his voice unusually husky.

"I meant our jaunt last night to be a sort of farewell party, but when the time came to tell you I couldn't bring myself to spoil it all."

Mary clutched at the shreds of her pride.

"Why should you think I should be so upset?" she said stiffly.

He looked at her, and his mouth twisted helplessly, while his eyes, eloquent and piteous, met her own.

"I'm leaving right away," he said. "I don't suppose I shall come back ... here. I just wanted to thank you tremendously. You've made this life bearable for me, you see, and I can't possibly explain to you how very grateful I am. Good-bye."

A strong brown hand was suddenly thrust out across the table to seize her own. For a moment she felt its pressure, fierce, urgent and despairing, and then without a word he got up and went out of the room, leaving his breakfast cold and untasted.

Mary sat very still for a moment. She felt numb and unsteady. There was a great weight in her chest, and a chill crept up and down her spine.

Outside the window the autumn leaves whirled like a flock of sparrows in the wind, but their warm colour seemed to have deteriorated, and the room within felt damp and musty.

Mary could not taste her coffee, and she swallowed it with difficulty. She was not in love with Peter, not disappointed and heartbroken because he was running away, she explained to herself reasonably, but she was frightened because she was alone. The dreadful vista of a lifetime of silent, lonely meals spread out in front of her like the pathway to eternity, and she felt her eyes filling with helpless tears.

Across the room Miss Campbell-Smith caught sight of her and came edging forward, her bright eyes fixed upon Peter's empty chair and untasted breakfast. Mary gulped. She felt she could not stand barbed insinuations at the moment, and, rising to her feet, she threaded her way quickly among the tables towards the hall doorway.

But Miss Campbell-Smith was not to be cheated. She reached the girl's side just as they came to the foot of the stairs.

"Mr Muir hasn't eaten his breakfast," she began in her soft voice with the little croak in it. "Is the poor boy ill, Miss Coleridge?"

Mary glanced about her wildly for deliverance, and it came in unexpected form. At the top of the stairs a most unlikely apparition had appeared, and now it came slowly down towards them, completely and complacently conscious of the sensation it was creating.

Mary saw a big, red-faced sandy-haired girl wrapped in a black lace negligee which would have been considered a little overexotic in a Hollywood boudoir. It was obviously outrageously expensive and was predestined to look out of place almost anywhere, let alone the slightly dingy front hall of Merton House.

Miss Campbell-Smith gasped audibly, and the newcomer smiled, revealing unexpected good humour.

"Good morning," she said. "Where's the breakfast room?"

She had a deep, pleasant voice and a broad Australian accent.

"Miss Mason—" Miss Campbell-Smith's tone was tinged with hysteria— "you can't breakfast like that—here!"

"Oh? Who says not?"

The stranger's broad cream forehead, on which golden freckles were scattered like stardust, ruckled into angry folds, and Mary became aware of a personality both forceful and forthright and beside which Miss Campbell-Smith's spiteful little temperament took on a mosquitolike quality.

"I paid good money for this, and I'll say it suits me."

The stranger turned round on the stairs, mannequin fashion. The negligee was even more sensational at the back, and Miss Campbell-Smith twittered helplessly.

Mary looked at the splendid barbaric figure, so distressingly vulgarized by the sophisticated insinuations of the creation, and took a step forward.

"It does," she said impulsively. "You look magnificent. But you'll feel awfully uncomfortable if you go in to breakfast like that. You see, this isn't the right sort of place. It—It'll be like going into a railway station."

The other girl seemed to notice her for the first time, and she peered through the gloom of the hallway at her face. Finally she laughed.

"I get you," she said. "I've come to the wrong party. All right, kid. What you say goes. Send my food up to my room, will you, Granny?"

Miss Campbell-Smith started back at the appellation as though stung, and an even deeper crimson stained her cheeks. The vision in the lace negligee was retreating slowly up the stairs, however, and she thought it prudent not to remonstrate, at least at the moment. Still bristling, she strode back to the dining room while Mary followed Miss Mason upstairs.

On the grey landing the other girl paused and looked back.

"What a dump!" she said expressively. "You certainly said it, kid. A railway station just about hits it off—the sort of station where the trains don't go any place. I thought there was something queer about it when I booked in last night, but I was too darned tired to be particular. Well well, I'll be seeing you."

She turned into her room with a little friendly wave of the

hand, and Mary caught a last glimpse of the disturbing negligee as its black lace folds floated out behind her.

Mary went to her own room and put on her hat. As she turned to go out again she saw herself in the mirror and was startled by the pathetic little figure with the pale face and burnt-out eyes who confronted her.

She looked at herself for a long time, and gradually the conclusion which was to poison her faith in herself took shape in her mind. She saw the truth, she told herself bitterly, and might as well face up to it. Peter had been amusing himself with her and had suddenly suspected that she was growing fond of him. In his alarm he had taken the rather drastic step of running away.

She reproached herself for being so frank with him. Most men were conceited, but he might have seen that she only needed a friend, someone to talk to sometimes. Her eyes began to smart ominously, and she rubbed them angrily as she hurried down the stairs.

She was not late for her work, but she walked quickly because she did not want to think, and arrived at the green door in the wall of Mrs Leonard Armstrength's Improved Kindergarten at twenty minutes to nine.

She had passed through the bright new garden schoolroom, which always smelt of paint and wet sand, and was in the little cloakroom hanging up her hat when Jenny, the Armstrengths' parlourmaid, came to tell her that "the master" would like to see her in his study "up at the house."

As Mary walked down the narrow stone path through the garden to the back of the old-fashioned Hampstead house she was mildly curious. Leonard Armstrength, whose books on his advanced theory of child welfare were largely responsible for the success of his wife's school, did not often condescend to speak to the three ladylike but underpaid girls who were supposed to put his somewhat impractical notions into effect, and she knew him only as a thin, arty looking person with thick eyebrows and a grey, stringy neck and chin who walked about among the mothers at the termly displays, talking of reflexes in a fluty voice.

She was astonished, therefore, to find him seated at his desk, his grey face suffused with dull crimson and his long fingers twitching with suppressed fury.

"Miss Coleridge," he began before she was well into the room, "Miss Coleridge, will you kindly explain to me why you intend to ruin my wife's entire life work? Have you no control at all?"

He was so angry that his entire body vibrated and his voice was cracked and uncontrolled.

Mary stared at him.

"I don't understand," she said. "What have I done?"

Leonard Armstrength fought with himself to find speech, and the girl, with the odd irrelevance which comes to one in time of stress, found herself wondering if the single lock of white hair in the front of his coarse black curls could conceivably be artificially bleached.

The man swallowed.

"Mrs Peeler visited me last night," he said, "Mrs Stukely Peeler, the mother of little Rodney. Standing in this very room she told me that yesterday afternoon you actually struck the boy."

"I slapped him, yes," said Mary briefly. "In the circumstances it seemed the only thing to do. That child will be murdered when he goes to a preparatory school unless he is taught now that he can't do exactly as he likes."

"My good girl—" Leonard Armstrength rose to his feet— "had I known when Mrs Briden recommended you for the responsible office which you have held here that you were an uncontrolled type of pronounced sadistic tendencies I would rather have cut off my right hand than have put you in charge of lit-tle cheeldren."

Mary's face flushed. The mention of Mrs Briden always moved her to anger. She was the squire's wife in that far-off village in Sussex who had so condescendingly obtained a post for the nineteen-year-old daughter of the widowed doctor, who had worked himself to death without being able to save a penny towards the future support of his orphaned girl.

"That's nonsense, Mr Armstrength," she said. "Rodney Peeler is nine years old. He is thoroughly spoilt, overfed and precocious. Yesterday afternoon he called me by a name I can only hope he learned in the street and not at home. When I told him it was wrong he laughed at me and repeated it. So I slapped his arm and sent him out in the garden to cool his heels. He was not hurt. There was not even a red mark on his arm."

"A red mark on his arm?" screamed Mr Armstrength. "Good heavens, girl, do you realize that Mrs Peeler has had a nerve specialist at her house half the night? What about the poor little fellow's repressions? An incident like this may cause a fixation which will throw his whole subconscious out of gear."

"The sooner he has a fixation that it's wrong to swear the better," said Mary before she could stop herself.

Leonard Armstrength took a deep breath.

"A manic type," he said. "That I should have had you in the school ... I can never forgive myself. You will leave this place at once of course. Never expect to get any sort of reference or recommendation from me. Indeed, I shall feel it my duty to see that you are never again employed to take care of innocent children, and I flatter myself that my name carries some weight in scholastic circles. You may go."

Mary turned on her heel. The injustice of his accusation was so great that it left her speechless. In those few minutes she had seen the man as he really was, a crank with a great sense of his own importance and a streak of meanness which would lead him to hound her from post to post if she attempted to enter his world again. She knew without making a fight for it that her career as a schoolmistress was ended.

She had reached the doorway when he called her back.

"Miss Coleridge."

"Yes?" She swung round to see his thin lips parted and his small eyes dark and narrow.

"I shall find it my duty to write to Mrs Briden and report to her the way in which you have repaid her kindness."

Mary looked at him steadily. He was enjoying himself, she noticed, and the sight of his secret pleasure brought home the helplessness of her position more strongly than anything else could have done. He laughed at her expression.

"You're beginning to think now, are you?" he said. "You should have done that before you gave way to your terrible impulse to torture a child. Look for work but don't expect me to help you. I'm afraid you may have some difficulty: jobs are not easy to find."

Mary fled. In the hall Jenny was waiting with her hat and gloves.

"The mistress told me to give these to you here, miss," she said, "and to tell you that you wasn't to go down to the school-room among the children. Oh, miss, is there anything wrong?"

Mary took the hat and fixed it on her curls with shaking fingers.

"Everything, Jenny," she said in a voice which made the little girl stare at her. "Everything in the world."

2

NOTHING TO LOSE

I t was late afternoon when Mary came slowly up the stairs at Merton House. Her visits to a dozen employment agencies had not been very encouraging. She could neither type nor write shorthand, her knowledge of dressmaking was elementary, and her complete lack of references made the astute women behind the big desks raise their eyebrows dubiously.

She was frightened. Long afterwards, when she looked back upon it, it seemed to her that it was then that the first manifestation of the terror that was to come appeared to her. At the time she thought it was the helplessness of her position which gave her that odd apprehension of horror to come. She was alone, terribly alone. The loss of her job meant more to her than mere temporary loss of employment. Mrs Briden was a powerful person in her own small way, and Mrs Briden was going to be very angry with her. A small village may often be entirely ruled by its squiress, and, searching round in her mind for someone to whom she could turn for recommendation or advice, the girl realized with a sudden thrill that there was no one, no one at all, no one in the world. She longed helplessly for

Peter; not the Peter of this morning, embarrassed, frightened of her, but the Peter of last week who had been a friend.

He had gone already. Old Stephen had told her the news with ghoulish relish the moment she entered the door, and Mary had fled on up the stairs, unable to face the old man's inquisitive glance.

There are moments in everyone's life when the ordinary misfortunes and antagonisms which are part of the business of living total up or, crowding too quickly upon one another, produce a formidable array before which the mind panics, but fortunately it is not everyone who at such a moment is confronted by an opportunity to take a great risk.

It was at the moment when Mary, frightened, helpless and temporarily demoralized, paused outside her own door that the shadow's wing passed over her and she stepped into a darkness from which there might never have been any escape.

Someone was in the room, someone who sang softly to herself in a deep throaty contralto. Considerably astonished, she opened the door, which was unlocked, and went in.

Miss Mason, clad in a golden evening gown, was parading in front of the mirror, while at her feet, over the bed and on every chair was strewn a profusion of dresses and underclothes.

She looked up as Mary entered and raised a strong brown arm in mock salute.

"Hello, Lovely," she said. "Look at me."

"It's beautiful." Mary was too surprised to make any other comment.

"You're telling me," said Miss Mason complacently as she twisted round to see her bare shoulder blades framed in the metallic folds of the gown. "I hope you don't mind me coming in here. I didn't know it was your room. The mirror in my cabin has got chicken pox under the glass, and this is the only decent one on the floor. I tried 'em all."

"But how did you get in?"

The spectacle of any of the other boarders on the floor, the nervous Mr Clark, the prim Mrs Fisher or the irascible Major Breen discovering such an apparition in their bedrooms temporarily took Mary's breath away.

"Oh, all the locks are the same. My key fitted them all," Miss Mason explained airily. "I bet you've lived in this dump for years without finding that out. That's what comes of having a trusting disposition. Now you won't feel nearly so safe tucked up under Granny's little old skin rug, will you? Still, we needn't tell the boy friends. Sit on the bed, Pretty. Heave that junk onto the floor. I will say it for Granny, she keeps this old morgue of hers plenty clean."

Mary sat down on the edge of her own bed, and Miss Mason took off the gold dress and scrambled into another.

"I'm going to light out of here tomorrow," she said, a frown appearing for an instant on her forehead. "Got to go and see my auntie and plod all over ploughed fields. Am I delighted! The thought of smelling wet earth after a sight of this little village just makes me sick."

Wet earth. Mary's mind jumped involuntarily to the wide fields and rain-soaked woods of a little Sussex village, so far away now that it might have been at the other end of the world, a village where the bonfires sent spirals of sweet acrid smoke floating up through the valley and where there was a shabby old house with paraffin lamps and red curtains and a tired country doctor coming home through the dusk to his tea. Her eyes filled with irrepressible tears, and she suddenly swung round and buried her face in the pillow.

"Holy Joe!" said Miss Mason, bundling a train of green satin under her arm and striding across the room towards her. "What's the matter, kid?"

Half an hour later Mary was bathing her eyes at the ancient washstand in the corner and Miss Mason was sitting upon the bed, her knees drawn up to her chin and her green satin train wrapped round her large, shapely feet.

"Tough," she was saying. "Plenty tough. No kin at all, you say? No friends, and now your job going back on you. Any boy friend anywhere?"

"N-no," said Mary. "Not—I mean, not now. He never was a boy friend, really—not what you mean, a sweetheart. Anyway, he's gone."

Miss Mason cocked an eye at her.

"Ever thought of the stage?"

Mary was astonished.

"The stage? Oh no, I wouldn't be any good on the stage. I'd never get on, for a start."

"I shall," said Miss Mason with conviction. "And when I get there I'm going to stick, believe me. The trouble is it's got to be done in a hurry. It's only this darned family trip that's holding me up. Unless—I say, I've got it!"

She got off the bed and went over to the other girl. She was excited, and her big hands gripped Mary's shoulders with unsuspected strength.

"How old are you, kid?" she demanded.

"Twenty-two last August."

Miss Mason considered.

"Ten months younger than me," she said. "Look here, Lovely, you listen to me."

She sat down on the bed again and began to talk.

"I'm Marie-Elizabeth Mason, and I was brought up in a little one-horse town called New Bolton in New South Wales. I was quartered with a family called Hendricks when I was a kid, and they looked after me. The only kin I have is an aunt and her husband over here in England, and I guess they're pretty wealthy. However, they're old and sort of quiet. Understand?"

Mary nodded. There was a forcefulness about Marie-Elizabeth Mason which could not be ignored.

"Well, this old aunt, Mrs de Liane—Aunt Eva, I call her—has been badgering me to come over and see her for two years now. Said she'd send the fare 'n' everything. But I wasn't so keen. You see, there was an actor back home who …" She paused and regarded Mary reflectively. "I guess I needn't go into that just now. Anyway, I didn't want to leave home just then for any visit. However, three months ago she wrote kind of urgent. She was getting old and wanted to see her first husband's sister's child before she died, and so on. And she sent the cash. It was a lot of money; return fare, first class, and a bit over. I got a grand idea. I came over steerage. I didn't buy my fare back, and I spent a lot of cash buying these clothes. I'm going to get on the stage over here in the short time I have before the money gives out. The only thing that's stopping me is this darned visit to the country. The old girl may expect me to stay with her the whole time while I ought to be getting busy. Now do you see where you come in?"

"No," said Mary violently.

"You're going on that visit instead of me," said Miss Mason in a tone of certainty. "We'll swop identities."

"No," said Mary again. "Don't be silly. You can't do things like that in England."

"Can't I?" said Marie-Elizabeth Mason, and laughed as she spoke. "You just watch me."

Mary looked at her and marvelled. There are people who are possessed of some indefinable power of personality which lifts them out of the common, and as the younger girl glanced at this tall red-headed young savage she knew of a certainty that here was the sort of person who might get away with anything.

"Look here, kid," said Marie-Elizabeth Mason persuasively, "there's an old woman living in the country with an older husband. She's sentimental and dull as ditch-water. She hasn't seen me since I was three months old. She doesn't know a thing about me because I hate writing letters. I sent her cables over this visit business. She hasn't seen a photograph because I've never sent one, and, above all, she wants to like me. She wants to find me a dear, sweet, innocent little girl who will feed the pigeons and take Rover for a walk and say howdy to the neighbours in a good little dress with a high neck. Why the heck shouldn't you go? You're what she wants!"

Mary hesitated. There was a forthrightness about Marie-Elizabeth which made her reasoning sound like common sense.

"If she was important I wouldn't suggest it," she went on, "but she's not. She's just a poor old woman who wants to see something young of her own family in the house for once, and may leave me two or three hundred quid in a year or two if she likes me. Now, look at me. ... She won't just not like me: she'll have forty fits. I can see that. But if she sees you she'll be as pleased as Punch and die happy. You'll be doing it for her sake, poor old girl. Here's the proposition. You're out of a job. You need a holiday and a spot of home life. You go down there for the month that I'm supposed to be in England, play the sweet little innocent you are and take whatever comes along. Don't do anything to queer my chances of a legacy, but you're welcome to any present or pickings you can get out of the business. I don't mean to put it as crudely as that, but you see what I mean. You please the old lady, and if she cares to give you a pair of diamond earrings that belonged to her great-grandmother you take 'em and hang onto 'em. Anyway, stay for a month, and that'll give me time to see how the land lies in the theatre world. If I strike lucky, as I shall, you'll have done me a great service. If I don't you needn't worry about me. I'll work my passage back as a stewardess. I'm that sort of person.

"Come on, kid, what have you got to lose?"

It was the final appeal which decided Mary. "What have you got to lose?" The question fitted in so well with her mood.

"Nothing," she said bitterly. "Still, It'll be rather awkward for both of us if I'm found out."

20

"There's nothing for anyone to find out," said Marie-Elizabeth. "Remember your name and don't talk too much about Australia, and you'll be okay. I'll give you all the facts you have to know. Come on, do it for Auntie. Think how she'll feel if I turn up in answer to her prayers. I'm not a riot in an advanced boardinghouse, so the Lord knows what effect I'd have in the unspoilt country. Besides, I like this town, and now I'm here I'm going to see it. If you won't go I'll wire her I'm not coming and risk losing a legacy and breaking the old dear's heart. I'd half made up my mind to do that this morning."

Mary looked up.

"Do you mean that?"

"I certainly do."

For some time Mary sat silent. A recklessness completely foreign to her nature was slowly creeping over her. She thought of the old woman in the country, anxious to mother someone so different from the vigorous, independent figure at her side, and she saw herself alone and unfriended and so very suitable for the role of homecomer.

Presently she stirred and uttered a decision which was to lead her into a labyrinth of sorrow and fierce joy undreamed of.

"I'll go," she said.

3
BARON'S TYE

T he mistress sends her apologies for not coming to meet you, miss, but the doctor doesn't advise her to drive in the damp."

A chauffeur in neat livery bent before the girl as he spoke and picked up her suitcase from the wet stones of the deserted little railway platform.

Mary nodded to him, smiling mechanically. She was speech-less, not with fear as she had anticipated, but with an indefin-able sense of homecoming which took her breath away. She had not realized before how different was the warm, dry air of the city from this soft elixir of country breath, sweet with the tang of wet ferns and oak leaves rotting cleanly in the grass. Here in this quiet wayside station Merton House, Leonard Armstrength and the magnificent Miss Mason seemed to be the dream and this familiar piece the reality.

In the back of a huge old-fashioned Daimler, whose age had added to rather than detracted from its dignity, she leant among the cushions and tried to prepare herself for an ordeal. But her mind refused to consider her project in any other light than a return to sanctuary.

It was a long, lonely drive through a maze of wet yellow and red leaves. Great oaks and elms hung over the path, and on either side of the road the deep chocolate of the newly turned earth spread out until it mingled with the misty distance.

Mary clutched her handbag, which contained her new identity, but her mind was not upon the story she was going to tell, nor did it rest upon the future at all. She was enthralled by the magic of the present.

"The mistress is looking forward to seeing you, miss." The chauffeur spoke over his shoulder. "It's lonely for her and the master down here, so far from everyone. There's the village. The house is just down here. Baron's Tye," he added, not without a certain pride, as he swung the car down a narrow gravel pathway between two immense cedars which made an archway over high wrought-iron gates.

Mary caught her first glimpse of the house through the trees, and her heart turned over. The long, low lines of Baron's Tye, lying gracefully in a nest of trees, were gracious and lovely. It was a house whose original builder had been inspired to create a home, and generations of successive owners had caught some of his passionate spirit, so that each alteration and addition had been made lovingly and with thought.

The great door stood wide above a long low paved terrace, and, as Mary stepped out of the car and moved timidly up the shallow steps, a silhouette appeared in the arched doorway, and a voice as gracious and as welcoming as the house itself cried impulsively:

"Mary, my dear!"

The girl found herself clasped gently by the shoulders, and a little old lady who appeared to be an incarnate bundle of real lace, black satin, gold chains and eau de cologne kissed her softly on the cheek

"Come in," she said. "Come in. Tea's ready. Dorothea, take

23

Miss Mason's bag up to the blue room. Well, my pet, let me take a look at you."

A long, low room with carved beams, a stone fireplace enclosing a log fire, soft hangings, prim, old-fashioned maids in starched lace caps who hovered and fussed, warmth and a smell of old wood, sweet, clean stone floors and dried flowers, these multiple impressions crowded on the girl and overwhelmed her. She looked round, shy and frightened, her eyes wide and the colour bright in her thin cheeks. Her hostess peered up at her, and Mary took a deep breath.

She saw a little old lady with bright, laughing blue eyes, soft grey curls and a placid face which told of great beauty long ago. She seemed quite overjoyed to see her visitor, and the girl's conscience pricked her unmercifully.

"Mary here at last!" said Mrs de Liane, linking her arm through her visitor's possessively. "You don't mind me calling you Mary, do you, dear? It's so much more English than Marie-Elizabeth. Besides, my own daughter—" She stopped abruptly and shook her head. "That's an old sorrow, my pet, an old sorrow."

She looked away, and the girl heard the ghost of a sigh at her elbow. Long afterwards she remembered that a slight emphasis on the word "old" and the sigh were the first indications she had that all was not well in the great house.

The next intimation followed almost immediately when a woman in a grey cotton dress and a white apron appeared for a moment at the top of the stairs. Old Mrs de Liane looked up at her anxiously, and she smiled back, pityingly, Mary thought, and entered one of the doors just visible over the carved balustrade.

Mrs de Liane opened her mouth as though to make a confidence, but thought better of it.

"Tea," she said decisively. "Tea next and see your room afterwards. I do so want to hear all about my little girl. You're like your mother, dear."

"Am I?" said Mary guiltily.

"Exactly. The same hair and so pretty, so very pretty. Any sweethearts yet?"

"No," said Mary, wondering what Miss Mason's reactions would have been to this pathetically eager welcome.

"None? Well, what are the young men thinking of? But I expect you're very choosy, is that it?"

In spite of the conventional words Mary had a distinct impression that the old lady was pleased. Her soft hands gripped her arm affectionately.

"Now come and see your uncle," she said, adding in a confidential whisper, "He's a little worried today, I'm afraid, poor darling. But don't mind. He's as glad to see you as I am."

She piloted the girl into a big candlelit drawing room where tea was set before the fire. Seated in the depths of a winged needlework chair Mary made out the figure of an old man. He was leaning back but not asleep, and there was something odd in his attitude when they entered—a tenseness, almost a listening pose. But he sat up and blinked at them as his wife brought the girl forward.

Mary saw a white, harassed face, pale hazel eyes and a petulant mouth. Then an unsteady hand was thrust into her own and a faraway voice, as nervy and indeterminate as its owner, muttered:

"Pleased to see you, my dear."

And Marie-Elizabeth's uncle Ted got up and walked out of the room.

Mrs de Liane's grip on the girl's arm tightened, her old mouth twisting as the candlelight fell on her face and her bright blue eyes filling with tears.

"He's worried, poor man," she said, "terribly worried. Never mind him, dear. Sit down to your tea. Do you know, I've been so anxious about you," she went on, settling down behind the teacups. "I thought living out in one of those—those primitive little towns you might have grown up coarse, self-willed and—well, difficult. I thought you might find it so dull and narrow down here, do you know."

She bent her bright eyes on the girl, and Mary spoke involuntarily out of the depths of her heart.

"I think it's like home," she said.

4

THE DREADFUL THING

At ten o'clock that evening Mary sat alone in the drawing room fighting with her conscience. Ever since she had come to Baron's Tye she had reproached herself. It did not seem right that she should be so happy. Aunt Eva was so kind, so pathetically eager to love her, and the whole atmosphere of the place was what she had longed for in her years of exile in the city.

The deception itself had been childishly easy. Uncle Ted had not reappeared, even for dinner, and certainly at her first meeting he had not seemed particularly inquisitive. As for Mrs de Liane, she was so pleased at finding her niece the sort of girl she liked it had clearly never entered her head to doubt her authenticity. Besides, it was evident that she had something else on her mind.

Dinner had been an elegant meal exquisitely served, and afterwards they had sat over coffee in the candlelit drawing room and listened to the wind in the trees and the peace of the quiet old house: not very exciting for anyone—deadly from Marie-Elizabeth Moon's point of view—but water in the desert to the little country girl who had been cooped up for two years in the urban discomfort of Merton House.

During the first part of the evening the impression that something was very wrong had not presented itself with any certainty to Mary's mind. A distraction in Mrs de Liane's manner, her whispered conversation with the grey-clad woman in the hall after dinner, and Uncle Ted's nonappearance had been the only real evidences of disturbance until half an hour ago, when a startled maid had entered to say that "Mrs Jane" would like to see Mrs de Liane for a moment, and then the old lady had sprung up with a muttered exclamation and had hurried out of the room.

Since then there had been a great deal of bustle to and fro. A car had driven up to the front door, and there had been urgent voices in the hall.

It was the first time Mary had been alone in Baron's Tye. Outside the wind roared in the trees, and through a narrow strip of open window the warm, moist air poured into the room, bearing the sweet smell of wet leaves. The girl took deep breaths of it greedily, never guessing how that haunting savour was to linger in her nostrils in the days to come.

Around and above her the quiet house crouched like some great sleeping animal, lovely in line and texture but in temperament utterly unknown.

Since the car had gone there had been other sounds, quick pattering footsteps over polished wood and the murmur of lowered voices. Idly she wondered how many servants there were, and the vague thought that there sounded to be a great many to look after one old lady and her husband passed through her mind.

But the peace and beauty of the room soothed her and drugged those inner senses which warn and prepare the mind for revelation.

Suddenly, however, her contentment was shattered as effectively as if the ground had opened at her feet. Whether it was the startled cry of a night bird in the trees or something even less tangible she never knew, but she found herself sitting up stiff and breathless, a cold fear utterly unlike anything she had ever known gripping at her heart.

Something was wrong.

She knew it with all the vividness of certainty. Something was wrong in this quiet, lovely house, something inexpressibly horrible, something cruel.

She sprang to her feet and stood taut and breathless on the white rug, her eyes trained upon the door. Even as she looked it opened quietly and the old lady came in.

Instantly Mary's own fears were forgotten. Her vision of the shadow, a glimpse which might even then have saved them all, had gone, and she was herself again, her round grey eyes alight with sympathy.

"Why, Mrs d—I mean Aunt Eva, what's the matter? My dear, don't upset yourself so terribly. Sit down."

She lowered the sobbing figure gently into a chair and stood before her helplessly until the old woman put out a trembling hand and drew the girl towards her. Her eyes were closed, and Mary was fascinated with pity at the sight of the round tears squeezing out between the closed lids and rolling down the finely wrinkled face.

"It's so terribly cruel. So young—so very young!"

The words broke from the old lips involuntarily.

Mary dropped on her knees beside the chair.

"Tell me," she said softly.

Mrs de Liane pulled herself together with an effort and wiped her eyes.

"I didn't want you to know, at once—your first evening. I thought I could be brave just for the first little while. Ted knew it was beyond him, poor man, but I tried so hard. Now the doctor's been and—and ..."

Her voice trailed away, and she pressed her little handkerchief into her eyes.

"Who is it?" Mary hardly recognized her own voice.

"Richard." The whispered name uttered so lovingly hardly reached the girl. "My dear dear boy. My Richard."

Mary was silent. Marie-Elizabeth had not mentioned a Richard, and she felt a sudden disgust at herself. Here was she, an impostor, intruding into a terrible grief.

She opened her mouth to speak, but the old lady's next words silenced her.

"Thank God you're here, my dear. Without you I should be alone. You haven't heard of Richard, have you? He's my son, my only boy. I didn't mention him in my letters because—because, oh, I had a foolish idea that you two dear children might fall in love and marry. He's only a cousin by marriage, you see, and I didn't mention him because you know how girls are. They like to find their man themselves. I thought if he came as a surprise to you you might—Oh, dear God, how foolish we are when we plan things!"

A fresh paroxysm of weeping shook her, and Mary laid her hand timidly on the tiny heaving shoulders.

"Is he very ill?" she murmured.

Mrs de Liane wiped her eyes and looked down at her wrinkled hands.

"Richard is going to die," she said softly. "Nothing in the world can save him. His spine is broken. Tomorrow, or it may be the day afterwards, he will be dead. That car which came to the door just now brought the last specialist we could call, the highest court of appeal. He says ... no—no hope."

Her voice trailed away, and there was complete silence in the big room, the old woman staring down at her clasped hands, the girl kneeling by her chair.

"Three days ago—" the old voice was scarcely above a whisper— "he went out very early in the morning, cubbing. He never reached the meet. They found him down in the valley, lying in the bracken, his poor horse standing over him.

"He was so young," she went on, her eyes resting on Mary's face. "So young and so full of life."

She rose unsteadily to her feet and for the first time since they had met looked searchingly at the girl.

"Mary, my dear," she said, "will you come and see him?"

"Why—why of course, Aunt Eva, if you want me to." The girl stammered over the words, and a faintly pained expression passed over the elder woman's face.

"He's not ... horrible," she said. "Come with me."

As Mary entered the brightly lit bedroom behind the old woman her heart was pounding unhappily. She knew now that come what might she could never look this tragic, lovable old lady in the eyes and confess that she had lied.

The woman in grey was sitting by the fireplace as they entered, but she rose at once and slipped out of the room, her white apron crackling as she moved.

Mary dragged her eyes fearfully towards the old-fashioned canopy bed which faced the two tall windows. Over Mrs de Liane's shoulder she caught a glimpse of a narrow mound in the white coverlet, lying pitifully stiff and still, and then an unexpected voice said softly:

"Hello, Angel."

"Richard, my dear boy." Mrs de Liane was holding herself in check with difficulty, for her voice quivered pathetically and she pulled the bed curtain on one side with a hand that trembled. "Here's Mary," she said.

The girl moved forward quietly and looked down into the bed. Lying very stiffly among the crisp white pillows was a man in his late twenties. She noticed his lean brown neck against the whiteness of the linen and the clean line of his jaw. He was smiling at her, and she was aware of a dark, vivid face with his mother's dancing blue eyes and crisp black curls shorn so tightly that his head seemed covered with karakul. A wave of dismay passed over her. This man was alive, so much more alive than millions of his fellows. It seemed a monstrous, unbearable thing that he should be going to die.

His smile broadened, and a shadow at the back of his dancing eyes alone betrayed his helplessness.

"How do you do, Mary," he said. "Sorry I can't get up."

The old lady turned away with a little inarticulate sound, and a frown passed over the brown face on the pillows.

"Sorry, Angel," he said unsteadily. "Look here, you go and warm your toes before your bedroom fire for half an hour and leave us. I want to talk to Mary."

"But Richard darling, you'll tire yourself." The old woman was all compassion.

"No I won't," he said, and added half under his breath, "Anyway, what does it matter? I'm going to have a long rest."

Mrs de Liane touched Mary's arm.

"Humour him," she whispered, and moved towards the door.

Mary caught a fleeting glimpse of her little figure, bowed with grief, as she vanished into the gloom of the hall.

"Sit down. I can't get you a chair, but you can perch on the end of the bed if you like. You can't hurt me. My poor old Red Jenny has done all the needful in that direction."

There was a laugh and underlying bitterness in the voice from the pillows, and Mary accepted the invitation simply, seating herself at the far end of the bed, where the light shone on her face.

"How's that?" she said.

"Fine." There was a tinge of admiration in his voice. "This is too bad, you know. Has Mother told you? I'm for it any time now. My legs have gone already, and my arms are pretty nearly paralyzed. Soon I'll get sleepy and then—"

"Don't," said Mary, "oh, don't!"

He blinked at her and smiled impishly.

"You can't be nearly as sorry for me as I am for myself, my dear," he said in a tone that was meant to be light and sounded inexpressibly weary. "Did you know Mother meant to marry us off? Rotten for the old dear, isn't it? Think you could have liked me if I—I hadn't died?"

The wistfulness in the terrible words was unbearable. Mary slipped off the bed and went up to him.

"Please don't," she said gently. "Please, please."

He smiled at her, and she noticed that his mouth turned down at the corners ridiculously to make little folds in his cheeks.

"Forgive me," he said. "I'm so utterly miserable, and there's so little time. There's something I've got to tell you at once, because no one else will, and I may not be able to if I leave it. My mother has plenty of money, but she doesn't own this house. She's lived here all her life, and she loves it more than anything else in the world except me. It belonged to her father, and he left it to me for my own and my wife's lifetime. When I die it goes to his stepson and his wife."

He paused, evidently weary, but his blue eyes rested searchingly on her face.

"I understand."

"I wish you did," he said bitterly. "But you'll have to take it from me that these people, Percy and Ethel Denver, are horrible. They're appallingly rich, and they're the sort of people who pull down and rebuild. They've had their eyes on this place ever since I can remember. I've turned down fantastic offers from them. And now they're going to get it and turn Mother out.

"Don't you see," he went on passionately; "as soon as I'm dead it goes to them, and Mother will have to leave her old home or stay in the village and see it mutilated. Help me, Mary. You're the only person I can ask because you're our family, if not our kin, and I can trust you to let her stay here always until she dies."

"What do you want me to do?"

The girl's voice was very quiet because she knew his answer, and it frightened her.

"Marry me. Marry me at once before I die. Then the house will be yours for your lifetime. You're young, you're strong, you're kind—you are kind, aren't you, Mary? Have pity on me. I can't do anything. I've got to die and know I can't save her home for her. Haven't you ever loved a house?"

"Yes." The passion in her voice silenced him for a minute. She was thinking, her thoughts chasing each other in nightmare ride.

He went on, his young voice pleading:

"You'll be a widow, but does that matter so much nowadays? That's all It'll cost you. You'll be young Mrs de Liane instead of Miss Mason. And when Mother dies you can sell the house, even to the Denvers if you like. I shan't know or care then. Will you? Will you, Mary? Time's so short."

The girl sat very still. She had no doubt of what Marie-Elizabeth would do in similar circumstances.

"We could trust you," the voice went on from the bed. "You wouldn't turn her out even if it meant refusing the finest offer in the world."

Mary started. It was true. Although he could not know it he could trust her implicitly, even more perhaps than the real Marie-Elizabeth, who might just possibly not understand the tentacles which an old house wraps round one's heart. There would be no difficulty about the name either. A marriage is one of the few contracts which hold good whatever pseudonym is used.

She looked at the man lying there, so young and so unutterably piteous.

"Could it be done—in time?"

"I think so. I've been talking to the doctor. There's a private chapel here, and it's only a question of getting me down there and paying the necessary fees for the special licence. Will you, Mary?"

His voice was growing fainter. He smiled at her wanly, and again she noticed with a curious tug at her heart the two little folds in his brown cheeks. His eyes danced.

"Oh Mary, be my widow," he whispered.

The girl's eyes suddenly filled with tears.

"Yes," she said resolutely. "I will."

Richard de Liane lay still and stared at her.

"You're sweet," he observed unexpectedly. "What a damned shame!"

"A shame?"

The man closed his eyes.

"A damned shame I'm going to die. Call Mother, will you? We must get this fixed up quickly."

Scalding tears on her cheeks and a sensation in her heart she never before had known, Mary crept silently from the room.

5

"... AND TO HOLD ..."

... "U ntil death you do part."

The young clergyman brought up from the village to perform the ceremony in the tiny sixteenth-century chapel at Baron's Tye faltered over the words. It was a heart-rending moment: the young man lying on the hospital stretcher, his face powdered to hide the greyness of his cheeks, and the girl beside him, pale and tremulous, fully conscious of the grim drama of the early morning scene.

Mrs de Liane knelt behind the couple, two of her maids and the woman in grey at her side. The only other witnesses were the tall man with the grave face, who Mary understood was the doctor, and the two sturdy farm workers who served as stretcher bearers. Uncle Ted had not appeared. Aunt Eva explained that he adored his son and the tragedy had broken him completely.

The tragic little ceremony was soon over. Mrs de Liane gave the parson a ring off her own finger, and he slipped it upon Mary's hand. The old-fashioned circlet of gold and small diamonds shone in the sunlight pouring through the chapel windows as the girl signed Marie-Elizabeth's name.

She stood back when the young priest approached the stretcher and watched while Richard's nerveless fingers were taught to hold the pen. She felt breathless but not afraid. In the face of this development her own deception seemed as nothing. Already she had made her plans.

As soon as what had to be had happened and the legal business came up she would sign away her interest in the house to Mrs de Liane and slip off back to London. Then there would be no need ever to explain, and when the truth had to come out at least the old lady would have no cause to remember her with anything but thankfulness.

Richard's voice recalled her to the nightmare present.

"Mary—where are you, Mary?"

She hurried to his side, frightened a little by the stab in her heart at the sound of her name on his lips. He lay smiling up at her.

"I want to kiss the bride."

She bent over him, her cheeks crimson and her eyes swimming, and kissed him gently on the lips. When she stood up again she caught a curious expression in his eyes. It was not exactly pity and not quite regret. She did not understand it until long afterwards.

"Angel," he said and closed his eyes.

On Mrs de Liane's advice Mary lay down in her room after the ceremony. Mrs Jane, the woman in the grey dress, and the doctor had been concerned in getting their patient up to his room again and were anxious not to have too many amateur assistants, who at such a time may so easily be a danger rather than a help.

Mary threw herself down on her big blue bed and tried to compose her thoughts. Emotions she had long thought dead in her had been aroused by the nearness of tragedy, and there was a pain in her throat much worse than tears.

Sunlight poured in through the window, and she rose from

the bed to stand for some moments looking out across the wooded parkland now stained red-gold with fallen leaves.

There was a river at the foot of the valley and great slopes of bracken beyond, all scintillating in the clear autumn air. It was beautiful, and she thought of the man on the stretcher, the man she had married and who was going to die. Richard loved this view. He rejoiced in the freedom of the fields, and his blood thrilled at the feel of the springy turf beneath his feet.

She put up her hands to blot out the scene and turned away, but she was back at the window in a moment, throwing its casements wide to let in the air. There was a small balcony outside running round the back of the house, and she stepped out upon it and walked along, her eyes upon the landscape. A voice arrested her.

It came out through the open window of a room a little farther along the balcony. She hardly recognized it as Mrs de Liane's at first, it was so brisk and coldly matter of fact.

"My dear Ted," it was saying firmly, "there's nothing to worry about at all. It's going splendidly. Richard can get well very slowly, and the girl will never question the genuineness of the whole story. She's a nice simple little thing, just the type to make the whole thing possible."

Mary stood quite still, her eyes blank with bewilderment. Just as she was convincing herself that the voice was part of an hallucination she heard Ted de Liane's querulous murmur in reply.

"You've done some wicked things in your time, Eva, but this business is too dangerous for me. This girl may not be the fool her mother was. When she finds she's been tricked into marriage with a cock-and-bull story of saving the house she's going to make trouble. As for Richard, she's probably guessed by this time that he's as fit as I am."

Mary gripped the balustrade for support.

"Richard played his part magnificently," said the voice of the strange new Eva de Liane. "And anyway, what can she do? She's here in a strange country with no friends and married. Richard can get well very slowly. You'll see, she'll be delighted."

"And her mother's fortune?" sneered the old man.

"Her mother's fortune," said Mrs de Liane with indescribable complacency, "will remain in the very good hands in which it has always been. We only just did it, though. She's twenty-three in two days' time."

Mary stood quite still.

It was one of those moments when the ordered procession of probable incidents which is life seem to take on an element of madness and go careering off into the absurd. It is at such moments that the mind trembles as strange and terrible doubts assail it.

As the girl clung to the rail of the balcony and stared out over the rolling country, which a few minutes before had seemed the most beautiful sight on earth, she felt the world of reality slipping beneath her feet.

It was not true. Her ears had lied to her. Old Mrs de Liane with her gentle voice and sweet placid expression, her tear-filled eyes and trembling hands, could not have spoken the words she had just overheard. It was not possible. All her experience of life, so pitifully inadequate had she only known it then, convinced her that there are some appearances which cannot lie, and she found herself remembering those round tears forcing themselves between the closed lids and rolling down the lined cheeks. If these had not been genuine where then was reality?

Shivering and suddenly weak, she crept back into her own room and sat down on the big blue bed. Through the open window the lingering scent of wet leaves followed her and was mingled for the first time with a sense of stark terror, with which it was ever afterwards to be associated in her mind.

If it were true...? She thought of her own position, of

Marie-Elizabeth's broadly smiling face, of her own deception and helplessness, and then, suddenly before her mind's eye, she saw a picture of the man on the stretcher, the clean line of the brown jaw and the laughing, dancing blue eyes.

She looked down at her hand. The narrow band of gold studded with small diamonds bit into her flesh. Impulsively she tried to draw it off, but only an agonizing pain rewarded the effort, and she sat staring at her hand, a thrill of superstitious terror stealing through her heart. The ring would not move.

As she sat looking at it a new and terrible supposition crept into her mind. If her senses were misleading her and her imagination were playing her tricks, what then?

A wave of alarm sweeping over her brought her back to the sober world of every day, and in consternation she remembered every detail of her own behaviour since that fateful morning when Peter had told her he was going away. She had consented to exchange identities with a girl she had only just met. She had come down to a strange house, palmed herself off as a relation, and had actually married a dying man. Regarded in this cold, unemotional light, it did not seem credible that she, Mary Coleridge, could possibly have done such things unless she had taken leave of her senses.

The final suggestion brought her to her feet, breathless, her cheeks burning.

Her inclination was to run away, to fly out of this strange old house whose very graciousness seemed to have changed into something sinister, and to get back to London, that cold unyielding city which yet had the comforting quality of being completely logical and comprehensible.

She was halfway to the door, no clear intention in her mind but the urge for flight strong upon her, when someone tapped softly on the panel and Mrs de Liane came in.

She had changed her black dress for one of stiff mauve watered silk, which rustled expensively as she moved. Her tiny white hands peeped out of soft ruffles of real rose point, and round her throat, hanging on a heavy gold chain, was a locket in which, Mary could guess, there reposed a miniature of a child with crisp black curls and laughing blue eyes.

The girl shot her a single searching glance, and her frightened eyes took in the calm, placid face, the delicate mouth, and the blue eyes so like those other eyes which she did not want to remember.

The old lady moved forward, her lips parted and her eyes soft with tears.

"My dear little daughter," she said quietly. "My Mary, back again."

The girl could not trust herself to speak. If this was acting, then Eva de Liane was a past mistress of the art.

The old woman linked her arm through the girl's.

"Now, my dear," she said, "you must come down to lunch, you really must. This has been a shattering experience for us all. It still is. But we must be very brave, my pet, very, very brave."

The ghost of a sigh escaped her, and it seemed to the girl that a chill air ran round the sunlit room.

"Come, dear," the gentle voice repeated. "Come, my poor brave little bride."

Mary sat through the meal in the big oak-panelled dining room at Baron's Tye. At any other time the polished wood, open fire and fine old silver must have filled her with a sense of well-being, and the glimpse through the tall windows of a wide lawn studded with red-gold leaves have satisfied her, but now the great wing of the shadow was over her, and she felt the undercurrent of terror which ran secretly through the old house like the bacillus of a plague.

Mrs de Liane in her mauve dress presided over the table, a pathetic little figure of tragedy, and at the other end of the shining oaken board her husband sat fidgeting with his food, waving away each course untasted and speaking only at odd intervals, and then in a jerky spasmodic fashion, his pale eyes never meeting those of the person he addressed.

Mary sat on his left, and the only other member of the strange luncheon party was the woman in grey, to whom she had not yet been introduced.

During the many silences she had leisure to observe her and was struck by something she had not noticed about her before. The woman was either in the last stages of nervous exhaustion or she was in terror of her life.

Mary made this discovery quite suddenly. She was watching the strong, by no means unhandsome face beneath the severely arranged fair hair, when Mrs de Liane sighed again, and all at once the woman in grey grimaced horribly. Her mouth twitched and sagged open, and she squinted, the pupils of her eyes nearly meeting at the bridge of her nose.

In a moment she had recovered herself and, looking across at Mary, had smiled at her timidly, the colour coming into her pale face. But it had happened, and once again the girl felt something of the same sensation which she had experienced on the balcony outside her window, a sense of the reality of something unbelievable, something that could not be true.

It was at this moment that Mrs de Liane began to talk. As an exhibition of gentle bravery in the face of overwhelming tragedy her conversation was masterly. Mary, who did not consider herself particularly impressionable, found that she was listening to it with pity and admiration, even though the memory of that extraordinary conversation which she had overheard still rang in her ears.

The old lady did not once refer directly to her son or to the extraordinary ceremony of the morning. Instead she related little incidents of her early life in the old house, conveying without actually saying so her gratitude to the girl who had saved it for her.

It was towards the end of the meal that the little scene occurred.

"I must show you the garden soon, my dear," said the old woman, leaning forward, her gentle eyes on the girl's face. "We have a cherry orchard. It is so—so unutterably lovely in the spring. You'll be enchanted. We shall be able to sit out there together and listen to the nightingale."

There was a muffled exclamation from the other end of the table, and Mary swung round to see Ted de Liane staring at his wife. His weak, harassed face was paler than usual, and there was something the girl did not recognize just then in his pale eyes.

"Are you so sure that Mary intends to live with us during her ... widowhood?" he demanded brutally.

There was a moment of frozen silence, and then Mrs de Liane pulled out a tiny handkerchief.

"Oh—Ted!" she said with such piteous reproach in her voice that Mary felt her sympathies called upon as clearly as if a direct appeal had been made.

"Are you?" the old man repeated, leaning forward across the table. "Are you?"

Mrs de Liane stretched out a hand and took Mary's own.

"My little daughter and I understand one another," she said simply.

Ted de Liane uttered a single explosive word and, thrusting back his chair with a clatter, strode out of the room. The old woman looked after him in silence and, as the door closed with a shattering slam, smiled bravely at the girl.

"Can you blame him?" she said softly, her eyes filling with tears of pity. "Can you blame him? His only boy."

Mary's brain was reeling. She opened her mouth to speak, but at that moment something so incongruous happened that the hesitant words died on her lips. From the room directly above their heads came a burst of wild music. Someone was playing the piano with skill and an emotional abandonment which was somehow terrifying.

Mary recognized one of the lesser known Liszt rhapsodies, and an expression of astonishment spread over her face. Ted de Liane could not possibly have reached the room above in the time, and neither the performance nor the moment suggested a servant.

But if she was astonished the effect upon her hostess was extraordinary. The old lady stood as though transfixed, and Mary, glancing at her, saw that her face was completely expressionless. The laughing blue eyes were blank, the gentle lips closed and unemotional.

But the change lasted only an instant. The next moment she was herself again.

"That naughty girl!" she said. "You haven't seen my maid Louise, have you? Such an extraordinarily accomplished young person. I really don't know why she wastes her time looking after a dull old woman like me. Excuse me a moment, my dear, will you?"

She hurried out of the room, set purpose in her face, and, although there was nothing in her actual movement to suggest as much, Mary felt instinctively that she was angry.

She also realized that the other person the room contained had been temporarily forgotten.

She remained in her place looking down at her dessert plate until the music suddenly ceased in the middle of a bar. It did not end with a jangle of notes but broke off smoothly, as though the player's hands had been lifted unexpectedly from the keys.

With its ending a silence fell upon the room, so complete as to be oppressive. The very house seemed to be holding its breath.

For a moment Mary sat staring idly at the red pheasants on her plate, and then the next thing happened. From somewhere very close to her a voice she scarcely recognized as being human in its soft intensity said quickly:

"Go away. Get out of here as quick as you can. It's your only chance. Leave your things behind you. Go now, through the window."

She looked up. The woman in grey was staring at her without expression, and it was only because she saw her lips actually forming the last few words that Mary realized that it was she who had spoken.

Instinctively she lowered her own voice.

"What do you mean?"

An expression of terror appeared in the other woman's eyes, which were, Mary noticed incongruously, as grey as her dress.

"Hush," she said so swiftly and with such pleading that any further question was impossible.

Her eyes still fixed upon the younger girl's face, the woman in grey rose quietly to her feet and pushed back her chair.

"Excuse me please," she said in a perfectly ordinary voice and walked out of the room.

For a moment, as she sat there alone in the big dining room, Mary seriously considered taking the strange advice whispered so passionately in her ear. Long afterwards she was to remember that impulse and wonder at herself and her fool-hardiness.

The broad lawn looked inviting, and one of the tall windows which came down nearly to the ground was open at the bottom. It would have been so easy, so very easy ... then.

As it was, she walked over to the window and looked out. The garden was as beautiful as the house itself. There were long tree-lined walks, dense shrubberies and a walled flower garden. It was not far to the station. She knew the way. But something made her stay, something which she would not admit at that moment even to herself: the recollection of a man lying help-lessly on a stretcher in the grey light of a little sixteenth-century chapel.

All the same, she was by no means unmoved by the strange warning she had received, and she made up her mind then to take a very serious step and one which was to have strange consequences.

She was still standing there, her knee on the low window sill, looking out on the lawn, when Mrs de Liane appeared. The old woman's arrival was completely unexpected. She came round the side of the house, treading softly on the dense grass, and it was not until she had practically reached the girl's side that Mary saw her, yet such was the power of her personality that in spite of the suddenness of her appearance and the thoughts racing through the girl's mind her sweet smile completely subdued for the moment the dark suspicions the girl had entertained.

The old lady was radiant.

"He seems a little better," she said. "Oh, I know it's so silly of me to say so, but I was so happy that I had to come out here and walk by myself before I could bring myself to talk to anyone."

There were tears in her eyes, and she dabbed them away petulantly.

"He wants you to go up and sit with him. It—it may be for the last time. Oh, my dear, it's all so tragic!" she went on, as Mary climbed out onto the lawn and went to meet her. "He's so brave and so young. You—you do like him, don't you, just a little bit?"

"Why, of course I do," said Mary, trying to convince herself that she was merely being polite.

Mrs de Liane closed her eyes.

"If only it hadn't happened …" she said. "But we mustn't think of it. Come, dear, I'll take you up."

As Mary entered the big bedroom with the dark hangings once again she was conscious of a strange tightness about her heart, and once again the overwhelming sense of tragedy which she had experienced the night before descended upon her. But this time there was a difference. Now she had had time to collect her scattered wits and to realize that that dreadful conversation she had overheard must be explained if there was to be any sanity left in the world.

The old lady parted from her at the door.

"The doctor said not *too* many people," she murmured. "Not *too* many people at once."

The heavy velvet curtain rustled as it dropped back into its place over the door, and Mary crossed the thick pile carpet to the bed.

She had nearly reached it when a voice from the other end of the room startled her.

"Hello, Angel, I'm over here. I'm not going to die in my bed after all."

She swung round to see the man who she could hardly realize was her husband lying flat upon his back on a divan which had been pulled up under the window so that he could catch a glimpse of the rolling country outside.

He smiled at her and stirred a lean brown hand which lay upon the coverlet.

"Sit down, young widow," he said lightly. "Where shall we go for our honeymoon? Heaven or the other place?"

Mary stood looking at him. It could not be true—it could not be true! The words drummed in her head. How could he lie there and deceive her? It was not possible. And yet she found herself thinking with something deep and primitive in her nature, which she realized with a shock was hope, that it might indeed be so.

He blinked at her, and she saw again with a little catch at her heart the two deep creases in his cheeks.

"Seeing a halo round my head?" he enquired. "Or is it flames? Sit down and talk to me. A widow's first duty is to her husband. I like you, Mary. Let it be a comfort to you in the years to come to know that your first husband—poor blighter—

liked you very much. He thought you were sweet—he did really."

She did not answer, and he frowned, the amusement dying out of his bright blue eyes. He wrinkled his nose at her like a child.

"Don't look so serious, sweetheart—or mustn't I call you that? Aren't you going to smile at me, Mary? No? Well, ought it to be Marie-Elizabeth then?"

Mary took a deep breath.

"I am not Marie-Elizabeth," she said. "I'm not Marie-Elizabeth Mason."

"Of course you're not, Angel. You're Mary de Liane. Didn't we write it all down, with a nice little parson to hold my hand?"

Mary felt as though her heart must burst. A great wave of self-disgust passed over her. She rose to her feet.

"You don't understand," she said, her voice quivering. "I'm telling you the truth. I am not Marie-Elizabeth Mason. I never was."

The man lay looking at her. There was no expression upon his face at all, and she was reminded with a stab of apprehension more justified than she could ever have hoped to know of Mrs de Liane's face when she had heard the Liszt rhapsody.

After a long pause he smiled, and once again amusement danced in his eyes. But this time there was wariness there also.

"Trying to make my last hours exciting?" he enquired. "I said talk to me. No need to mystify me."

Mary closed her eyes. When she opened them again he was still looking at her with the same half-amused, half-cautious expression.

"I am—or rather I was—Mary Coleridge," she said. "I've never been near Australia in my life. I changed places with Marie-Elizabeth Mason in a London boardinghouse three or four days ago because she didn't want to come down here and I had nowhere else to go. I'm afraid I've deceived you all, but I was so sorry for your mother last night that when I saw I could help her I did what she asked. I am willing to sign away any interest I may have in this house and to go away quietly."

There was utter silence when she had finished speaking. The man was looking at her steadily, an expression in his eyes she had never seen there before. It was not anger or amusement, but something she did not understand.

"Is that the truth?" he enquired quietly.

"All of it," she said.

Richard de Liane whistled. It was an astonishing sound in the circumstances and, as she afterwards discovered, completely typical of him.

"All the truth?" he said. "Oh, my dear young friend...!" And then, with a movement which took her completely unawares, he sat up in the bed, slipped lightly out of it and, striding across the room, pulled the old-fashioned tapestry bell rope.

Far away in the grim old house the terrified girl heard the sound of a peal of alarm.

6

THE MOUSETRAP

R ichard!"
        Mrs de Liane stood in the doorway, her husband behind her, and behind him again the woman in grey.

Looking at them, Mary experienced a wild desire to laugh, but the hysteria was checked upon her lips before the expression on the old woman's face.

Eva de Liane was still charming, still gentle, but there was about her a strange new force which the girl found absolutely terrifying. Her blue eyes were veiled, and her lips were set in a firm, hard line.

"Richard!" she said again and came quietly into the room.

The young man stood where he was, the loose folds of his dressing gown showing the long, strong lines of his figure. He was very tall, and there was a new arrogance about him which had not been apparent on the couch.

He looked at his mother defiantly.

"I'm sorry, darling," he said, "but in the circumstances I didn't see the point in going on. You see, this isn't Marie-Elizabeth Mason."

For some seconds the old woman remained looking at her

son, and it seemed to Mary that there was some strange method of silent communication between them. As they stood facing one another it was almost as though they were arguing without words, and while she watched she saw the man gradually convince the woman that he told the truth.

It was then, after that extraordinary exhibition, that Mary first saw Eva de Liane as the astonishing person she really was. She stood in the centre of the great room, less than five feet tall, a little scrap of a person bundled up in silk and lace, with her grey-white head held high and her shoulders set, and dominated them all as though she actually outstripped them in stature and physical strength.

Very slowly she turned away from her son and looked at Mary. The girl trembled. Although the old lady had not moved forward it was exactly as though she had suddenly come within a few inches of her.

"You are an impostor?" she said softly. All the gentle friendliness had gone out of her tone. Her voice was cold and practically without expression.

Mary found herself explaining, pouring out her story in frantic haste. The words stumbled over one another, and she felt her cheeks blazing and her eyes filling with tears. And she was afraid, that was the extraordinary part about it. Although her motives had been of the best from the very beginning, she was afraid. Her forehead was damp, and a cold trickle of fear played round her spine.

The old woman waited until she had finished. Then she raised her chin.

"You tricked us," she said, and the contempt in her voice was such that it completely blinded the girl to the utter injustice of the remark, although the evidence of that much greater trickery stood lounging by the fireplace.

"I meant to help." The words were wrenched from the girl.

"You deceived me."

As the frozen words left the old woman's lips a thin trickle of laughter, more horrible than any screaming, sounded from the other side of the room. Ted de Liane was leaning against the carved door of a great armoire, his face contorted and his eyes half closed. He laughed and laughed. The tears streamed down his face, in which was no amusement, only the havoc of taut nerves suddenly snapped.

Mrs de Liane looked at the woman in grey.

"Take him away," she said imperiously, and the woman left, the old man clinging helplessly to her arm.

Mary was left alone with the old woman and her son. The man took no part in the ensuing conversation. It seemed almost as though he had no interest in the business in which he was so intimately concerned. He walked over to the bedside table, helped himself to a cigarette from a box and, lighting it, wandered over to the window, where he stood looking out at the sweeping landscape beyond.

"Sit down."

The words were sharp and commanding, and the girl obeyed instantly. Mrs de Liane came over to her and stood looking down at her face.

"Where is Marie-Elizabeth Mason now?"

"At—at the Imperial Palace Hotel. She left the boardinghouse at the same time that I did. She's got all the rest of my things. I've got her passport. I—I'm sorry. I only did it to help."

Mary was trying to get a grip on herself. Somewhere in the back of her mind there was a calm, reasonable self which was desperately angry at the trick which had been played upon her, but the personality of the old woman, combined with the emotional upheaval which she had gone through, to say nothing of the grim influence of the house itself, was too much for her. She heard her voice quivering as the ridiculous words poured out of her mouth. "I only did it to help!"

"The Imperial Palace Hotel? She is staying under your name, I suppose? Mary Coleridge, you said? Very well."

There was an extension telephone in the room, and, leaving her victim, Eva de Liane sat down before it. Within a few minutes she was through to the hotel bureau.

Mary marvelled at the change in her as she spoke to the booking clerk. Once again she was the old lady, fragile, gentle, charming. The sweet voice enquired after her dear niece, explained that it was a trunk call, and agreed prettily to wait until it had been ascertained whether Miss Coleridge was in the hotel.

"She *is* staying there?"

For the first time Richard de Liane took an active interest in the proceedings. He strolled across the room as he spoke and stood before his mother. The old woman looked up at him, nodded and signalled him to leave her.

Mary looked at the two of them. Even in that moment of desperation, when the whole world seemed to be rocking crazily about her, she found herself thinking what a curious pair they were: the man so handsome, so heart-breakingly attractive, and the old woman so dominant, so strangely impressive.

Suddenly Eva de Liane began to speak again:

"Just gone out? Oh, thank you so much. I wonder, would you mind asking her if she will ring up her aunt, Mrs Eva de Liane, Baron's Tye, Heronhoe, Bedfordshire? Heronhoe 26. As soon as she comes in. Will you? Thank you. You won't forget? Goodbye."

She hung up the receiver and turned towards the girl. Richard looked at her too, and for a moment the pair of them studied her thoughtfully.

Mary never understood quite what it was that was so utterly terrifying about that calm, speculative gaze. They were not angry, not frightened, but they looked at her thoughtfully, consideringly, not as though she was a human being, much less the wife of one of them, but as though she were some negligible object which had become momentarily difficult. She felt her heart contracting, and it was not all fear, not all exasperation. There was something else there too, a bitter disappointment, a sort of shameful despair, and it was because of the man.

Mrs de Liane rose. "You will go to your room, Mary—Mary Coleridge, and wait for me until I come."

The girl rose nervously to her feet and took two or three stumbling steps towards the door.

Richard de Liane reached it before her and pulled it open with mock courtesy. As she passed he gave her a little ironical bow.

"Can I take it as a compliment?" he murmured. "Don't cry, my dear; I may die yet."

Mary hurried from him blindly and threw herself face downwards on the bed in her own room. The sun had gone in, and there was a tang of rain in the air. The terrible scent of wet leaves seemed to permeate the room, and there was a cold melancholy about the old house, which had seemed first so lovely and afterwards so sinister.

For some minutes she lay there sobbing, but gradually her good sense reasserted itself. After all, it was she who had been tricked quite as much as Eva de Liane. It was she whose sympathy had been falsely aroused and she who had married.

The last consideration stunned her as she realized its significance. Marriage with a dying man is one thing, but marriage to a live man is a contract which cannot lightly be overthrown by either side.

She sat up on the bed and worked feverishly at the ring upon her hand. It would not move. Hysterical and more than a little frightened, she tried to file it off with a nail file, only to realize how inadequate an implement it was. In desperation she resorted to violent wrenches, and not until her finger was torn and bleeding and the ring remained exactly where it had been placed did she desist.

It was at this moment of despair that she remembered Peter. She longed for him desperately. At least he would have understood her motives. He would have done something to save her from the terrible predicament in which she found herself. She thought of him, square, fair-haired and smiling, sitting opposite her at the dingy little table at Merton House.

A wild desire to get back to that unfriendly but at least not sinister atmosphere came over her, and she pulled herself together.

There was only one thing for it: she must get away.

Slipping off the bed, she went over to the wardrobe and took out her hat and coat. Instinctively she moved silently and with caution. Ten minutes later, dressed for the street, her small suitcase in her hand, she let herself quietly out of the bedroom door and crept down the thick-carpeted corridor to the broad staircase.

Before her, across the wide hall, she saw the open front door. Instinct warned her to take to her heels and fly, but caution prevailed, and she set off down the stairs, feeling her way carefully lest she should make the least noise.

She had reached the bottom step when she stopped abruptly, a chill shooting through her heart. Mrs de Liane had appeared before her on the red flags of the hall. She had come with the same quiet unexpectedness with which she had appeared on the lawn outside the dining-room window. There was something uncanny in this habit of hers of materializing suddenly in the path of flight.

She looked the girl up and down and opened her mouth to speak, but before the words had left her lips the telephone bell in the library on the other side of the hall began to ring and Richard's voice from the doorway remarked that he would answer it.

The two women stood listening intently to the scattered

scraps of excited conversation, and then the man reappeared. He was still in his dressing gown, and his face, Mary saw, was white and strained.

"It was the police," he said. "The London police. Marie-Elizabeth Mason was killed in a car smash this afternoon. She was joy riding, with some stage folk apparently. The police have rung us up as her only known relatives. Your phone call did that. They want us to go and identify the body. I said we'd go, of course. What shall we do?"

Through Mary's impressionable mind there shot a vision of the tall, red-headed, good-tempered girl who had meant to get on the stage, but before she could realize that the reckless primitive spirit was actually gone, Mrs de Liane had spoken, her voice calm and matter of fact.

"Did they say 'Marie-Elizabeth Mason?'"

Richard caught his mother's meaning.

"No, of course not. They think she's Mary Coleridge. They said 'Mary Coleridge.' They got her name from the hotel."

A sigh escaped the old woman.

"Mary, my dear," she said, turning to the girl at her side, "Mary de Liane, you mustn't think of leaving us, my dear. Your place is going to be here, by your husband, more than ever now."

There was a quiet intensity in the gentle voice, much more alarming than anything the girl had ever heard before. One of Mrs de Liane's frail hands closed round her wrist and held it with soft, insinuating pressure.

"But what are we going to do?" demanded Richard, his voice for the first time rising out of control. "What about the police?"

The old lady eyed him calmly.

"Your father will go to London and identify the body of Mary Coleridge," she said quietly. "After all, as she has told us herself, she has no other relatives, no friends."

The quiet words slowly sank into Mary's mind. At first they had no meaning. She stood bewildered, still crushed by the death of the girl who had made such a great impression upon her during their brief acquaintanceship, but gradually, as the steady pressure on her arm increased, she became aware of the old lady looking up into her face, her blue eyes unexpectedly bright, her old lips parted enquiringly.

Then the full force of the outrageous suggestion which had just been made descended upon her, and she stepped back.

"I won't." The words escaped her huskily, and the blood rushed into her face. "I won't," she repeated. "You'd make me a criminal if I did that. I must go to the authorities and explain everything."

Mrs de Liane laughed. It was a gentle sound, musical and amused, yet it set the echoes jangling round the old house, and it seemed to the overwrought girl that the very walls repeated her derision.

"What a sweet child!" The old hand drew Mary's arm through Mrs de Liane's own, and another little hand, glittering with a single marquise, patted the girl's wrist. "She's a dear girl, Richard," the old lady went on. "A dear girl, this little wife of yours. But a little stupid, just a little stupid. We shall have to educate her, the sweet pet."

Mary glanced sharply at the man. The momentary alarm which the telephone message had inspired in him had vanished, and he was himself again and very much the son of his mother. He too was looking at her with an amused smile, and she realized with something very like panic that they were not at all afraid of her or of anything she might do. Their confidence in their own ability to deal with any opposition which she might put up was supreme.

It was a terrifying experience, comparable, Mary thought suddenly, with being held up in the hands of giants. Afterwards she remembered with a sort of awe that even then, at that moment when she saw them frankly revealed in their true colours, she was conscious of their charm.

Baron's Tye would have been a beautiful house even at the moment when a murder was committed in it: so it was with its owners. Even at the moment when Mrs de Liane calmly suggested that Mary should take a principal part in depriving Marie-Elizabeth's heirs of their heritage and Richard smilingly abetted her, they remained delightful people.

Mrs de Liane was still gentle, still frail and gracious; Richard was still gallant, still handsome and still curiously and disarmingly friendly.

Mary felt that she was drowning, that her natural honesty, her scruples, her very personality were being slowly submerged and overwhelmed by an irresponsible but charming force. She made a desperate stand, but it was the old woman herself who gave her the cue.

"My dear," she said, "look at Richard. You've tricked him into marrying you and he's not angry with you—not in the least. He finds you delightful, and so do I. You two dear young people should be most happy together. Why do you want to go and spoil everything? Look at this beautiful house, think of the lovely garden. What a place to live and make love!"

"But it was *you*," said Mary, gripping reality with the frenzied urgency of the drowning. "It was *you*. *You* persuaded me to marry Richard. You told me he was going to die, you made me *believe* he was going to die. You tricked the clergyman, the stretcher bearers, everybody.... How can you hope to keep up the lie?"

"My dear!—In the hall, where everyone can hear you? Think of my poor servants."

Mrs de Liane's tone was only mildly reproving. She did not seem in the least perturbed by the reproaches.

"But I want them to hear me," said Mary. "I want everybody to hear me. You married me to Richard thinking I was an heiress, and now you find that I'm not—"

"I still find you a very acceptable daughter-in-law, my dear," said the old lady calmly. "I am a very reasonable woman, and I hold marriage vows sacred. I am very hurt to find that you don't. There there, my dear, you're overwrought. You must go and lie down."

She led the girl slowly towards the stairs as she spoke, and it was only at the last moment that the girl seemed to realize what was happening and wrenched herself away.

"You can't keep me here by force," she said. "You wouldn't dare."

The old woman looked down at herself and laughed.

"Child, child," she protested, "aren't you being rather absurd. You are a nice, strong, healthy young woman, and I am very old. No, my dear, you shall go if you want to. Force doesn't come into it. But what are you going to do? You're married. The vows you made to Richard this morning are binding. Marriage is a very serious contract, you know."

Mary put her hands over her ears.

"I won't listen to you," she said. "I shall go to the police and explain who I am."

Somewhat to her surprise neither the old woman nor Richard made any attempt to bar her passage to the door. Instead Mrs de Liane smiled.

"And what makes you think they will believe you?"

The question was put quietly, but Mary caught the sense of it and the gentle tone sent a thrill of terror through her heart.

"I shall explain to them how I was tricked into this marriage, and they'll help me to get it annulled. Marriage in circumstances like that can't be binding."

"I think you may find the circumstances a little hard to prove. Richard is so well, you see."

Mrs de Liane was smiling frankly.

"Don't let me dissuade you from any project you may have in mind, my dear," she went on. "But I feel it's my duty to point out that if you, a friendless, unprotected girl, go to our local police or even to the London people with the story which you insist on believing is the truth, I can't help feeling that what they will do is to ask you to sit in one of their offices very quietly until your husband—your lawful husband, my dear—very kindly comes and promises to take care of you until you are feeling more yourself. The police are very reasonable and deferential towards husbands. I've always thought that one of their nicest attributes."

The quiet words uttered in the reasonable, conversational tone had the awful ring of truth, and Mary began to realize just how far the great wing of the shadow had swept over her, and for the first time she saw herself in the pitiless trap which had been prepared for her.

She stood looking at them in the great hall with the mellow stone floor and the rich dark carving, the blood slowly draining out of her face and her eyes widening.

"But there were witnesses," she said. "Witnesses who can't be corrupted. Witnesses of standing whom someone must believe."

She paused. For a minute it seemed to her that a flicker of something vaguely resembling anxiety had appeared in Mrs de Liane's face. It was very momentary, however. The next instant the old woman was smiling again, placid and irritatingly superior.

But it had been there, Mary felt sure of it, and she pressed her advantage.

"There was someone," she said, "someone there who can prove the truth of my story."

The words died upon her lips, and a shadow fell across the hall as a car drove up the path and stopped at the foot of the steps.

Mrs de Liane stepped forward with a curious half-arrested gesture as though she would wave the girl aside, and the next moment a tall, grave-faced man whom Mary had taken to be the doctor, and who had been present at the wedding, came lightly into the house.

He paused on the threshold, and his expression of bewilderment as he caught sight of Richard was too spontaneous to be anything but genuine. Mary saw her opportunity and snatched at it. She brushed past the old woman and threw herself before the man.

"You," she said, "you were there! You can prove my story to the police."

"Mary!" Mrs de Liane's voice expressed outraged protest. "Please go to your room. I am afraid the little bride is hysterical, Doctor."

"I'm not! I'm not!" Had it not been for the agony in the girl's eyes the tears on her cheeks might have belied her words. "You must listen to me. Please—please! I've done a silly thing, but these people are mad. I want to get away. I want to go back to London."

The man stood looking down at her, astonishment on his face. He seemed too surprised to take in the full purport of her incoherent words. She caught his arm in her anxiety.

"You're a professional man. Your word carries weight. You must help me. You can't stand by and see them do this to me. You'll hear me, won't you?"

"Really, Mary, this is ridiculous." Mrs de Liane sounded very tired and very gentle. She came forward and took the girl's arm. "Dr Beron will prescribe a sedative, I'm sure. I'm afraid the strain has been too much for her, Doctor. This has been a very strenuous day, full of surprises and unusual excitement. Come with me, my dear."

Mary still clung to the man's arm.

"Listen to me. Hear me. Just hear me—you can't refuse that."

In her desperation she infused a note of passionate appeal into her tone which it was very difficult to resist. The man

61

looked at her and saw a pale, beautiful face, two grey tear-filled eyes and a tremulous mouth. He seemed to makeup his mind.

"I think if you don't mind, Mrs de Liane," he said quietly, "I should like to have a little talk with this young lady."

He ignored Richard, although it was quite evident from his expression that he had seen the young man and was preparing himself for other explanations later on.

Mrs de Liane uttered a gentle protest.

"Really, Dr Beron, the little girl's quite all right. Just slightly hysterical. Nothing more."

"All the same I should like to speak to her."

There was a command under the quiet statement, and the girl felt rather than saw the old woman shrug her shoulders. She led the way to the library and threw open the door.

Mary still clung to the doctor, and, as though reading her thoughts, the man cleared his throat.

"I think if you don't mind, Mrs de Liane," he said, "I should like to see this young lady alone for a moment."

The old woman did not look at him. She swept away with considerable dignity, her rustling moiré skirts billowing behind her.

The doctor closed the door.

"Now, young woman," he said sternly, as he turned to Mary, "you made an extraordinary exhibition of yourself just now. What's the trouble?"

The big library at Baron's Tye was an unexpected room. Its cedar-panelled walls were interspersed with high bookcases which reached from floor to ceiling, and its three long windows were hung with heavy plum-coloured curtains. On any other occasion its quiet, gracious dignity, its sense of peace and drowsy gloom must have been impressive. But now Mary received only a confused impression of books and old furniture as she allowed her mind to be absorbed by the man in front of her.

He was something between forty and fifty, heavily built and distinguished-looking, with dark hair greying at the temples and a grave, clever face, the forehead high and intellectual. Fierce eyebrows almost hid the sharp, dark eyes beneath them, which now peered out at the girl inquisitively.

He did not sit down or suggest that she should do so, but placed himself on the hearthrug with his back to the blazing fire and regarded her severely as she stood nervously before him. He repeated his last words.

"What's the trouble?"

Mary felt safe. Here at least was a reasonable person, someone belonging to a reasonable world untouched by the strange topsy-turvy magic of Baron's Tye. Here was someone who would at least understand, if he could not condone.

An intelligent person herself, she knew instinctively that it was no use prevaricating in any way, no use whitewashing her own part in the story or trying to put herself in a favourable light. The time had come for a showdown, and she was determined to go through with it.

However, because she was frightened and because her mind was still reeling, she did not begin at the beginning but picked up the story at the point which interested her most.

"Mrs de Liane told me her son was dying. She told me that to save the house from relations who would pull it down he must have a wife. And so I agreed to marry him, so that I could make the house over to her."

She paused. He was staring at her, a slightly amused expression on his face.

"Did you believe that? It was rather an extraordinary story, wasn't it?"

"Was it?" she said. "I—I suppose it was in cold blood, but she made me believe it. She's a most extraordinary person. Anyway, I did it to help her. Now I find her son's not dying, and in fact it's all a trick to get me to marry him because they thought I was somebody else."

The little dark eyes blinked at her.

"You think I'm mad, don't you?" she said helplessly.

"On the contrary." There was a new inflection in the deep voice which she had not heard there before. "I find you very interesting. Because you were somebody else?"

"Yes," Mary floundered on. "Because she thought I was Marie-Elizabeth Mason, her niece. And I'm not. I changed places with Marie-Elizabeth Mason. She took my identity and I took hers, because she wanted to get on the stage and I was miserable and had nowhere to go. And now she's been killed and they want me to go on being her and that's criminal and I won't. You will bear witness that I thought Richard was dying when I married him? You will help me to get this dreadful marriage annulled? You will? You must ..."

Her voice broke on the last word, and the man raised his hand to silence her.

"Did you think my patient was actually dying?"

"Yes, of course. Didn't you?"

He laughed. "Why no, of course not. I may not be a very good doctor, but I'm not as bad as all that! Richard de Liane had a nasty spill, and I told him for his own sake that he ought to lie flat on his back for at least a fortnight. I don't know what he's doing roaming about now. I was appalled when I saw him in the hall just now. This is a very extraordinary story of yours, young lady. On your own showing you came down here as an impostor."

"Yes, I know I did." Mary was very appealing in her despair. "I know I did. But I came down here to help Marie-Elizabeth, and when this extraordinary story was put up to me I went through with the marriage to help Mrs de Liane."

She stood looking at him, her hands stretched out in unconscious appeal, and he took a sudden decision.

"It's the most extraordinary thing I've ever heard in my life," he said, "and if your story is true you've been the victim of a most outrageous trick. As a rule, you know, medical men make a point of not interfering in the private business of their patients, but this is really amazing. I'll see what I can do."

Mary sank down in a chair.

"Oh, if only you would!" she said. "I only want somebody to back me up, someone to explain that I'm telling the truth when I say that I was married to a man on a stretcher who appeared to be dying. I only want to get away. I don't want to be revenged upon anyone. I only want to be free."

The man laughed. "Taken a fancy to young Richard?"

"Oh no," she said breathlessly. "No. Of course not."

"I see. You just want to get out of it as quietly as possible?"

"Yes."

He sighed. "Very well. You stay here for a moment, and I'll go and see Mrs de Liane. I think with a little persuasion from me she may see what an extraordinarily dangerous game she's playing and that I may get her to see everything quietly and satisfactorily arranged. You wait here and don't worry."

He took her hand for a moment, shook it, and went out of the room, closing the door quietly behind him. Mary leant back and shut her eyes. If Peter himself had suddenly appeared and taken charge of her difficulties she could not have felt more content.

She dared not think about Richard. She found it much easier to keep him out of her mind altogether. For the first time since she had come to Byron's Tye she felt almost at ease. The doctor had been so sensible, such a reasonable everyday sort of person. He had not even been unduly surprised.

It was beginning to occur to her that he had probably had his suspicions about Mrs de Liane for some time and was speculating upon the exact line he would take with the old lady, when a faint movement on the other side of the room brought her to her feet as the glass front of one of the bookcases slowly swung open to reveal that its contents were false and hid a small doorway in the panelling.

Through the doorway came the woman in grey. She had discarded her apron but still walked quietly, with a nurselike step. She shut the bookcase door quietly behind her, locked it and slipped the key in her pocket, and then, still without speaking, sat down in the chair nearest her on the opposite side of the hearth.

Mary did not speak immediately. Her appearance had been so unexpected and so quiet that it seemed hard to believe that she had not been sitting there by the fire all the time.

Mary resumed her seat. She felt that she had a champion and that there was no point in entering into conversation with any member of the household.

After a moment or two, however, the woman's steady stare got on her nerves, and, looking up, she met her eyes deliberately.

"You should have gone when I told you to," said the woman in grey. Her voice was as quiet as her movement, and there was no expression in it.

Mary shrugged her shoulders. She checked the impulse to say "Oh well, it's going to be all right now," but her attitude conveyed the remark as clearly as though she had spoken.

The woman in grey smiled. It was not a pretty sight. Her upper lip rose, disclosing pale gums above her strong white teeth. There was weariness, a hint of despair and unmistakable contempt in the expression.

"You little fool," she said, still in the quiet, inflectionless tone. "You poor wretched little fool. Dr Edmund Beron is Mrs de Liane's eldest son. His father died in Australia, leaving most of his fortune to his sister, Theresa. Her daughter was Marie-Elizabeth Mason.

"You think he sympathized with you," she went on with

sudden passion, doubly terrifying after the apathy she had hitherto displayed. "I tell you, Mary Coleridge—or whatever your
name is—you might as well expect sympathy from a fox or
kindness from a wild beast as from Edmund Beron. I ought to
know. Do you know who I am? I'm Jane Beron, his wife."

Mary looked about her wildly. For the first time she noticed
that the steel frames of the windows were locked and barred.
She fled towards the door, and as she reached it the woman's
voice, placid and expressionless again, said monotonously, "He's
out there with that mother of his, deciding what they're going to
do about you. He didn't want to give himself away until he knew
how much you knew."

Mary's hand closed over the doorknob, but it did not turn.
She tugged at its solid panels helplessly. Behind her the woman
in grey laughed.

7
THE WIFE

Mary awoke with a start to find herself in half-darkness. She was still in the big green leather armchair by the side of the fireplace in the library, but the blazing fire had died down to a handful of white ashes and a few glowing coals.

She had no idea how long she had slept. Her last recollection had been of drinking a cup of coffee and nibbling a piece of buttered toast which the woman in grey had brought to her when, exhausted by her recriminations and a fit of helpless weeping, she had sunk down in the chair, weariness overcoming every other emotion.

She lay still among the green cushions, gradually assimilating the facts of that amazing day, and then somebody sighed.

The little sound sent a thrill of horror through her, and she remembered with a startling vividness the scene at lunch when just such another sound had produced such an amazing effect upon Jane Beron.

She turned her head, and there was a rustle of silk as a little figure, terrifying in its very smallness, came quietly towards her from the shadows round the doorway at the other end of the room.

"Awake, my dear?"

There was a faint element of amusement in the question, and Mary sat up unsteadily.

"I was drugged," she said, growing conviction in her tone.

"My dear … my dear …" The repeated words expressed first astonishment and then reproach. "Dr Beron prescribed a sedative, and I sent it to you."

"Dr Beron is—"

Mary opened her mouth to make the accusation but thought better of it. After all, there was no point in getting the woman in grey into unnecessary trouble. In her own position the more friends she had the better.

"I've come to take you up to bed. I thought you might feel a little shaky."

Mrs de Liane's tone was solicitous, and Mary could see her blue eyes dancing with friendliness only a few feet away from her.

The girl dragged herself to her feet. She knew instantly that she was in no condition to make any bid for safety at the moment. Her legs and arms felt heavy, and her head was swimming.

As the old woman led her across the room she talked affably.

"Dr Beron and my husband have gone to London to investigate the death of that poor girl we heard about this afternoon," she said. "I do think these motorcars are so dangerous, especially if they're driven by—well, by wild young people in an excited state. Here we are, my dear. I've changed your room. Will you come up here?"

The bookcase door opened to reveal a narrow flight of steps, and, with the old woman following her, Mary stumbled up a little dimly lit, thickly carpeted staircase for what seemed several flights.

They came at last into a small hall in which there were but three doors. Slipping past the girl, the old woman threw open the centre one and ushered her into yet another of the magnificent apartments which Baron's Tye contained.

It was a fine old bedroom, white-panelled and gilded, lit by a gleaming lustre and containing an ornate Louis Quinze bed, two tapestried settees and a draped dressing table.

"You'll be very happy here, my dear. It's so pretty, isn't it? This is the best suite in the house. Good night."

She touched the girl's arm lightly, a caressing gesture unbearably distasteful, and turned towards the door, her skirts whispering as she moved.

Mary looked round her, and her eyes rested upon another door on the other side of the room. Suddenly the significance of the apartment dawned upon her and she swung round, her cheeks blazing and outraged indignation in her eyes.

"Mrs de Liane, what is this?" she demanded.

But already the door was closing behind the little old lady, and her only reply was a laugh and the gentle grating of a key in the lock.

Mary stood where she was, looking out across the room. The other door stood open, and the little room beyond was brightly lit. Because she was too angry to be frightened she made no sound when a shadow fell across the threshold and her husband appeared in the doorway.

He stood looking at her, a curious smile upon his lips, and for some moments they eyed each other in silence. Then the man laughed shortly.

"Mother's too delightfully old-fashioned, don't you think?" he said. "It's amazing, isn't it? Seventy-two years old and still romantic...."

He did not attempt to move, and his smile did not fade when she continued to stare at him with cold animosity. Instead he went on talking with the same ease and charm which still fascinated her in spite of her anger.

"All your things have been brought up here. My mother's

maid, Louise—such a dear soul, you'll like her—has stowed them all away in the cupboards over there by the fireplace. They're built into the panelling."

He paused, and still she did not speak. He laughed again, and the deep creases at the sides of his mouth appeared.

"Cheer up," he said. "It's three times a widow and never a bride—not once. Or am I talking about bridesmaids?"

Mary was helpless, exhausted, dizzy from the "sedative" which Dr Beron had so thoughtfully prescribed, and now strange emotions which she refused to recognize were trying to take possession of her.

Suddenly she gave up the unequal struggle, and, throwing herself on her knees by the side of the bed, she buried her face in the coverlet and burst into tears.

She wept undisturbed and unmolested for some minutes, and then a voice said pleasantly, "Coming over," and she looked up at the moment that a large white handkerchief landed neatly on the bed in front of her.

She took it, feeling indescribably foolish in spite of her misery, and rubbed her eyes.

Richard de Liane regarded her from his stance on the threshold of the smaller room.

"I do hope you're not getting worried on my account. I'm not an exacting husband. I've never had a wife before, but I'm not going to let it change my beautiful personality.

"I suppose you're absolutely livid with me?" he went on. "I don't blame you. I'm much too lively for a corpse. You mustn't blame Mother too much, though. Try to think of her as a hard-working woman trying to bring her boys up decently."

Mary sprang to her feet.

"How can you stand there talking such rubbish?" she burst out passionately. "How *can* you? You—you—"

"Unspeakable cad?" he suggested. "Or monster? Both nice epithets if spoken with the right spirit. My dear girl, be reasonable. Or don't be. That's not a bad idea. Just lie and scream. Nobody can hear you, I am long-suffering, and It'll do you a power of good."

The words had the desired effect upon the girl. They cut through her hysteria and left her dull and quiet in her exasperation. She sat down on the end of the bed.

"O God," she said brokenly, "what am I going to do?"

The man stood looking at her bent head, and for a moment the amusement died out of his eyes and his long, thin lips twisted pityingly. The next instant, however, he was himself again.

"You probably won't take my advice," he said, "but I should make the best of it. I don't wish to appear vain, but as a husband I might be worse. I might be drunk or offensive or even affectionate, but as it is I'm quite reasonable. I've made myself up a little couch in this dressing room. You can have the key of this room. I really don't see that you've got much to grumble at. I should have a good sleep."

She raised her head and looked at him.

"Is that a bet?" she said.

"Of course it is. I'm sorry I let you in for this instead of the jolly funeral I promised you, but when you get to know Mother better—as you will, my dear girl; don't run away with the idea that you're going to shake her off: she's the kind of acquaintance that sticks—you'll see how impossible it was for me not to back her up. Anyway, don't be upset. It's not worth it. You may even get to like me. You don't feel that coming on yet, do you?"

"No I don't," said Mary violently. "I loathe you. I can't tell you what I think of you."

"I see," he said, and grimaced at her, his eyes dancing. "I rather thought that was the case. You've got a way of conveying it, you know. Well, I'll go back to my camp bed. The key's in the lock of this door."

He turned on his heel and had half disappeared when he looked back.

"Would you mind a personal question? Are you in love with anybody else? It's sheer inquisitiveness on my part, I know, but you *are* married to me."

Mary thought of Peter. He seemed so far away now that he might have belonged to another world.

"No," she said.

"You hesitated?"

He was standing in his doorway looking at her, a faintly wistful expression on his face which long afterwards she tried hard to forget.

"I said No. I mean No. And if you were the last man on earth I would never fall in love with you. Good night."

He sighed. "I really do believe you mean that," he said. "However, I still think you're sweet. Good night."

He went into his room and closed the door behind him. The key was sticking out of the lock, as he had said, and she took a childish and unworthy satisfaction in turning it noisily.

Then she went to bed. She did not sleep for a long time, although the old house was silent as a tomb. Even here the smell of the wet leaves percolated, and on her finger the little gold and diamond ring cut into her soft flesh.

She cried until she could cry no more, and when her emotion was exhausted a new sense of reality settled down upon her and she saw herself trapped. In her heart she knew that Mrs de Liane had spoken the truth when she described the probable police reactions to any story she might tell them. A husband's rights were strong, especially when the girl had no relations and no friends.

There was no sound from the little room. Richard de Liane had evidently taken his own advice and was sleeping soundly, probably with the innocent sleep of a child, she told herself with grim amusement. But she dragged her thoughts away immediately. She did not want to think of Richard de Liane.

At last she fell into a light sleep herself, tossing and turning in the great bed, her lips moving feverishly and little disjointed phrases escaping her as she relived in dreams the fantastic episodes of the day.

She awakened with a start to find that it was dawn and that the long curtains were glowing and the room was full of sound. At first she could not understand what it was. The shrill yelping of dogs was broken by excited shouts and the thud of horses' hooves on the turf.

She sprang out of bed and hurried over to a window, catching up her dressing gown and throwing it over her shoulders as she went.

She was pulling aside the curtains when the completely unexpected happened. A door in the panelling whose existence she had never suspected burst open, and Richard, his hair tousled, his eyes dancing with excitement, came hurrying out, tying the girdle of his gown as he ran.

"It's the hounds!" he said. "Come on, let's lean out of the window."

"But the door ..." The words died on the girl's lips.

He laughed and slipped his arm through hers.

"The back of the cupboard in one room goes into the cupboard in the next," he said. "I didn't mention it because I thought you might get needlessly irritated. But I just couldn't miss the hounds. Come on!"

He threw up the window sash and she realized at once how impossible escape that way would be. It was a sheer drop of three stories to a gravel path below.

On the other side of the path was the turf, stretching down towards the river, and across it, in full cry, sped the pack, the field streaming out behind.

It was an exhilarating sight. In spite of her troubles the girl was excited by it. She leant out, and Richard put his arm over her so that he supported himself on the farther lintel.

He was shouting with excitement, and one or two of the riders glanced up at him as they passed. One man was having trouble with his horse, a huge thoroughbred bay who danced off the turf onto the gravel as his rider avoided a speeding chestnut.

Something familiar about him made Mary catch her breath, and at that instant he looked up and she stared down into the face of the last man she expected to see. The man she knew as Peter Muir. Recognition was instantaneous. She saw him glance at the man at her side, and then, as the colour vanished from his face, the bay swerved and dashed off after the hounds, who were fast disappearing in the fold of the valley.

Mary stepped back into the room. She was white and breathless. Richard looked at her.

"That fellow recognized you," he said.

"Did he?" Mary strove to speak lightly with the urgency of despair. "I don't think so. I've never seen him before."

Richard de Liane smiled, and the creases in his cheeks deepened.

"You're no wife for a De Liane," he said. "You're not even a good liar."

The girl's grey eyes darkened. It did not occur to her that she looked beautiful standing very stiff and straight in her severe man-tailored dressing gown, her red-gold hair in disorder and unexpected colour in her cheeks.

"I fully realize I don't come up to the standards of the family," she said bitterly, "but you all seem to have a degree of perfection in that respect that I should never attempt to imitate."

"Splendid." He was looking at her with admiration in his dancing blue eyes. "Splendid. You've got a spot of fire too, have you, Angel? That's great. I may be able to love you after all."

Mary raised her hand. It seemed to be the only retort. The blow caught him squarely on the cheek with much greater force than she had intended. He stepped back, and for a moment she recoiled before the fury in his eyes.

Almost at once he was himself again, laughing and gently ironical. But there was a new note in his voice when he spoke to her, and she realized with sudden terror just how angry he could become.

"I should go back to bed," he said. "They'll bring you your breakfast."

He walked over to the door of the room and, taking a key from the pocket of his dressing gown, calmly let himself out. On the threshold he paused and looked back at her.

"When did you meet that man before?"

Mary met his eyes squarely. He really was extraordinarily good-looking—the thought sprang into her mind incongru-ously—but his anger had increased his arrogance, and there was something primitively satisfactory to her in the sight of the crimson mark which her hand had left on his cheek.

"I don't know what you're talking about."

He laughed explosively. "You're learning, Angel," he said. "You're learning fast."

And, stepping quietly out of the room, he locked the door behind him.

8

THE INGENUITIES OF MRS DE LIANE

In a bright, sunny room whose windows opened onto a terrace overlooking the southern lawn, whose walls were hung with an ancient Chinese paper and whose furniture was graceful Queen Anne walnut, Mrs de Liane sat up among the lace-covered cushions of her enormous four-poster bed and went through her morning's correspondence.

She made a delightful picture. Her small figure was wrapped in a white embroidered Chinese shawl, and a little cap of rose-point framed her gentle face.

She looked a charming person, her small mouth pursed pityingly as she read the contents of the long overnight telegram which had been delivered with her letters.

Although she was quite alone in the room, and no one, save possibly the fat pigeons perched on the balustrade of the terrace, could have seen her, she did not relax her pose for a moment. She was playing the part of a pathetic, affectionate old lady grieved by the message she had just received.

She read it over to herself for the second time, murmuring the words aloud.

"DEAREST MOTHER:

"I am afraid I have sad news to report. Ted and I arrived at the Imperial Palace to find that the poor girl we had come to see had been taken to a mortuary. I went down there, and both Ted and I were much overcome to find that our hopes were dashed in that no mistake had been made. There is no conceivable doubt but that it is our poor Mary. I am arranging everything, and the authorities are being most kind and helpful. The funeral is fixed for this afternoon, and since we are the only relatives I am letting it be a quiet affair at Leabridge Cemetery. We shall return tomorrow, bringing back her few belongings. I am afraid the poor girl was in low water, for she seemed to have very little money and to have become mixed up with a wild stage set. We both send our love to you.

"Yours,
"EDMUND."

Mrs de Liane sighed, patted with an ivory hand the three telegraph forms on which the message was printed, and murmured "dear boy" in an audible tone. Then she laid them aside and picked up another letter. Her expression changed as she reread it, and the gentleness faded from her blue eyes, leaving them shrewd and contemplative.

"DEAR MRS DE LIANE:

"Your telegraphed news is indeed surprising, but if as you say your niece is the impulsive young person she certainly appears to be I can understand that you had to agree to the hurried match. I hope you will convey my congratulations to both the young people. I realize that your niece will not want to be bothered by business affairs on her honeymoon, but I am afraid I must remind you that she is also your ward and that a certain amount of responsibility must attach to your position until we have her affair settled. It is now the twenty-fifth and, even allowing for the twenty-four hours' grace, I am afraid I must insist that both you and she visit this office before the twenty-seventh. It is a formality that really must be complied with.

"With kind regards and best wishes for your own health,

"Yours very sincerely,
"LEONARD J. LATCHER."

Mrs de Liane sat looking at the signature for some moments, and then, stretching out her hand, she took a little silver mirror from the bedside table. She was still contemplating herself with grave eyes which had at least nothing of vanity in their depths, when there was a tap on the door and Richard came in.

"Hello, Angel, you look wicked," he said, laughing. "I don't like you when you eye yourself in the mirror. Oh, I see, a line from old Latcher.... You're disgraceful, at your age, my dear! You twist that poor respectable old bird round your finger as though he was still a young articled clerk."

Mrs de Liane set down the mirror and regarded her youngest son thoughtfully.

"He's suspicious, Richard," she said. "I know he's suspicious. We must be very, very careful. That girl must be taught her part."

Richard's hand caressed his cheek involuntarily, and he murmured something under his breath.

"What?" His mother glanced up at him sharply. "Is she going to be difficult?"

Richard avoided her eyes. "I don't think so," he said, and picked up the telegram.

As he read it through his face changed, and an expression

that was half astonishment, half contempt flickered through his eyes.

"There's something about Edmund," he said, "that makes me sick. There was no need for this. Who's likely to read a telegram?"

Mrs de Liane's eyes blazed. "You're a fool, Richard," she said. "It's Edmund's care, Edmund's attention to detail that makes him so valuable. You lie," she added calmly, "but Edmund believes what he says."

Richard wandered over to the window and spoke over his shoulder.

"All the same I don't like him," he said.

His mother regarded his lean, boyish frame tolerantly.

"My dear, don't be childish. How is your wife?"

The man did not answer immediately but stood staring out across the garden, his hands thrust deep in the pockets of his dressing gown. Presently he swung round.

"You know that fellow at Heronhoe Hall?" he said slowly. "That fair chap who spends most of his time abroad and only turns up for the hunting? He came past here this morning."

Mrs de Liane was gathering up her letters from the folds of the embroidered counterpane and did not reply immediately.

"A fair boy?" she said at last. "Sir Peter Muir-David?"

"That's him. Mary and I were looking out of the window when he came past. He glanced up, and they recognized each other—I'm sure of it."

"Richard!"

The word broke from the old woman's lips in a startled whisper, and he swung round to see her crouching over her letters, her head twisted and her eyes piercing. The arrested movement was much more expressive than any gesture she could have made.

"What are you saying?" she demanded. "What are you saying?"

A frown appeared on the man's forehead.

"They recognized each other," he repeated. "I saw it. But it wasn't merely recognition. I don't think he noticed me, but I had a good opportunity to see his face. As soon as he caught sight of her the colour went out of it, leaving him as white as paper. And then his horse, which was behaving pretty badly, carried him off."

"And she? What does she say?"

"Oh, she lies." He shrugged his shoulders as he spoke, and his frown deepened. "She behaves as though she was in love with him," he said, and there was a hint of irritation in his tone. "But he looked as though he was frightened to death of her."

"Richard!" Mrs de Liane's voice was momentarily uncontrolled in her exasperation, and she looked a very old woman. "Have you gone off your head? Do you realize what you're telling me? This girl has got to lose her identity. No one must recognize her. Otherwise—"

She broke off, and one of her small white hands rose in a helpless half-finished gesture.

"But you were mistaken," she went on with a sudden change of tone. "Of course you were mistaken. I must have a little talk with her. Did you lock her in her room?"

He nodded and opened his mouth as though he would have spoken, but a glance at the old woman evidently made him think better of the words, whatever they were, and he turned away.

For some time Mrs de Liane was silent. She sat up in the great bed, looking like a compact little ivory carving. Only her blue eyes were alive and thoughtful.

Around her the great house rustled and echoed the early morning sounds; the rattle of milk pans in the yard, the soughing of brooms vigorously wielded on heavy carpets, and the subdued voices of busy servants.

It was a pleasant and cheerful house, peaceful, elegant and

comfortable, but the power of the little old woman sitting up in the bed dominated it with sinister influence just as the sweet, acrid smell of the wet leaves dominated every other perfume pervading the gracious old rooms.

Presently the woman stretched out her hand.

"Richard," she said, "ring for Louise and then go back to your own room on the first floor. Your wife and I must have a chat this morning."

The man did as he was told but paused after he had pulled the heavily embroidered bell rope which hung down by the chimney.

"Although I hold no brief for Mary," he began deliberately, "I hope you won't misunderstand me, Angel, when I say that I really shouldn't like to see her reduced to—well—Jane's condition. —No drugs."

Mrs de Liane's eyes hardened.

"Jane was a very foolish, obstinate girl," she said. "Edmund agreed with me that she had to be taught."

He still hesitated, and she spoke to him sharply:

"This little impostor is a very pretty girl, Richard. Don't make a fool of yourself."

The man laughed and, going over to the bed, kissed her lightly.

"Sometimes you're almost human, aren't you?" he said. "Almost funny."

He went out of the door without another word. Mrs de Liane glanced after him thoughtfully, but then, as heavy footsteps sounded down the passage, she leant back among the cushions and composed her face into a sad, appealing smile.

The woman who came into the room was not young. When Mrs de Liane had referred to her as a girl she had spoken euphemistically. Short, square and miraculously neat, Louise Lafouchardière had all the French peasant's reserve and silent patience. The small black eyes set too closely to the broad, full-bladed nose were dull and secretive. She came in quietly, only her big starched white apron crackling as she advanced across the room.

She paused by the bedside and regarded her mistress without speaking. Mrs de Liane leant back among the cushions and smiled.

"So tired, Louise," she said with pretty helplessness. "So terribly tired. I'm growing old. You must take good care of me, my child, or I shall die, and that would be very awkward for us all, would it not, Louise?"

The words were spoken so lightly and conversationally that it seemed impossible that they could express anything deeper than their obvious meaning, but the dull colour came into the other woman's face and she murmured "Oui, madame" as she bent to find the tiny quilted bedroom slippers beneath the chair.

Mrs de Liane made a careful but extraordinarily hasty toilet. While the woman arranged her hair she kept up a constant stream of chatter, all of it in the same vein.

"Time is growing short, is it not, Louise? Still, I am not weak, you see. I have my wits about me. Don't worry, dear child. You can rely on me. You know that, don't you?"

The last words were put sharply, and the old woman turned her head to look up into the dark face above her. Just for a moment a piteous expression appeared behind the small dull black eyes.

"I hope so, madame. Sometimes I give up hope. Only one more little year and then—"

She broke off, her voice quivering.

Mrs de Liane patted one roughened hand.

"Louise, don't be foolish. I have given you my word. The child shall be found before he returns—that is, if it is still alive."

She uttered the last words with such gentle deliberation and her eyes were fixed with such curious satisfaction upon the other woman's face that no one who had seen the little old woman just then could have thought the thrust was anything but deliberate.

The other woman closed her eyes, and her lips twisted.

"I have thought of that, madame."

"Of course you have, but you mustn't." Mrs de Liane rose and surveyed herself in the cheval glass opposite the window as she spoke. "You really mustn't. You mustn't be morbid." One tiny white hand smoothed the heavy grey silk of her skirt. "I am doing everything that can be done, and if I can't succeed there is nobody in the world who can. Oh, Louise …"

The last words were uttered with a complete change of tone.

"Mr Richard and his new little wife … I am curious about my son, naturally, Louise. You would understand that. I want to know how they get on together, what they talk about when they are alone. There is nobody who could help me there better than you, my dear. After all, Louise, you have listened at doors before now."

A wooden expression crept over the other woman's face.

"I—am growing a little deaf, madame."

One of Mrs de Liane's small white hands rested on the maid's arm, and not with light pressure.

"Then recover, my dear Louise," she whispered. "Recover. If you want me to help you you must help me. Just their attitude towards each other—that is all I want to know. If they quarrel it does not matter, but if they should stop quarrelling, Louise, come and tell me at once. Do you understand?"

She peered into the woman's wooden face, and evidently something she saw there reassured her, for, with a last glance at herself in the mirror, she rustled off to the wide staircase, her tiny high-heeled shoes clicking on the parquet.

Louise Lafouchardière stood watching her, and it was not

until her little figure had disappeared round the carved stairhead that a very odd thing happened.

Her sombre, unutterably patient expression vanished, and there appeared in its stead another containing such passionate depth of hatred that her whole face seemed to be transformed into a mask of living fury.

9

THE AMATEUR

S ometimes during a great emotional crisis the mind rallies. The gentlest spirit sometimes revives as though it had received from some unsuspected depth a new lease of courage and endurance.

It is at such times that hitherto helpless, unsophisticated souls goaded by circumstances so terrible as to be almost outside their comprehension make an unexpected stand, receiving from their reserves a small measure of that exhilaration in the face of danger normally possessed only by their stronger brethren.

As Mary strode up and down the enormous Louis Quinze bedroom, her bare feet sinking into the deep pile of the Aubusson carpet and the skirts of her severely tailored dressing gown swinging with the vigour of her stride, she was past terror.

Her mind was working with feverish clarity. The shock of seeing Peter—and it really had been Peter, that was the amazing part of the whole incomprehensible incident—had been followed by another discovery.

Not only was she a prisoner, but her clothes, her shoes and her handbag containing the little money she possessed had disappeared. Someone had entered her room during the night and removed them silently while she lay tossing helplessly in the great bed.

It was this discovery, the realization of her physical helplessness, combined with the moral and legal web which surrounded her, which had driven her to a point of despair at which she must either have collapsed or rallied. As it was, she summoned her slender reserves and steeled herself to make an attempt at freedom.

Once she could get away from this terrible old house, whose very graciousness had something spurious and dangerous about it, she felt certain she could discover some way to dissolve the legal tie by which she was bound to Richard. But the first and main thing was to get back her personal liberty.

A careful examination of all the windows of the rooms composing the suite had forced her to the conclusion that direct methods were not to be contemplated. The only other way, then, was by strategy.

Mary was an amateur at deception. Never during her short life had she been confronted by the need for it. But now she composed herself resolutely to her task, never realizing, mercifully, the hopelessness of pitting her gentle subtlety against that past mistress of the art, Eva de Liane.

Her schemes were only half formed in her mind when a soft knock at the door disturbed her. She swung round to face it.

The door opened gently with a rustle of silken curtains, and the old woman came in. Seeing her with new eyes, Mary had time to wonder at herself afresh. Mrs de Liane looked as charming, as utterly guileless as she had done at their first meeting.

She came forward with a little impetuous movement of welcome, so spontaneous that it seemed incredible that it was not genuine. Even knowing what she did know, Mary yet felt her heart warm involuntarily before that infectious smile.

"I'm afraid you're cross with my poor Richard." Mrs de Liane took the girl's hand and drew her down onto one of the ornamental settees. "But you deceived me, you know, and not only about your name."

There was no reproach in the remark; only a quiet playfulness which Mary found mystifying. Her expression betrayed as much, and the old woman hurried to explain.

"You told me you had no sweetheart, and now I hear you've found an old one on our very doorstep."

The attack was so sudden that the blood came into the girl's face unbidden.

"I—I don't think so," she said.

"Oh, my dear, don't be shy. We pretty women have lots of sweethearts."

A dimple appeared in the faded cheek as she spoke, and Mary found herself fighting against the charm of that extraordinary personality.

"No wonder you're cross with poor Richard—although I do think it's most tactless of an old flame to turn up on one's honeymoon morning."

The quiet voice rambled melodiously on.

"A titled sweetheart too! And very wealthy, my dear. Did you know that?"

Mary was genuinely astonished, and her expressive face showed it as clearly as if she had spoken.

Mrs de Liane looked at her sharply.

"I didn't know you'd been abroad—or did you meet Sir Peter Muir-David in England?"

"I met Peter Muir in a London boardinghouse," said Mary, startled out of her caution. "I don't know any Sir Peter Muir-David."

The bright, dancing blue eyes opened a fraction wider than was their wont.

"But how romantic!" Mrs de Liane saw her advantage and pressed it hard. "And did you know each other well?"

"No," said Mary desperately. "I—we—that is, we shared the same table for six or seven months. But we were acquaintances, that's all. I think you're quite wrong about the title, Mrs de Liane. I did see a man I thought was Peter Muir out of this window this morning, but I was probably mistaken. Please forget the whole incident."

"Why, of course I will, my dear, of course, if it's like that." Mrs de Liane cast down her eyes, and a faintly prim expression appeared on her face.

Mary was goaded into further explanation. She was too overwrought, too completely swayed by the experience and ingenuity of the other woman to realize the dangerous path she was mapping for herself and, incidentally, for Peter. Long afterwards she was to remember the conversation and to wonder at herself, but at the moment she was completely taken up with her new project. Mrs de Liane must be lulled into a false security.

"You don't understand," she said with an attempt at cautious confidence. "We just met for meals. There was no question of him being my sweetheart, as you call it. We just discussed everyday things, and he can't possibly be the man you seem to think he is, because he was just an ordinary London worker. I think he spent his time in some sort of office; I never knew what it was. He was the last person in the world to have a title or a fortune. Anyway, I've completely forgotten him."

There was a pause while she watched the other woman anxiously. To her relief Mrs de Liane seemed to accept her explanation.

"Of course, my dear," she said. "You know best. It was just

some story of Richard's, I suppose. I'm afraid you're going to find him very jealous."

"Jealous!" The word formed on Mary's lips, but she did not utter it. What right had Richard de Liane to be jealous, of all ridiculous things! With an effort she dragged her mind away from her wrongs. Mrs de Liane was a lunatic, one who had to be humoured, to be managed, and very timidly she set out to make the overtures on which she had decided.

"I—I've been thinking," she said. "I'm afraid I may have behaved very stupidly. I was flustered by everything, you see. You—you made a suggestion to me yesterday, Mrs de Liane, and frankly it frightened me, but I—I'm not a fool and I've been thinking it over and I want to tell you that—well, that you can rely on me."

The ill-told little lie was over, and Mary took a deep breath. Mrs de Liane was not looking at her. She had turned her head away, and the girl did not see the smile at the corners of the gentle mouth.

"My dear Mary," she said, "what a very sweet child you are! Do you know, as soon as I saw you I knew we were going to be great friends. I'm so glad you've decided to be sensible. It's so much easier in the end. You may even grow to love Richard in time…?"

She paused, her voice ceasing on an upward inflection, and at the question the girl answered in spite of herself: "Oh, I don't think so, I mean—well, all that can be arranged later, can't it?"

Mrs de Liane turned, took her hand and looked into her eyes.

"Yes, of course it can, my dear," she said. "Of course it can."

There was another pause, during which Mary looked out across the beautiful room and saw the glint of sunlight on the yellow leaves beyond the window. It was a beautiful morning, bright and clear and fresh, the last day on earth for the extraordinary drama working itself out inexorably in the mellow old house.

Mrs de Liane's voice startled her by its crisp practicalness.

"Since you've made up your mind to be reasonable, my dear," she said, "I may as well tell you my plans for today. We are going to London, you, Richard and I. I shall take you to see an old friend of mine who, for family reasons, may be extremely interested in your identity as Marie-Elizabeth Mason."

She paused and eyed the girl thoughtfully.

"Last night you left your handbag downstairs," she said deliberately. "It was brought to me, and quite by chance I found the passport which my niece lent you. It seems perfectly in order. Fortunately the photograph is extremely bad. Really, I don't know how they let these things pass. There is no actual resemblance, of course, but I think with a little care, hairdressing and the right sort of clothes it will be possible to make you resemble it quite closely enough to pass by the rather foolish old gentleman whose eyesight has been none too good these last ten years. The description is easy. Your hair might easily be described as auburn, and the difference between grey eyes and grey-blue is a debatable point.

"Now if you use your intelligence and are guided by me the whole interview can pass off most satisfactorily. If you are sensible you will find that I shall be a good friend to you. Do you understand me?"

"Yes," said Mary with a little more force than was strictly necessary.

Mrs de Liane's smile appeared again.

"Very well then," she said. "I shall rely on you. Louise will bring you your things, and we will drive up to my flat in London. There we can make the necessary alterations, and then we will go and see this very old friend of mine."

Mary heaved a sigh of relief. It was going to be much more

simple than she had dreamed. Once in London she was sure they could not hold her.

Just for a moment she allowed her triumph to show in her eyes, but it died instantly as she caught sight of the old woman watching her. There was nothing definite in the look, nothing actually malignant or even unfriendly, but there was something there which sent a cold chill creeping slowly up her spine, and after Eva de Liane had gone she remained crouching on the settee, trembling and afraid.

10
THE CITY OF SHADOWS

The day, which had begun so brightly in the country, had deteriorated into an afternoon of cold, misty rain when Mrs de Liane's big car, driven by a stoical chauffeur, reached the outskirts of the city.

From her position between Richard and his mother on the back seat of the limousine, Mary caught glimpses of dank pavements, slate-coloured with the wet, and the drab fronts of rain-soaked shops.

Their way into the city led them through the mean streets, and here the chill gloom was everywhere. Even the slowly moving traffic looked sullen and half moribund in the discomfort of the day.

Richard was very silent. All through the long drive from Heronhoe he had barely spoken. Mary hated him with an intensity she had never before experienced towards any living thing. She glanced at him now, his handsome profile outlined against the dark curtains of the car window, and wondered if he knew how much she loathed and feared him, and then, inconsequentially, if he knew whether he would care.

But he remained quiet, arrogant, and if anything a little bored.

Mrs de Liane chattered. Mary forced herself not to listen to that quiet, engaging voice, so subtly attractive. The carefully chosen hints concerning "new clothes … a little jollity … something to amuse your wife, Richard" passed her by. She refused to hear them. She was waiting breathlessly for an opportunity, a chance to escape. She had made up her mind to take it as soon as it presented itself. She knew she would be alone, penniless and friendless in a city which had always frightened her, but at least she would be free.

At the junction of a wide road, which yet managed to look mean and shabby, the chauffeur turned and addressed his employer.

"It's nearly half-past, madam, but I can just make it. Shall I turn?"

"Yes, I think so, please, Walker. You needn't go right in. Just pull up somewhere near the small gate."

Mrs de Liane spoke gently, but there was an underlying excitement in her tone which Mary was quick to notice. It was Richard whose reaction to the words was most marked. As the car swung round to take a narrower road whose far end was lost in the misty distance he stared at his mother, frank disgust upon his face.

"Mother, you're not actually going to…?"

His voice failed him as the old woman met his gaze steadily with dancing eyes so like his own.

"I think it best, dear," she said placidly. "Ah, Walker, here we are. Anywhere here will do."

She leant forward as she spoke, obscuring Mary's view, and it was not until the great car had come to a standstill against the curb that Mary, peering beyond the driver, saw a dismal stone gateway with an illegible notice-board nailed upon each post.

On either side wet shrubs and naked trees lined the high iron fence.

The mist was thicker here. Its clinging vapour crept round the car, trying with long white fingers to pierce the warmth within.

With her handkerchief Mrs de Liane wiped the frosting glass, and over her shoulder the girl saw the gleam of something whiter than the mist and a thrill of superstitious alarm assailed her.

The car was drawn up outside a cemetery, and it was the headstones she could see gleaming through the bushes.

"Come, Mary." Mrs de Liane's voice was very soft. She bent forward and opened the door of the car. The cold damp air rushed in, and with her heart beating wildly Mary allowed herself to be thrust gently out onto the pavement.

Mrs de Liane took one arm and Richard, cold and rigidly disinterested, the other, and they walked together into the great gloomy field of death beneath the dripping trees.

Their feet crunched upon the gravel, and the old lady led them on to the trim grass among the rows of pathetic little mounds, so silent beneath their burdens of sodden, withering flowers.

At last she paused.

"Look, Mary," she whispered.

They had reached a rise in the ground, and from where they stood they could see a group of dark figures motionless round something less than fifty yards away.

It was a lonely little funeral, the girl thought involuntarily. Two mourners stood bareheaded beside an open grave while a clergyman read solemn words over the burden which four bearers had just lowered into the ground.

Her own visit was so unexpected that its possible significance did not dawn upon the girl immediately, but as her gaze rested upon the lonely scene one of the mourners caught her attention and she strained her eyes to see his face.

Suddenly he looked up, and even at that distance she recognized him as Edmund Beron, Mrs de Liane's eldest son, and the truth burst upon her in all its elemental horror.

"Who?" The word broke from her lips involuntarily, her eyes wild and questioning.

Mrs de Liane smiled up into her face.

"You, Mary," she said softly, and there was an ineffable complacency in her tone. "Poor Mary Coleridge, killed in an accident. Dead, my dear; dead and buried."

"No!" The word was a scream.

Maddened, driven beyond all endurance, Mary wrenched herself free from their restraining arms and flung herself headlong down the incline towards the group.

"Stop!" Her own voice sounded strange and out of control. "Stop! You're making a terrible mistake! I am Mary Coleridge. I'm alive. You're making a mistake."

And as the scandalized clergyman lowered his book and the bearers and gravediggers gaped at her in shocked amazement the gaunt trees took up the echoes of her frenzied words:

"You're making a mistake—a mistake!"

The clergyman moved with unexpected swiftness, and stood so that his surpliced figure with arms outstretched was immediately between the girl and the thing that lay behind him.

Mary came to a full stop on the wet turf to find herself looking up into a grave old face now shocked into unwonted colour, and two very stern grey-blue eyes which peered down into her own.

The sight of him in all his venerable dignity brought the girl out of her hysteria sharply, but his sternness added to the unspeakable horror of the situation.

She heard herself explaining in a husky, frightened voice unsteady with tears:

"That's not Mary Coleridge. I am Mary Coleridge. I can prove it to you if only you'll let me. These people—" she indicated Beron and Ted de Liane— "are deceiving you. They're making me a prisoner. They ..."

Her voice ceased. There had been no response from the calm, shocked face, no softening of the steely grey-blue eyes.

The clergyman did not speak. If only his voice had broken the awful helpless silence she might have been less awed by him. As it was, she had time to become aware again of the rain and the heavy drops falling from the naked branches of the trees.

It was Edmund Beron who stepped forward and took her protectingly by the shoulders. There was studied emotion in his face, and his words were husky.

"Marie-Elizabeth, my dear, you're beside yourself. Come away."

He tried to lead her back towards Mrs de Liane and Richard, who were both hurrying up, but she wrenched herself free and with tears streaming down her face made a last appeal.

"Only hear me! You're making a terrible mistake. Please!"

The priest raised his hand. He still said nothing. His mind was engaged in preserving the sanctity and the dignity of the task which he was performing.

It was that gesture, so utterly unaffected in its majesty, that silenced her, and at that moment Richard came up. He took Mary in his arms.

"Oh, my dear, you shouldn't have done this," he said, and, although she knew what a consummate actor he was, the note of genuine reproach and regret was so strong that it momentarily overcame her.

Holding her arms with a grip of steel, he looked over her head at the old man in the surplice.

"This is my wife, sir," he said. "She was a friend of the dead girl's. The tragedy has—has *shaken* her."

He put into the one word "shaken" an unmistakable mean

97

ing, and Mary, struggling to free herself from his hold, caught a glimpse of the face of one of the bearers. In it she read some of the natural pity and disgust which the normal man feels towards the insane.

It was too much. It was the last straw. She felt her knees giving under her, and the next moment she was being hurried along towards the car, one of Richard's arms round her shoulders and the other gripping her inner elbow.

Behind them a scene dreadful in its duplicity at such a time and in such a place was being enacted. Mrs de Liane, a pathetic figure in her black gown and coat, was weeping silently while her eldest son held her arm, supporting almost all her slender weight.

It was Beron who explained and apologized.

"We are all so sorry," he said. "So terribly sorry. I particularly asked my brother not to bring his wife. We knew, of course, how deeply she was affected by the suddenness of the death of her friend, but we did not dream that anything like this would occur. She was so anxious to come that I suppose my brother gave way to her."

He paused, and as the old clergyman's face softened in sympathy towards the two dignified and sorrowing figures he made a last point that was to save the De Liane family forever from any embarrassment by enquiries from this particular source.

"This is not her first delusion," he said, dropping his voice on the word. "I'm afraid she has a medical history."

The old man bent forward.

"I understand. Your brother is greatly to be pitied," he said. "Now, shall we go on?"

Mary suffered herself to be led back down the sodden gravel path to the dilapidated stone gateway where the big car awaited them. The moral effect of such an incident ending in such a way was devastating. She felt dazed, too frightened even to speak.

The face of the bearer, open-mouthed, half smiling, half revolted, hung in her memory with a vividness that was to haunt her for months to come.

The insane have no friends. They are outcasts more surely than any leper in a banished colony. The weapon Beron had used was invincible: she saw it. The discovery annihilated her, stifling her, keeping her silent.

Richard did not let her go even when they sat together in the back of the big car. The chauffeur was standing in the road with his back to the bonnet. At a sign from Richard he had not even come forward to open the door but remained where he was, staring down the road. Looking at his broad, unresponsive back, Mary knew instinctively that there was no help there. She must find some other way.

They waited for some minutes in complete silence, and then the girl looked up timidly at her captor, whose arm was so very strong and unyielding about her slender shoulders.

He too was staring in front of him like the chauffeur, and his face still wore the expression of cold disinterest mingled slightly with distaste which had distinguished it ever since they left Baron's Tye.

She tried to wrench herself free, but his grip tightened, and, looking up at his face, she saw that his lips had narrowed, that his eyes, deep blue and terribly like his mother's, were angry.

Suddenly she heard herself pleading:

"Let me go. Oh please, please, if you're human, let me go! I swear I'll make no trouble. Only let me go!"

He took no notice of her. She might never have spoken. Only his grip tightened about her.

"They couldn't blame you if I got away." The words came with a soft urgency from her lips. Frenzied despair made them blurred and expressionless. "Just let me get out of the car. You'll never see me again. You'll never even hear of me. Let me go. O Richard, let me go!"

The sound of his name on her lips seemed to startle him. For the first time he showed some anger.

"Be quiet," he said. "You've made enough trouble. Be quiet."

But she had got him to speak. At least that was something. She tried to argue, she tried to plead, but it was useless. He held her there rigidly.

"Suppose I scream? This is London. Someone'll come. Suppose I scream?"

He took a deep breath. "I don't like having to explain that my wife's insane," he said. "If you insist on carrying on like this I shall begin to believe it."

He would do it. The realization came to her again. They would all of them do it. They had done it. They had got away with it once and they would get away with it again. She was married to Richard, that was the hold. That was the terrible, unescapable fact.

She lay back. Her head lolled against his shoulder, but she was too broken, too exhausted to care. She closed her eyes, and the helpless tears trickled slowly down her pale cheeks.

Passers-by glancing in through the windows of the big car saw a young girl in tears outside the cemetery, comforted by a young man staring stonily in front of him, fighting, no doubt, with a grief of his own.

After a long time two people dressed in black and walking slowly came out through the stone gateway. Mrs de Liane leaned on the arm of her eldest son, and he bent over her protectingly. He helped her into the car very gently and, when the chauffeur had taken his place at the wheel, got in himself, sitting on the small occasional seat which let down in the front of the tonneau.

Glancing across at Richard he remarked quietly:

"Ted's seeing to the rest up here."

Richard nodded, and the little party sat in complete silence until the big car had travelled down the wide, wet road and turned once again into the noisy stream of East End traffic.

Then there was a change. Edmund Beron bent forward towards the girl.

"Now, look here," he said. "We don't want any more tricks like that. Understand? Get it into your head that you can't escape; you're to do as you're told and you're to do it quietly. Otherwise—" he shrugged his shoulders—"we'll have to find some other means of dealing with you."

Mary raised her eyes and looked at him. She was frightened by what she saw in his face. Richard was only like his mother in her lighter moods, but about Edmund Beron there was something of the same cold power which she had seen in the old woman only once before.

She said nothing. Once again her original resolution was forming itself in her mind. She must get away. She must get away quietly. She must be as cunning as they. Direct appeal to strangers was useless—she had found that out—but some opportunity must come when she could escape quietly. She composed herself to wait.

11

THE CONFIDANTS

Y ou did very well, my dear boy, very well indeed. I was
quite impressed."

Mrs de Liane leant back in the shell-shaped, satin chair in
the small boudoir of her London flat. She had changed her
gown for a slightly more elaborate affair of pale grey watered
silk with touches of real lace at her throat and wrists. Her hair
was freshly dressed, and the soft curls framed her sweet, gentle
face, the deadness of their colour lending a new brilliance to her
dancing eyes.

"It was excellent," she murmured, stretching out one
elegantly shod foot to the blaze in the grate. "I am very proud of
you, Edmund: you have brains."

Edmund Beron glanced round the gracefully furnished room.
Heavy velvet curtains of old rose, the gleam of silver and the rich
pile of a priceless Chinese carpet counteracted the cold grey
misery of the London day. All the same the man was clearly not at
ease. He strode up and down the room with quick, nervous steps,
his hands folded behind his back and his eyes sharp and anxious.

"It might have been very dangerous," he said.

Mrs de Liane laughed, and the little tinkling sound seemed to suit the eighteenth-century elegance of the room.

"But it wasn't," she said. "Thanks to my two dear boys it wasn't. I quite liked the clergyman. Such a dear, sympathetic old man. I'm sure he really felt for us all."

The man paused in his stride to look at her, and a faint smile appeared for an instant upon his heavily handsome face.

"You're wonderful," he said. "I believe you really think that."

"Oh, but I do," she said, and opened her eyes wide at him. "I do. It was a most distressing incident, most uncomfortable for us all, but I'm glad it happened. It inspires confidence, you know. Besides, she'll never dare to try it again. Did you see her face when she saw that everybody thought she was mad—or, well, shall we say doubted her full control? It was most illuminating."

She laughed again, and this time the sound was not so pleasant.

Edmund Beron shook his head as though to drive the echo out of his ears.

"All the same she's not to be trusted," he said quietly. "I've been watching her as we came along in the car. Her nerves are beginning to show serious signs of wear. A woman in that condition may do anything. She might even try to get herself certified. We've got to be very careful, Mother. Old Latcher is no fool, and if, as you say, you think he's getting suspicious we don't want any hitch there."

Mrs de Liane did not answer immediately. Instead she settled herself back in her chair and looked down at her small white hands folded in her lap. The stones in her rings caught the light and winked like tiny spurts of fire.

She spent some time contemplating them, or appearing to do so, her soft mouth pursed and her eyes downcast. Finally she looked up.

"Latcher is the only *good* man who ever really liked me," she said. "I wonder if that proves he's a fool?"

Beron shook his head. "It's no good, Mother. Latcher's getting old. He's got his reputation to think of. He daren't risk it. If he smells a rat he's bound to investigate."

"Ah," said Mrs de Liane quickly, "we don't want that."

Her son looked at her sharply, but there was not the glimmer of a smile upon her lips.

"She *has* married Richard, that is one thing," she said. "That's important. That will carry a lot of weight with Latcher."

Beron nodded. "It's got to. Well, suppose we get away with it—and we're going to—what does that mean exactly? The entire fortune is in her control, I suppose?"

"And in her husband's." Mrs de Liane was complacent.

The man picked up her words.

"Do you mean that, literally?"

The dancing blue eyes were raised to meet his own.

"Well, no. But she is in the control of her husband and incidentally in mine. Once this identification business is settled I don't think it will be very difficult to persuade her to sign any documents we care to put before her. After all, she doesn't understand the position, and anyway she's not the person to be unpleasantly interested in detail."

He looked at her admiringly. "You have it very neatly planned out, haven't you?"

"I have considered it," she said gently.

"Her husband's control …" Beron repeated the words slowly. He made an impressive figure standing on the hearthrug, his hands still clasped behind him and his chin raised a little, his eyes fixed upon the farther wall. His mother looked affectionately at the flecks of white at the sides of his smoothly brushed black hair.

Suddenly he turned and looked down at the woman.

"She's an attractive girl," he said, a note in his voice which made her look sharply at him. "A very attractive girl. With the right clothes and makeup she could be a beauty."

He was silent again, and then, just as she had framed a cautious question in her mind, he answered it himself, dispelling her momentary anxiety.

"Do you trust Richard?"

To his relief she did not laugh, and he realized that aspect had been considered by her also.

"Yes," she said deliberately. "Yes. Richard has never been impressionable, and I don't think his good sense is deserting him now. However, if it should, I would know immediately."

He dropped a hand on her shoulder.

"Wonderful woman," he said lightly. "Wonderful woman."

Mrs de Liane patted the hand resting so affectionately on the sleeve of her gown, and at that moment anyone who had seen them could not have helped being impressed by the charming picture of filial and maternal affection which they portrayed so clearly.

They went on to discuss the girl. The confidence they had in each other and the obvious bond of something that could only be called affection which held them together added to the chill horror of that dreadful conversation.

After a moment of silence Mrs de Liane mentioned the name that was so prominently before both their minds.

"Latcher ..."

He nodded. "Half-past four. That's the time of the appointment, isn't it? It's hopeless to reason with her. She'll agree to anything and then go back on it. Where is she now?"

"With Louise. I sent the girl up by train this morning. I showed her the passport photograph, and she thought that with a fringe and one or two slight alterations—fortunately girls do makeup so heavily these days—quite a passable likeness could be achieved."

Beron shrugged his shoulders.

"I only saw the other girl when—well, after the accident. The face was practically pulped and—Sorry, my dear."

Mrs de Liane had put up her hand appealingly, and he was all apology.

"It doesn't matter in the least," he said. "After all, it's the photograph Latcher will see. How is she taking to the idea?"

"Very well. She was quite calm and subdued when I told her."

He nodded. "That's a bad sign. I—I wonder if I dare ..."

The remark was so unlike him that the old woman glanced up at him questioningly and he explained.

"There's some stuff called hembutal," he said slowly. "It's really an anæsthetic, but rather different from the ordinary kind. They use it in cases where the assistance of the patient is required. It produces a curious effect. It destroys memory—not from hour to hour but from moment to moment. It might make him think her a little queer, but I don't think it would occur to him ... D'you see what I mean?"

"It sounds excellent," said Mrs de Liane with composure. "I leave all that to you, my dear Edmund. You understand these things. Is there any other effect?"

The man hesitated. "I've had it on my mind for some time," he said. "There's only one thing."

"And that?"

"Frankly, it's dangerous. It has rather gone out of fashion lately because of the deaths. Some people die under it, and some people don't. They can't explain why. Shall we risk it?"

Mrs de Liane looked up at him, and her eyes danced. There was a gleam of something that could only be called excitement in them.

"Why not?" she said.

12

THE OPEN BOOR

Mary stood looking at herself in the full-length mirror in Mrs de Liane's austerely furnished bedroom at the flat. Outside the window rain was pouring down on the noisy streets, turning them to muddy rivers. A thick overhead fog had materialized, and although it was barely half-past three the street lamps were lit, and the glaring bulbs in the bedroom showed her the results of Louise's handiwork.

She, who had known Marie-Elizabeth in the flesh, could not help smiling at the complete falsity of her impersonation of that vigorous, unforgettable creature.

However, when she thought of the photograph in the passport she realized once again how very clever they were. Although a suspicious observer might have detected several flaws in the likeness, no one who merely glanced at the girl and then the photograph would hesitate to pronounce them the same.

She had allowed Louise to cut a fringe and to dress her hair in the style the real Marie-Elizabeth had affected. The heavy makeup bothered her, but she put up with it and had climbed into the new clothes which had been brought to her without objection.

Louise had been silent to the point of sullenness all through the preparations, and now she stood looking at the girl, an inscrutable expression on her square, heavy face, her dull black eyes betraying nothing of the personality behind them, the existence of which the girl did not even suspect.

Mary had been glad that the woman had not talked. It had given her time to think. Now that the hour had come she had made up her mind what to do. She had decided to assist Mrs de Liane and her sons in every way and await her opportunity to escape.

She did not allow herself to think further than that lest her heart should fail her. No money, no friends; only London waiting for her, a cold, wet, unresponsive London which would swallow her up in its muddy skirts.

Alone with the Frenchwoman, she had persuaded herself that she had nothing further to fear from Mrs de Liane now that her mind had been made up to take the vital step. Once that remarkable personality was out of sight she found it easy to think of her as merely a very clever and dangerous old woman, and yet when the door opened softly behind her and she heard the rustle of the silk dress her heart turned over in her side even before the gentle voice had spoken.

"Oh, clever, Louise, very clever. You're a good girl. I shall not forget it. You may go now."

"Oui, madame." The words were whispered, and the woman fled on silent feet, leaving the two together, the old woman and the transformed girl.

"My dear, how very interesting."

Old Mrs de Liane held the passport in her hand, and her eyes travelled over the girl's slender figure clad in the new rough tweed costume, and then travelled up to the face again and the red-gold hair peeping out from under the small brown felt hat.

"It is the eyebrows," she said. "Yes, definitely, the eyebrows. Louise is a genius. You're going to be sensible, Mary?"

The question slipped out unexpectedly in the midst of the stream of chatter, and the girl started violently. The old woman came very close to her.

"My dear, you were very stupid this morning," she said. "I hope you have learnt your lesson."

Mary took a deep breath. "Yes," she said unsteadily and shivered. Even now the memory of that sodden cemetery could chill her and the recollection of the bearer's face send a thin trickle of terror through her.

To her relief Mrs de Liane seemed in the mood to be easily persuaded. She even made friendly overtures.

"You won't come to any harm, you know," she said, "unless you bring it on yourself. I'm sure we're all very fond of you. I am—and Richard."

She watched the girl's face closely on the last word, but there was nothing in the grey-blue eyes to tell her if her shot had gone home.

Mary was forcing herself to think clearly. She realized she would need every ounce of her courage and intelligence to get away. The first opportunity of slipping silently out into the crowds must be seized, and there must be no mistake this time.

Meanwhile, she must be careful.

Mrs de Liane took her into the big living room of the flat where Richard and Edmund Beron sat waiting. Mrs de Liane looked round as the two men rose when she entered.

"Ted not back?" she said, and raised her eyebrows. "I hope there's been no trouble."

"Oh no, none at all. He telephoned." Beron spoke easily. "He'll be here waiting for us when we come back."

Mary had not noticed the incident. She was acutely conscious of Richard staring at her. She thought she read surprise and distaste in his eyes, and somehow the discovery pleased her. She did not allow herself to analyze the feeling, to face the fact that she was pleased because he obviously preferred her as herself.

Mrs de Liane beckoned him forward, and he came over sulkily, like a small boy, fumbling with something in his pocket.

Mary drew back when she saw the jeweller's box in his hand. Mrs de Liane took it from him calmly and, opening it, produced a small platinum wedding ring.

"Now, my dear," she said briskly, "Richard has brought you a proper ring of your own. You must give me back mine."

Mary laughed. The request touched her sense of the absurd, and, holding out her hand, she allowed them to twist and turn at the little diamond ring until they realized, as she had done long before, the impossibility of removing it save with a file.

It was when Beron came to help his mother and twisted her flesh so that she winced that Richard interfered.

"This is my prerogative, isn't it?" he said casually, and stepping forward, he took her hand from theirs and looked down at the little torn finger.

Mary glanced up and caught the expression in his eyes. She looked away hurriedly to find Mrs de Liane watching her furtively.

"I'm afraid that's impossible, Mother. We must put the new ring over it." Richard spoke perfunctorily, and, taking the platinum circlet from the old woman's hand, he slipped it onto the bruised finger.

"With this ring I thee wed," he said lightly.

Mary snatched her hand away, but she did not utter the protest which rose to her lips. Instead she contented herself with looking her dislike and hastily pulled on the new brown gloves which Louise had given her.

"We ought to start," said Richard hastily. "I'm quite ready. Marie-Elizabeth and I will wait here for you, shall we?"

A slow smile passed over Beron's face.

"I don't think so, Richard," he said. "I should like to have a word or two with Mary before we start. I want to give her a short lecture on Australia."

Richard hesitated. Mary caught a glimpse of him, his eyes bright and suspicious as his glance travelled swiftly from Beron to his mother. Quietly the old lady took him by the arm and led him unwillingly from the room.

When the door had closed behind them Beron turned to the girl.

"Sit down?" he said, pointing to a deep tapestry chair with its back to the window.

He spoke quite quietly, but there was a professional note in his tone, the command firm but impersonal. Mary obeyed him nervously. Mrs de Liane was an enemy, she knew, but this man was unknown. His suavity terrified her.

"Now," he began, placing himself directly in front of her and looking down into her face, "there are just one or two things that I want you to remember, Mary. You are not to forget them. They are to stay in your mind. Your real name is Marie-Elizabeth Mason."

The girl drew back from him. There was an intensity in his cold eyes which was alarming. To her relief he laughed.

"You're frightened, aren't you?" he said. "Well, there's no need to be. There's nothing to worry about, nothing at all."

He leaned forward, and his hand closed over her forearm.

"Look at me," he said. "I'm not going to hurt you."

She looked up at him again, and his eyes held her whole attention so that she forgot the growing pressure on her arm.

"You are Marie-Elizabeth Mason," he repeated.

Mary blinked at him, uttered a sharp cry and attempted to spring up in her chair.

"My arm!" she exclaimed. "My arm! You stuck something in my arm!"

Edmund Beron slipped the little silver hypodermic back into his pocket.

"You *are* jumpy, aren't you?" he said. "There's nothing to worry about, old lady, nothing in the world."

He was talking very swiftly now, as though time had suddenly become vitally precious.

"Nothing to be frightened of. Just remember your part. You are Marie-Elizabeth Mason. You married Richard for love. For love," he repeated, and it seemed to Mary that the word grew in enormous letters before her eyes. "You married Richard for love. You were glad to leave the Hendricks. They were nice people but not your sort. You are very happy at Baron's Tye. *You love Richard very much.*"

Mary sat stiffly in the chair, her eyes fixed upon his face in an unwavering stare. After a moment or so a puzzled expression came into her face. She looked down at her arm and rubbed it thoughtfully. Two minutes later she had forgotten it, forgotten the strange numbness which was creeping up her side.

"You are happy," said Edmund Beron steadily. "You have never been so very, very happy in your life before. That's so, isn't it, Mary? Isn't it?"

The girl frowned at him. Somewhere in the back of her consciousness she knew vaguely that something was wrong, but her main sensation was that of first waking, when the mind flits about from subject to subject and feeling is reduced to half-formed impressions too fleeting to be caught.

"You are happy."

"Yes," said Mary unsteadily. "Yes," she repeated with more conviction. "Yes, yes, I'm happy."

"You love Richard. He is your husband. You love Richard. You love your husband."

"I love my husband," she said, and it was as though an oppressive weight had been lifted from her heart. "I love my husband. I love Richard."

She had risen on these words and now, turning her head, saw the man of whom they were speaking standing in the doorway. There was an odd expression on his lean face. The creases in his cheeks had disappeared, leaving his mouth firm and his eyes unusually hard. Mary took two or three uncertain steps towards him.

"I love my husband," she repeated mechanically. "I love you, Richard."

The man strode across the room to face his brother.

"What the hell are you playing at now, Beron?" he said bitterly.

Edmund Beron glanced at his watch.

"We must hurry," he said. "It's nearly a quarter-past four. Besides," he added, glancing at the girl, "we haven't any too much time."

Five minutes later they came down the steps of the block of flats. Mary was clinging to her husband's arm, looking up into his face, unusual colour in her cheeks, her eyes dancing. Behind them Mrs de Liane walked, a picture of happy maternal affection, while behind her, a wary expression on his broad, by no means unhandsome face, came Beron, acutely conscious of the watch ticking away the minutes on his wrist.

The chauffeur held open the door of the car, and if he felt any surprise at the sudden change in the girl's demeanour he did not show it.

The rain descended in a cold, desultory fashion, soaking relentlessly everyone who ventured out into the gleaming streets.

But there was one lounger, one man in a light fawn raincoat who leant against the railings on the opposite side of the road, who was oblivious of the rain. Neither the girl nor her captors dreamed of his existence or his interest in them, but as soon as the great car slid away from the curb he sprang into a passing taxi and, after murmuring instructions in the driver's ear, crouched down on the rough mat within so that his eyes should not miss for a moment the tail lamp of the big black car in front.

Inside the car the four were silent. Mary sat by her husband's side, her arm through his and her eyes fixed upon his face with new interest.

On her other side Mrs de Liane leant back among the leather cushions and glanced under her lashes at the two young people, amusement and frank interest in her bright blue eyes.

Edmund Beron had resumed his original seat opposite the three of them, and he too watched the girl, but there was no amusement in his glance. His eyes were cautious, and there was anxiety upon his heavy face.

The tonneau was softly lit, and for the time being, at any rate, Mary entirely forgot the world of glistening streets without, her attention absorbed by the man at her side.

Richard de Liane did not appear to notice her. His easy, playful attitude had vanished, and he remained cold and ominously quiet. He sat staring straight in front of him, his mouth narrowed and his eyes bright and angry.

For some time the old woman watched him, and then, leaning still farther back in her seat, she spoke with studied lightness:

"You don't seem very happy, Richard. I do hope your attitude won't be misconstrued."

He turned to her impatiently. "You can rely on me when we reach Latcher," he said briefly.

Mrs de Liane laughed. "I was not thinking of Latcher," she said. "I was thinking of your brother and me."

The man stiffened, but although he controlled the angry retort which rose to his lips he could not prevent the colour rising slowly in his face.

Mrs de Liane glanced sharply at her elder son, and the look he returned to her was eloquent. Richard was aware of the little interchange, and a cautious expression flickered for a moment through his eyes.

"That's the penalty of being ... unconventional in one's business methods, Mother," he said. "One's apt to suspect everybody."

The old lady laughed. "Of course," she said. "You must forgive me, Richard. We all have nerves, you know."

Her tone was appealing, but neither of her sons believed for a moment in her confession of weakness.

The conversation had passed completely over Mary's head. She herself was undergoing one of the most extraordinary experiences of her life. Worry had left her. It was not that she was no longer conscious of the terrible situation in which she found herself so much as that she had ceased to think of it. She was living entirely in the present. She knew that the car in which she sat was comfortable, that she was warm, and she had the curious contentment which comes from wearing new clothes.

The man at her side delighted her. She did not think about him, but she knew that he was there and she knew that she was in love with him. Somewhere at the back of her mind there was a little warning note which sounded only at rare and still rarer intervals, but she paid no attention to it. The active part of her mind was not interested and had not the power to seize upon it, much less to analyze it.

She was very very happy.

Presently the car turned out of the wide stream of traffic and took a smaller road leading down into the City. Mrs de Liane drew a sharp breath, and the little sound was oddly expressive. Edmund Beron leant forward and touched the girl's hand.

She was aware of his face in the faint, warm light from the roof. It looked very large and anxious, and he moistened his lips with his tongue as though they were dry.

"You are glad to be in England," he said. "You are Marie-Elizabeth Mason, and you love your husband."

She laughed at him. It seemed such a silly thing to say. It was true, of course it was true, but his face looked funny and she had to laugh.

Beron sat back. Small beads of sweat had appeared on his forehead, and the hand on his knee trembled. Mrs de Liane glanced at him.

"You'd better stay down here in the car, Edmund," she said. "There's no need for us all to go up. It might even look a little suggestive. You wait here."

"Very well." The man seemed relieved. All the same he watched the girl nervously, and she smiled at him. She had quite forgotten who he was.

The car pulled up outside a dim entrance which had been elegant in the days before the City had crowded down upon it, forcing it into obscurity. A man in the uniform of the Corps of Commissionaires greeted them in the hall and conducted them down a long corridor to a white-panelled door in the heart of the building.

Mary still clung to Richard's arm. She was growing more and more lightheartedly irresponsible at every moment. She could not remember what had happened to her in the past and had no idea what was going to happen to her in the future, but meanwhile the present was delightful.

Mrs de Liane walked in front. Her small figure in the grey watered silk gown, the long squirrel cape and the fashionable hat was distinguished and in perfect taste.

Richard's face was set. There was something completely inscrutable in its lean, handsome lines. His anger had entirely disappeared, however, and his step was light.

The commissionaire opened the door and announced them, and Mary received an impression of a big walnut-panelled

room with a thick, bright carpet, a fine old fireplace, a great
many books and, in the centre, a big walnut desk.

The man who rose to meet them was slight and dapper.
Mary had only a most confused impression of him. She was
aware of white hair sleekly brushed, a pair of friendly eyes
behind horn-rimmed spectacles, a big white collar, unusually
shiny and somehow odd in pattern, and a voice which was thin
and precise and sometimes a little squeaky.

Leonard Latcher came forward and with old-fashioned
curtesy took both Mrs de Liane's hands in his own.

"My dear lady," he said, "how very nice to see you. Younger
than ever, if I may say so."

Mrs de Liane laughed. "You're disgraceful," she said. "You
flatter a poor old woman. My dear man, where can I sit down?
You're looking disgustingly young yourself."

Mr Latcher laughed. It was a nervous, depreciatory little
sound which had nevertheless a touch of excitement in it. Mrs
de Liane had that peculiar gift of flattery which even age does
not seem able to destroy.

Proceedings were held up for several minutes while the
elderly Mr Latcher saw his client safely established in the
largest chair. It was a long business involving many compli-
ments and a great deal of moving about.

Having settled herself in a high-backed Queen Anne fauteuil,
in which she looked like a vivacious Queen Victoria, Mrs de
Liane waved her hand toward Mary and Richard.

"Well, my dear man," she said, "there they are, the wretched
children! Married and done for. Don't blame me for the inde-
cent haste. I ran away to get married myself, but that was far too
long ago for me to remember any extenuating circumstances."

Little Mr Latcher, already considerably flustered by the irrepressible personality of the woman who had never ceased to
fascinate him, glanced at the young people.

Richard seemed young, handsome and embarrassed, while

the girl looked up into his face with an expression so unmistakable that Mr Latcher felt quite uncomfortable and rather old.

"Mary, come here," said Mrs de Liane. "We call her Mary," she explained boldly to the bewildered Latcher. "Marie-Elizabeth sounds so foreign."

The extraordinary thing was that it was the second name which made the girl stir. The three things which Beron had impressed upon her were the only concrete facts in her world.

She went across the room obediently. Mrs de Liane performed the introduction. Mary said nothing. She smiled and looked young and extremely shy. Mr Latcher received the impression that for a girl who was going to have so much money in her control she was a little over-youthful, and it occurred to him then, perhaps for the first time, that the marriage might prove to be a very good idea.

He began to talk to her, but his voice was not particularly interesting and Mary had not the inclination to try to follow his words. She glanced back over her shoulder at Richard, and he came over to her and slipped his hand into hers.

Mrs de Liane caught Latcher's eye.

"They're ridiculous, aren't they?" she murmured. "They've been like this ever since they set eyes on one another. I did hope marriage would cure it, but they seem to be worse than ever. Doesn't it make you feel old, Leonard Latcher?"

"I—er—I'm afraid it does," he said, laughing. "But we must get down to business, you know. This is a very momentous day for you, young lady. Three hundred thousand pounds is a very great fortune. Of course at the moment it is all very suitably invested, and if you're wise you won't make any rash changes. However, I shall come to that later. You and I must go into conference in a week or so. Just at the moment there are one or two—er—formalities."

"Of course," said Mrs de Liane hastily. "I really think she would have come without any papers at all. Love is a very terrible thing, Mr Latcher. But I have them all here. I'm afraid they leave all dull things like business to me. Here we are."

She placed a little black satchel on the desk and motioned him to open it, while the two young people looked on.

In such circumstances, perhaps, it is understandable that Leonard J. Latcher, that astute and sophisticated solicitor, should have been more preoccupied with the admittedly questionable business of the marriage between Mrs de Liane's son and her very wealthy ward than with the actual identity of the girl herself, which he was inclined to take for granted.

He glanced at the passport, saw the photograph, and looked through the other papers which the real Marie-Elizabeth had given to Mary for the purpose of deceiving Mrs de Liane.

It was while Mary stood there, her hand in Richard's and her eyes resting casually upon the old man bending over the satchel, that the little warning note at the back of her mind grew suddenly stronger.

Downstairs in the car Edmund Beron glanced at his watch. It was late, much later than he had thought, far too late for safety. He sat forward in the back of the car, his hands clasped and his face becoming strained and anxious as he thought of the scene going on in the office and wondered what its upshot might be.

Mrs de Liane was blissfully unconscious of the possible duration of the effects of the drug. Her mind was entirely absorbed with Latcher himself, and behind her dancing blue eyes there was a new shrewd expression, a watchfulness which the old man never suspected.

Presently he straightened his back.

"Yes, this is perfectly all right," he said.

"I should hope so," said Mrs de Liane drily.

The solicitor laughed apologetically.

"These formalities have to be attended to, dear lady," he said. "They're important, you know. However, that part of the business is settled. Now, Miss Mason—I'm sorry! Mrs Richard de

Liane—I'll keep this marriage certificate, if you don't mind, because your headstrong behaviour, young lady, has made me a lot of work. Then within a week or two I shall be able to give you all the documents relating to your affairs—unless, of course, you'd prefer to leave them with me, in which case I should be very glad to continue to act for you ..."

He paused questioningly, and Mrs de Liane leant forward.

"Oh, but naturally," she said hastily. "You don't want to leave Mr Latcher, do you, Mary, my dear?"

"No, no, of course not." Mary spoke mechanically. The warning note at the back of her mind was growing into a dreadful sense of foreboding. She was beginning to remember things vaguely—terrible, unbelievable things—while the room in which she stood, the old lawyer and his talk of papers, became foreign and incomprehensible.

Mr Latcher was too relieved to notice anything unusual in his young client. The account was an important one for him, and, although he had not anticipated any difficulty in retaining it, he was naturally very glad to be certain that it was in no danger.

Mrs de Liane, however, was not so unobservant. She caught the expression of mystification on the girl's face, and for the first time a gleam of alarm appeared in her eyes.

Mary looked at Richard and took her hand out of his. It was a very simple little gesture, but the man looked down at her, and she, looking up into his face, saw something there which added to her bewilderment and which afterwards she was to remember with mixed emotions.

Taken completely off his guard, Richard de Liane betrayed disappointment. He looked deeply and bitterly hurt.

The solicitor returned to his new client.

"I have opened an account for you at the bank, the same branch as your guardian uses. Here's a chequebook. You may draw up to five thousand pounds. This is your ordinary spending account. If you want any more—and I hope you're not going to be too extravagant—you must come to me, and in the interim the income from your estate will be paid into a deposit account. As that grows we will discuss further investments."

The voice rambled on, and if Mary did not express any delight or satisfaction it was because she did not hear or understand the words. Memory was returning to her and with it all the old terror, all the old sense of danger with which her life had been filled during the past few days.

She took the chequebook he offered her and, having no bag in which to put it, handed it mechanically to the man at her side. Mr Latcher looked appalled, and Mrs de Liane hurried to cover up the lapse.

"My dear, that's too touching!" she said. "I'm shocked. Put it in the pocket of your coat, child."

But Mary continued to hold it out to Richard, and in the end he took it and put it into his own pocket, smiling awkwardly.

Mr Latcher took a deep breath. "I see I must leave business until after the honeymoon," he murmured to Mrs de Liane.

She looked up at him and laughed. "I'm afraid you must, Latcher. I told you so. It's rather beautiful, you know. I didn't know modern young people fell in love like that."

She was speaking quietly, obviously with the intention of not embarrassing them. Mary heard the word "love," however, and looked up at Richard. The colour rushed into her face, and her anger and resentment against him returned to her mind all the more vividly because she was still aware of the strange passionate affection she had conceived for him during the period when she had forgotten his treatment of her and the many things she knew to his detriment.

She opened her mouth to speak, and the words, had they come, must have provided Mr Latcher with one of the most enlightening experiences of his life. But they were never spoken, for at that moment yet another veil was lifted from the shrouds which had enveloped her and she remembered something else. The De Lianes were her enemies. She must get away.

Looking back upon it afterwards she realized that had she made her appeal then, had she told her full story to Leonard Latcher, that old man would have been shrewd enough to discount even the powerful machinations of Eva de Liane. But at the time she was aware of him only as another man, another person who would be prepared to believe her insane, another person who would lead her back to her lawful husband and trust him gratefully to look after her.

The extraordinary thing was that she was not at all sure where she was or what had happened. As the effects of the drug wore off—and once it began her recovery was very swift—her mind went back to the time when she had sat opposite Beron in the sitting room at the flat, and everything which had taken place between that moment and the present was a complete blank.

She saw that she was in some sort of office and that a small, white-haired man who seemed to be a friend of Mr de Liane's was very pleased about something, but more she did not know.

She waited cautiously for a chance to get away. The interview was practically at an end. Mrs de Liane was anxious to leave and equally anxious not to show any eagerness. Mr Latcher came over to the girl.

"Well, Mrs Richard," he said, "hearty congratulations! It was a rash thing to do, but in the circumstances I think I must condone and approve. I hope you'll always be very happy."

"Thank you," said Mary. It seemed the only thing to say. He looked kind, but then so many people had looked kind.

She remembered suddenly that he must be the lawyer, and perhaps, had he not seemed so very friendly with the old lady, she might have made an appeal to him to see her alone, but she knew from experience that any friend of Mrs de Liane's was liable to prove dangerous.

"After the honeymoon, then," the old man said. "After the honeymoon I shall come down and see you. There's a lot of business connected with so much money, you know; a great deal of business."

He insisted on seeing them off the premises himself, a mark of special courtesy. Out of deference to Richard he walked with Mrs de Liane, and because the passage was narrow Richard and Mary went on a little ahead. The man had taken her arm and was holding her tightly, her forearm resting against his and her hand in his own.

Mary recognized it for what it was, the grip of a captor, and as she walked quietly at his side her mind was busy. It is a feature of returning consciousness that each stage is thought by the patient to be the final one. Mary did not realize that her memory was still imperfect. She knew that she was in danger, she was aware of some of the details of the whole fantastic business which had brought her to the present terrible situation, but she did not know that her mind still did not grasp the finer points of the matter. She did not realize her own strength. She did not understand that while Latcher was present she could force the De Lianes to take almost any step she chose. All she knew was that she was terrified and that she must get away.

Feeling very cunning and inexpressibly secretive, she made her plans and waited for her opportunity.

Beron was waiting outside the car when they came down into the street. When he saw Latcher he murmured a word to the chauffeur and hurried away into the crowds. It would certainly not look well if the whole De Liane family appeared to escort the heiress away.

Richard, Mary and the old lady stood for a moment on the steps of the building to make their farewells. The chauffeur stood holding the door of the car open some six or eight feet away across the pavement.

The girl did not listen to the brief interchange of civilities.

Her heart was racing in her side. A wild scheme had crept into her mind. She was the first to shake hands with Latcher, and, while Richard was doing the same thing, she moved across the pavement and climbed into the car.

Her departure was a little abrupt, but Latcher expected heiresses to be a little temperamental, and Mrs de Liane was too relieved that the initial ordeal had passed off so well to give more than a cursory glance after the girl to make sure that she had entered the car.

As Mary climbed into the limousine the opposite door seemed to rush to meet her. It was an old trick and so simple that the astute mind of the De Liane chauffeur never considered it.

Moving swiftly but with the caution of desperation, the girl turned the handle, slipped out on the farther running board, avoided an oncoming lorry by a miracle, and plunged across the greasy, rain-soaked road like a frightened hare.

The crowd on the opposite pavement received and swallowed her. Bending her head against the rain, stupefied by terror and spurred by the single blind desire to get away from the De Lianes, she ran on down the road, taking the first turning which presented itself, rushing she knew not where save that it was away.

13

THE CITY OF STRANGERS

The rain came down. It was not torrential or whipping and intermittent but a slow, quiet, steady downpour which had persisted all the afternoon and would probably go on far into the night.

At the rush hour, when the homegoing thousands poured into buses and tubes, the cold misery of the streets was accentuated, and even the bright lights winking down upon the oilskin capes of the policemen and glinting on the sides of the great red omnibuses seemed to add to the general discomfort.

Mary ran until she was out of breath and then slowed down to a steady walk, her head still bowed, her ears still strained for the sound of scurrying feet behind her.

After a while, however, her panic passed, and she began to realize the truth. She had left the De Lianes behind. She had escaped from them. She was free.

With this discovery there came another. She was free, but only in the most terrible way in the world. She was alone. Every one of the millions around her was hurrying somewhere: she alone had nowhere to go. She had no money, not even a purse.

The rain was soaking the shoulders of her new tweed jacket, and already her small feet squelched inside her brown shoes.

It was night, and there was no one in the world to whom she could turn. The discovery overwhelmed her. Anything, it had seemed, would have been better than being the prisoner of the De Lianes, but now she was the prisoner of something almost as terrible, the prisoner of London, the prisoner of a million strangers.

She dared not go to the police. That, she knew, would be to walk straight back into her husband's arms.

Plunging on through the maze of narrow streets bounded by high, dark buildings, she tried to pull herself together, to marshal her scattered wits, to find some way to establish herself once again in the civilized world. She was like a dancer out of step fighting desperately to get back into the swing.

She had not even a name. Somewhere out in that deserted cemetery there was a little mound to account for her very identity.

She thrust her hand into her pocket and, pulling out a hand-kerchief, wiped the makeup hastily off her face. At least she would look herself.

All the time she was walking. She was tired. The effects of the drug had left her weak and ill. That was another danger: if she should collapse she would be taken to a hospital and then Mrs de Liane would find her, she knew it instinctively. If it were humanly possible Mrs de Liane would find her somehow.

She thought of Merton House far away on the other side of London. She had no very high opinion of Miss Campbell-Smith, but at least she could identify her: that would be something.

She glanced up at the name of the street. She knew where she was. Merton House was miles away, but it was her only hope; at least it was somewhere to go. She turned on her heel and emerged at last onto Ludgate Hill.

She walked through to Holborn and straight on down

Oxford Street, intending to turn up Baker Street and get out towards Finchley.

By the time she turned off to go through Manchester Square she was very nearly exhausted. Her coat was wet through, and her feet were lagging, and all the time her heart was beating in terror lest the big black car should pull up beside her and Mrs de Liane's soft, horrible voice sound gently in her ear.

The man in the fawn raincoat was striding down the pavement towards her when he stopped abruptly and peered down into her face.

"Mary Coleridge!" he said.

The sound of her own name uttered in a strange but friendly voice brought the girl to a full stop, her eyes widening and her heart turning over in her side. She found herself looking up into the face of a big fresh-faced man nearing sixty. The raindrops glistened on the rim of his hat, and he had come along walking like a countryman, as if he enjoyed the weather. He laughed at her astonishment.

"You're going to tell me you don't remember me," he said.

"I don't," she said huskily.

"I'm hurt. I thought any daughter of Tom Coleridge would recognize me."

At the sound of her father's name Mary gasped, and to her horror tears rose in her eyes, while she sought anxiously in her mind for the recollection of any patient or friend of her father's who resembled the stranger in any way.

Meanwhile he was looking at her closely.

"My dear child," he said, "you're wringing wet! What are you doing striding about like this without an umbrella?"

Mary did not answer him. "Who are you?" she said.

"George Lissen, from Wickham. Don't you remember me? You didn't go out with your father much, did you? I lost a good friend and the best doctor in the world when he died."

Mary stood staring at him For the last hour she had been

alone in a strange and terrible world, a world in which she had no place, no right; and here, out of the thousands of strangers, had come one who had recognized her. The sound of her own name, her father's name, the name of the town which had been near her village home, were like talismans, and she stood looking at him, her lips quivering, the raindrops glistening on her soaked tweeds.

For the first time he seemed to notice that something was wrong, and he looked more closely into her face.

"What's the matter? Why, Miss Coleridge, you're crying. Anything wrong?"

Mary put out her hand to steady herself against the weakness which was fast overcoming her.

"No—no, I'm all right," she said unconvincingly.

He hesitated. "Look here," he said, "I'm an old friend of your father's; won't you come and have some food with me? Or—look, there's a tea shop over there. Let's have a coffee, and you can tell me the trouble. What about it?"

Mary nodded gratefully. As she sat at one of the little marble-topped tables in the tea shop she looked across her coffee at the man who had found her so opportunely, and her spirits began to rise in spite of herself.

Mr Lissen was plump and fatherly and indubitably respectable. His clothes were old-fashioned and good, and the same might have been said of his manners. At the moment he was looking at her with a puzzled expression, and Mary hesitated. When she considered the story she had to tell, nobody in the world would believe it, she reflected, much less this sturdy, conventional old gentleman who belonged to that other world, the world her father had known, the world where high adventure was considered not only improbable but rather unpleasant.

Suddenly an idea occurred to her. Here was the witness she wanted. Here was the heaven-sent respectable person who could vouch for her identity. She looked up at him.

"Mr Lissen," she said, "you do know I'm Mary Coleridge, don't you?"

He was naturally somewhat taken aback, but he laughed.

"Of course I do," he said. "The last I heard of you was from Mrs Briden. She said you were teaching at a kindergarten up here. Is that right?"

Mary could have wept with sheer relief. The De Lianes knew nothing of her life, and the foolish fear she had entertained that this stranger might in some way be connected with them was dispelled.

A few minutes later she was pouring out the whole story. She did not look at the man until she had finished. At any moment she expected him to get up and walk out, hurrying to get away from the young lunatic. But he remained silent, looking at her with kindly, shrewd dark eyes, and when the story came to an end he leant forward.

"Where were you going just now?"

She told him. "To Merton House. I must get hold of someone who knows who I am, mustn't I?"

"Haven't you any other friends?" he enquired. "No sweethearts?"

"No," said Mary, remembering with a tremor of alarm that other time when the same question had been put to her on the day when she had first visited Baron's Tye.

"I see. Well, it's a very extraordinary story." Mr Lissen spoke seriously and as though he meant what he said and not as if he doubted her integrity. "What do you want me to do?"

Mary thought she detected a note of suspicion in his voice and did not blame him for it.

"I don't know," she said. "Unless you'd come with me to the police. I daren't go alone, you see, or they'd give me back to the De Lianes, who would simply swear I was mad."

Mr Lissen was silent and appeared to be thinking.

"Look here," he said at last, "I have a friend at Scotland Yard.

I think he's the man we want. It's a very serious charge, you see. It involves kidnapping, false pretences and heaven knows what else. Did you ever meet my wife?" He answered the last question himself. "No, of course you didn't. But still, I'll tell you what we'll do. She and I are both staying at the Plantagenet Hotel in the City. I'm going along there now. I'll take you with me, and you can stay with her while I go down to Scotland Yard and get hold of my friend, and then I'll bring him back with me if I can and we'll all talk it over. How about that?"

Mary hesitated. "I—I ought not to bother you," she said weakly and looked up to find him laughing at her.

"My dear child," he said, "in a case like this one can't worry about the little niceties of polite society. You come with me."

Feeling wonderfully relieved and that her feet were at last on firm ground, Mary followed him out into the rain again and climbed into the taxi he hailed.

She found him a particularly comforting person because, oddly enough, she did not altogether like him. He was kind but he was pompous, friendly but sceptical, and altogether an ordinary genuine unsentimentalized sort of person, real and solid and everyday.

As they returned to the City again he turned to her.

"Look here, I've got to call in at my office, if you don't mind. I shan't be more than ten minutes or so, but there are one or two papers I have to collect and go over tonight for a business conference tomorrow. The delay won't take up more than fifteen minutes of our time. You don't mind, do you?"

"Of course not," she said naturally, and when the cab pulled up outside a large City building she got out and waited while he paid off the taxi.

"I could keep him," Mr Lissen remarked, "but I don't think I will. A penny saved is a penny earned, you know. I don't believe you young people nowadays think enough about that."

And with this observation he led her into the building. There was a night porter in uniform on duty who touched his cap very civilly to Mr Lissen and took them both up in the lift.

When they reached the second floor Mary followed her guide down a marble corridor lined with heavy mahogany doors. Taking a key from his pocket, the businessman let himself into one of the huge apartments at the end of the corridor, and the girl found herself in an office whose magnificence made Mr Latcher's walnut elegance look shabby and out of date.

The room was thickly carpeted, its white-panelled walls hung with valuable prints. The ashes of a coal fire still smouldered in an open grate. The desk was a miracle of modern efficiency, and the two leather armchairs were as big as Austin Sevens.

Mr Lissen waved to one of them.

"Sit down and wait for me," he said. "I shan't be a moment. The papers I want are just out here."

He went over to another door behind the desk and disappeared, closing it softly behind him.

Mary sat down thankfully, a wet, pathetic little figure in the midst of so much pretentious luxury.

She had just assimilated the odd procession of events which had led up to this unexpected solution of her affairs when a faint sound outside the door through which she had entered caught her attention. Her experiences of the past few days had made her suspicious, and springing to her feet, she went over and turned the knob quietly.

To her horror the door did not move. She tried it again and again, fear rising in her heart. It remained firm.

She turned and flung herself across the room towards the other door.

"Mr Lissen!" she called helplessly. "Mr Lissen!"

The last word died abruptly on her lips. The inner door had opened, and through it came a tall, cadaverous stranger dressed in the formal morning clothes of the elegant City man.

131

He paused, regarding her thoughtfully, and she, looking at him anxiously, was aware at once that he was a person of distinction and probably of considerable power and consequence.

"Ah," he said, and the voice was unexpectedly deep, "Mary Coleridge. Sit down, will you, Miss Coleridge? You and I have something very important to discuss. I have been looking for you for some time."

Mary stared at him. His appearance had been completely unexpected, and his opening words were frankly incomprehensible. For a lightheaded moment she wondered if she was suffering from hallucinations.

Meanwhile he remained with his back to the inner door, looking down at her steadily. There was a conventional smile upon his thin, distinguished face, and his narrow grey eyes were sharp and wary.

Her astonishment was so apparent that he attempted to dispel it by laughing pleasantly.

"I'm afraid my methods to ensure this interview were a little unconventional," he began, "but then, my dear young lady, you're used to unconventional people, aren't you?"

He eyed her as he spoke, and she was conscious of an insinuation in the final words. She did not attempt to follow it, however, and stepped back nervously. The light fell upon her bedraggled little figure, and the newcomer noticed for the first time that she was wringing wet.

"Won't you take your coat off and let it dry?" he said easily. "It's a wretched fire, I'm afraid, but perhaps we can do something to it."

He walked over to the fireplace and made it up somewhat inexpertly.

"Now," he said, waving her to one of the armchairs and planting himself squarely on the rug in front of her, "we must have our little talk, mustn't we?"

"Who are you?" Mary blurted out the words involuntarily, and he raised his eyebrows at her and smiled depreciatingly.

"I don't think that matters very much at the moment," he said. "You probably know that I'm one of—say—three people, but which one I am I don't think matters. What I want to assure you is that you can be perfectly frank with me and that I wish to deal with you as an independent agent. Now, Miss Coleridge, this is a point I want to make very clear. ...."

He paused, and she was aware of his sharp eyes peering into her own.

"You told Mr Lissen that you were without friends. Am I to understand that you mean that literally? You are entirely without friends? Real friends? You do mean that?"

Mary was completely bewildered. The man before her did not look like a lunatic: on the contrary he gave her the impression that he was talking very intelligently about something which she ought to understand, whereas she found him utterly incomprehensible. However, there seemed nothing to be afraid of in his manner, and she answered him truthfully.

"No, I have no friends at all."

"You mean that?"

"Of course I do. I have no friends. I'm alone."

The assurance seemed to please him, for he smiled at her.

"Oh well, that makes it very much simpler. If you really are an independent agent we can come to some arrangement. By the way, you don't hunt yourself, do you?"

The unexpected question was too much for Mary. She sat forward, the colour rushing into her face.

"I—I don't know what you're talking about," she began.

The man laughed. "You're a very transparent young person," he said. "Shall we say, then, that the answer to my question is that you prefer to watch? Well then, Miss Coleridge, I have a proposition to make to you."

Mary wriggled out of the deep chair and stood opposite the

man on the hearthrug. She was completely mystified, frightened, and had the uncomfortable impression that she was being persuaded to hint things which she did not understand.

"Look here," she said, "I don't understand you. I don't know what you're talking about. I met Mr Lissen, who was an old friend of my father's, and I told him of—of certain difficulties with which I am confronted and he promised to take me to see his wife while he went to find a friend of his at Scotland Yard. He came in here for some papers, and then you appeared. I don't know what you're talking about. I think you're making a mistake."

The stranger sighed. "You were being so reasonable," he said. "I had hopes of you. Why must you women be so difficult? I am being perfectly straight with you, perfectly honest, and you wriggle about as though I were trying to pin you down to something. Look here, Miss Coleridge, I know who you are. I know all about you. I know where you've been during the last two or three days, and I can guess very much what your relations with certain—er—certain people have been. Now you assure me that you have no friends, no loyalties to consider, and I am preparing to make you an offer."

The little touch of irritation in his tone awakened an answering flame in the girl.

"If you'll send for Mr Lissen and get him to take me to the police," she said, "I shall be very pleased. Or if you think you can prove who I am, if you'll take me to them yourself I shall be grateful."

The man raised a pale, carefully manicured hand.

"My dear young lady, no threats if you please," he said stiffly. "You came here with Mr Lissen because you were prepared to talk to me: get that into your head."

"But Mr Lissen was my father's patient and friend. He said so. He knew all about me. He—"

Mary's voice quivered and broke, and the man in front of her made an exasperated sound with his tongue.

"Why can't you be straightforward?" he said wearily, and, moving across the room, he opened the inner door and put his head inside. "Oh Lissen," he said, "come here a moment, will you?"

George Lissen, looking, if possible, even more respectable, more pompous and more elderly, came immediately. He stood just inside the room, his face wooden and unresponsive.

"Now Lissen—" the stranger spoke with authority—"I don't know what methods you've used to persuade Miss Coleridge to accompany you—they were certainly very effective—but she still seems to be under some misapprehension. I would like you to have a word or two with her. Oh, by the way, you'd better call me Mr Jones."

"Yes, sir." The deference in Mr Lissen's tone was as great as it was unexpected.

Mary could keep silent no longer.

"Mr Lissen," she said, "you knew my father and you promised to help me. What is the explanation of all this?"

The man looked at her steadily. There was a hint of severity in his manner which astounded her.

"Miss Coleridge," he said, "I never knew your father. I do not come from Wickham. All these things you must have known perfectly well during our brief conversation together. My advice to you is to be reasonable. Otherwise you are up against very powerful—"

"That'll do, Lissen," the man who preferred to be called Mr Jones cut in hastily. "We don't want any threats on either side. We both understand each other perfectly well. It's only that Miss Coleridge prefers to be a little more cautious than I think necessary."

Mary heard this extraordinary statement, but her mind did

not grasp its significance. She was only aware that the man she had thought to be her friend was repudiating her.

"But I told you," she said. "I told you what happened to me. I told you all my story."

For the first time since he had entered the room George Lissen permitted himself a smile.

"My dear young lady," he said, "you certainly told me a very extraordinary story, so extraordinary that I have not troubled to tell His—I mean, Mr Jones—the full details."

"But didn't you believe it? It's true!"

George Lissen shrugged his shoulders.

"A marriage to a dying man, a prisoner, another girl buried in your stead—don't be ridiculous. That sort of thing does very well in fiction, but this is real life, Miss Coleridge, and I am a reasonable businessman. That is the sort of story to tell to old ladies—some old ladies—not to me. Take my advice. If you are a free agent, as you seem to be, accept the proposition which is put up to you. If not ..." He paused significantly, and again "Mr Jones" intervened.

"Thank you very much, Lissen. You might wait for us in the next room, will you?"

Lissen took his dismissal gracefully and returned through the door by which he had entered. The man with the cadaverous face turned to Mary with a smile.

"There you are," he said. "You see. Are we beginning to understand each other, or are you still being very careful?"

Mary sat down in the chair again. Her head was reeling.

"But it's true," she whispered. "It's true. Look, there's the wedding ring on my finger."

He laughed. "A very pretty, touching piece of verisimilitude. Over the engagement ring too, I see. Really, Miss Coleridge, you ought not to go in for this sort of—adventure, shall we call it? It's not your line at all. Now shall we get down to business? We've wasted a lot of time, you know."

He was standing there smiling at her, and Mary marvelled at him. His poise and his ease were both magnificent. He spoke with that authority which is only achieved by those who have been used to it all their lives. And yet he was wrong. That was the thing which took her breath away. He was utterly, completely wrong.

Gradually, as she recovered from the shock, her mind began to work again.

She sat very still and waited. The man noticed her change in demeanour and beamed.

"That's very sensible," he said. "I thought we should get to understand each other eventually. We do understand each other, don't we?"

Mary hesitated. She did not understand, of that she was perfectly sure, but she also realized the impossibility of making him believe her when she said so. She shrugged her shoulders therefore.

"Yes," she said.

"Splendid," said Mr Jones, taking up his position with his back to the now brightly burning fire. "Well, Miss Coleridge, this is the offer. We—I and my friends—are prepared to give you the sum of three thousand pounds and your passage to Canada on condition that you go there immediately, signing an undertaking not to return for at least ten years. You must also promise not to communicate with anyone in this country or to enter into any litigation of any sort whatsoever during that time. When you arrive in Canada employment will be found for you in some capacity in which you are likely to succeed. There now, Miss Coleridge, you cannot say we have been ungenerous."

Mary did not speak. She could hardly believe that she had heard the words uttered so casually and pleasantly by the man in front of her.

Mr Jones misunderstood her hesitation.

"After all, you have not so much to worry about," he said. "I know it's a great hardship to leave one's own country for ten years, but you do see our point of view. In this way we safeguard ourselves completely. Do you agree?"

To get away! The words danced in front of Mary's eyes. To escape Mrs de Liane forever. To be safe from persecution! To start afresh with the dreadful nightmare of the last three days banished forever! It seemed too good to be true.

She looked at the man dubiously.

"I don't know why you should do this for me," she said.

"Still cautious?" He laughed. "Ah well, it's a very good fault. However, am I to take it that you accept?"

Mary hesitated. To her astonishment the person who came into her mind was the man she had married. But she put all thought of him from her instantly. Richard de Liane had proved himself despicable over and over again.

She thought of Peter and of his unexpected appearance. He had seen her in very compromising circumstances, however, and to the best of her belief he had run away from her in the first place because he had been afraid that she was growing fond of him.

There was nothing, therefore, to keep her in England. Rather, everything combined to persuade her to seize the first chance she received to get out of the country. Mrs de Liane had forced her to take part in a serious swindle. Her only hope was to escape the woman forever.

"Suppose we make it four thousand pounds?" said the man who called himself Mr Jones, softly. "That is a great deal of money. Will you go?"

"Yes," said Mary, startled by her own decisive tone. "Yes."

"Splendid." Mr Jones' manner became more and more friendly. "I'm sure it's a step you'll never regret. When I said you were not the type to be mixed up in this sort of affair I meant it. You're not. We shall have to take precautions with you, of course, but you won't object to that."

"No ..." said Mary dubiously. "What are they?"

To her surprise the man laughed at her. He seemed genuinely amused.

"I've never met such a suspicious person in all my life," he said. "You have had good training, of course. Still, in that case you will appreciate our own caution. As soon as you leave this office I want you to go to an address which I will give you. When you get there you will find a lady waiting for you. She will expect you and will know your name but not your affairs. She will engage you as a companion-help for her voyage to Canada beginning on Friday and will agree to pay you a salary. She will arrange your passport, and once you arrive in Canada will obtain a suitable post for you. When you leave this office I need hardly tell you that you will be followed, and once you have entered the employment of the lady to whom I am sending you you will not be permitted to make any communication whatsoever with anybody outside. Do you still accept?"

"Yes," said Mary. The fates seemed to be playing into her hands. She had no proof, of course, that the man was sincere, but on the face of it there seemed no conceivable reason why he should go to the trouble of making such a proposition if he had not a very good reason for it. Most convincing of all, he was obviously a person of importance, not used to wasting his time.

She made one last effort in the cause of sanity.

"I—I still don't understand you, Mr Jones," she said. "I accept your offer because it suits me, but I don't understand it and I see no reason at all why you should have made it. I do not know how you got to know so much about me, and the story I told to Mr Lissen, although it is extraordinary, happens to be true."

He held out his hand, and his eyes danced with amusement.

"Splendid," he said. "Game to the last. A little obstinate, perhaps, but a good fault. Now may I rely upon you to be a good girl and not attempt any monkey tricks? You will find that I'll keep my side of the bargain as long as you keep yours. When you arrive in Canada the money will be paid to you in lump sums over a period of three years—a further precaution—but if you are sensible you won't give us any cause to regret the line we took. Here is the address."

He sat down at the desk and, pulling a blank sheet of paper towards him, scribbled a name and address upon it.

"There," he said. "You will leave here in a taxi, which will be followed by another taxi. Mrs Mortimer will be waiting for you. Excuse me, but have you any money?"

"No," said the girl. "None at all."

Taking a key from his pocket, he unlocked a drawer in the desk. A few moments later he had counted ten new pound notes into her hand.

"There you are," he said. "That's a first instalment. Anything you will require for the journey will be given to you by Mrs Mortimer. Good-bye, Miss Coleridge. You'll find a taxi waiting outside the door downstairs."

He accompanied her to the lift.

"Good-bye," he said again. "Play fair, Miss Coleridge, play fair."

Mary walked out of the office in a daze, the money and address slip clutched in her hand. The cab was waiting, as Mr Jones had predicted. She gave the man the address from the paper in her hand: 12, Bacon Gardens. As the cab slid away from the curb she peered out through the little back window just in time to see another cab pull away from a dark doorway a little farther down the street.

14
SEARCH

Y ou should have stayed there." Mrs de Liane, seated at a
desk in the living room of her London flat, hung up the
receiver of the telephone which she had been using and looked
at her elder son coldly.

Edmund Beron flushed.

"I saw the landlady and made all arrangements. If the girl
shows up there she will phone you immediately. I assure you,
Mother, we can trust that woman."

"Trust her!"

Old Mrs de Liane's pale, beautiful face was transformed into
a mask of furious contempt. She made a very impressive picture
sitting there in her grey dress against a background of deep
Indian-red velvet curtains. Her small hands looked as though
they were made of ivory, and her bright blue eyes were no
longer dancing but hard and inexpressibly cold.

"I told you to stay there. We can trust nobody."

She touched a little bell on her desk, and when Louise
appeared she sent the Frenchwoman for Ted de Liane, who
came immediately. He looked paler and more dissolutely

unhappy than ever. His hands trembled, and his eyes were shifty.

"No sign of her, I suppose," he began querulously. "Now you've done it, Eva! I don't know why you're waiting here. Let's get out. Let's get out of here at once. We can leave the country, can't we?"

"With what?" demanded his wife coldly. "Your pittance, my jewellery, and heaven knows what charges hanging over our heads? You're a fool and a coward, Ted. I don't know which I hate most. We must find the girl, or when someone else finds her we must be ready with our story. Now pull yourself together. I have work for you to do."

The man stepped back. "Not me," he said. "I'm finished. I've stood by you on some mad schemes, but this is too much."

"Very well. Get out."

It seemed incredible that the words, spoken with such vituperant bitterness, should have come from that gentle mouth on which a sad, sweet smile so often lingered.

Ted de Liane crumpled. "I'm sorry, Eva. I'm rattled, that's all," he said abruptly.

"My good man, aren't we all?" There was a hint of the old arrogance in the woman's tone. "But we haven't all lost our heads, thank goodness. Now look here; you're to go down to that boardinghouse where she lived. Call yourself by some other name and take a room there. Spend your time sitting in the lounge and wait for her. As soon as she appears take her straight out of the house, put her into a taxi and bring her here. You can do that, can't you?"

"I don't know. The girl may refuse."

"It's your business to see that she doesn't refuse. Hurry. Every moment's precious."

The old man still hung back. "I quite like the girl. She's a nice girl. What d'you want to badger her for? She'd have played fair with us if we'd played fair with her. She was a nice girl."

"All the more reason to take care of her," said his wife impatiently. "Hurry. And remember this, Ted: if you fail, if you let her slip through your fingers …" She paused expressively, and for a moment their eyes met.

Ted de Liane went out quietly, and the old woman returned to the list of names upon her desk.

"I've been in touch with every hospital," she said quietly, and Beron, who had stood silent during her interview with her husband, strode restlessly up and down the room.

"It's the drug!" he said explosively. "It's the drug that's worrying me. I didn't see her, you know. You say she behaved quite well with Latcher?"

"Perfectly," said Mrs de Liane complacently. "There was no sign of weakness then. What are you thinking? That she may have collapsed somewhere?"

"I don't know," said the man huskily. "My God, Mother, do you realize that if she has It'll be—*murder*?"

For some moments Mrs de Liane was silent. Then she shrugged her shoulders.

"Your nerves are getting bad, Edmund," she said. "That girl is as strong as a horse and perfectly well. I only hope she may have lost her memory or been taken ill. Then we shall find her all the more quickly."

Beron opened his mouth to reply. There were deep lines round his eyes, and his heavy face no longer looked handsome. He was silenced, however, by the unceremonious arrival of his brother.

Richard de Liane threw open the door and strode into the room. There was a new tenseness about his tall, lean figure, and the high cheekbones stood out prominently in his brown face. He glanced at his mother questioningly, and on receiving her unspoken message threw himself down into an armchair and lay back, his lips compressed.

Alone in that household the old lady remained quiet, self-possessed and unshaken.

She looked at her younger son and laughed. There was a tinge of something that was almost jealousy in her gentle voice when she spoke.

"Quite the brokenhearted husband …" she said. "You really do it amazingly well, my dear boy."

A dark flush spread over the young man's face, and he rose to his feet and came quietly over to the desk, where he stood looking down into his mother's face.

"She had no money," he said. "No friends. And she was still dizzy from that filthy concoction Edmund had pumped into her arm. It was raining. It was the rush hour, and it was London. Good heavens, anything may have happened to her!"

The old woman's bright blue eyes darkened.

"It certainly makes a very pathetic picture when you put it that way," she said. "I only hope that she is not seated in some sympathetic policeman's office giving evidence that will send quite a number of people to jail, including her husband. I don't think you can have made very much of an impression upon her, my dear Richard. It's not a very complimentary thing to have happened, your young bride running away from you at the first opportunity."

Beron looked up sharply. "D'you think she may have gone to the police?"

"No," said Mrs de Liane calmly, "and if she has it doesn't matter. Fortunately she has a loving husband who is willing to take her back and forgive all. The only person I hope she hasn't gone to is Latcher."

Beron took a convulsive breath.

"Good heavens! Suppose she has? What do we do then? I'm almost inclined to say with Ted, let's get out of the country."

Mrs de Liane's blue eyes opened wide.

"And leave three hundred thousand pounds?" she said. "My dear Edmund, don't be absurd."

"She won't go to Latcher," said Richard from the hearthrug. "Poor kid! I don't suppose she even knows she ever went there. She was drugged and silly. She just walked out of the place and disappeared into the traffic."

Mrs de Liane looked at her younger son sharply, and Beron seized upon his words.

"There's a great deal in that. She wouldn't remember anything about the interview, you know, once the anæsthetic had passed off."

Mrs de Liane was not listening to him. Her eyes were still upon her younger son.

"We've got to find her," she said softly. "You've got to find her for your own sake, Richard."

Something in the quiet tone made him look up, and after seeing the expression in her eyes a new wariness crept into his own.

"I see that," he said slowly. "What shall I do? Go round to the police? Explain my wife is a stranger to London? I realize we must be very careful."

Mrs de Liane sighed, and there was relief in the little sound.

"Not yet," she said. "Wait till tomorow morning. We've got to be careful of Latcher, you see. You do realize our position, don't you, Richard? It would be better that she were dead than—well, than some eventualities."

The man met her gaze squarely, and the callousness in his face equalled her own.

"I agree with you," he said.

But afterwards, when he went out of the room and saw Mrs de Liane's satchel lying open on the hall table, he took up the passport which lay among the other papers and, turning it over, looked at the portrait within. Evidently what he saw there did not please him, for he threw it down again with a gesture of irritation and, taking up his hat and coat, strode out into the rain.

The light from a street lamp fell upon his face and showed for an instant the clean line of his jaw and the deep hollows of his eyes. Had Mrs de Liane seen him then she might well have had cause for disquietude, for there was conflict in his face—conflict and something like astonishment.

15

THE COMPANION

H ere you are, miss. That's the house."
Mary stepped out of the taxicab, and there was some little delay while the taximan found change. While he was getting it the girl had leisure to observe another taxicab draw up some distance down the dark wet road, and afterwards, when she had paid the man and entered the iron gate of the big Georgian house, it was still there.

It did not drive away until the door had opened and she had been swallowed up in the lighted hall beyond.

During the ride and up to the moment when she stood shivering on the doorstep of 12, Bacon Gardens, Mary had been too bewildered to think about this new turn her adventures had taken. She was aware, of course, that some mistake had been made. Now that she thought about it clearly that much was evident. But what it was, what exactly had happened, and who the man at the City office had been, she could not imagine.

Her heart was beating wildly when she pressed the bell of the large comfortable house in the quiet, fashionable street, and when the door opened and a manservant peered at her enquiringly it was with great difficulty that she restrained an inclination to run away. She knew that she must present a somewhat extraordinary appearance. Her new tweed suit was wringing wet, and she was clutching nine pound notes and a handful of silver, as well as a tiny scrap of paper.

But to her relief the man smiled when she gave her name.

"Oh yes," he said. "Will you come in? Madam is expecting you."

Mary followed him into a brightly lit formal hall glistening with white panelling and enlivened by a great bowl of flowers despite the season. She was conducted into a little room at the back of the house. Here the white panelling was continued, and she found herself in a little feminine study furnished with gilt and hung with tapestry.

The man motioned her to a chair in front of the fire and went out.

She was warming herself before the blaze when the door opened and a woman came in. Mary was conscious of a sense of surprise. The newcomer was a plump, brisk person, exquisitely dressed and very young looking despite her forty or even fifty years. She was in full evening dress and carried a velvet wrap over her arm.

She stood looking at the girl with a bright, birdlike glance which was inquisitive without being unfriendly. Then she held out her hand.

"So you're Mary Coleridge. Well, my dear, I understand everything's been arranged. You're to sail with me on Friday. Now don't talk to me about yourself: I don't want to know anything. That's part of the arrangement, isn't it?"

She rattled on, interspersing her remarks with occasional bright smiles, and it occurred to Mary that she was being studiously noncommittal.

She chatted for several minutes, and the girl realized that Mrs Mortimer was a very different person both from Mrs de

Liane and from the mysterious Mr Jones. Mrs Mortimer not only had nothing to hide but did not wish to know anything which she might have to hide.

She got the preliminaries over with all possible speed and steered away from the peculiar elements of the affair to the more practical side of the business with evident relief.

"You have no clothes, have you? Oh well, that doesn't matter. My daughter can lend you a nightdress and some toilet things for this evening. Then tomorrow one of us can take you shopping. Or perhaps you could go with Marie, my maid: I don't know, I must see about that. Anyway you shall have some clothes."

She looked at Mary as she spoke and suddenly put out her hand to touch the girl's shoulder.

"You're wet!" she said. "My dear child, you'll get pneumonia … Come upstairs at once. Evelyn, my daughter, can lend you something to put on and have your dinner in. Good gracious me, I don't want you ill on my hands! Come along."

Mary followed the woman up the staircase to one of the big bedrooms on the second floor. Mrs Mortimer tapped and called to her daughter.

"Evelyn, are you dressed? May we come in?"

On receiving a reply in the affirmative they entered to find a magnificent L-shaped room, one portion of which was curtained off with fine chiffon hangings to make a bedroom, while the other formed a boudoir.

A little sallow girl with dark hair and a petulant mouth was eyeing herself critically in a long mirror. Mary had never seen such a beautiful dress, and it occurred to her irrelevantly that the girl was not making the best of it.

Mrs Mortimer performed the introductions perfunctorily.

"This is Mary Coleridge, my new companion. She's sailing to Canada with me on Friday. She's wet through, hasn't any clothes. Do lend her some things, dear. Anything warm will do. I must run down now in case they come."

She hurried out again, shutting the door behind her, and the two girls looked at one another. Evelyn Mortimer seemed as embarrassed and as anxious not to ask questions as her mother had been, but she was not unfriendly. She seemed to find Mary's presence awkward but not unpleasant.

She opened a wardrobe door.

"Take anything you want out of here," she said. "We're about the same size."

Mary was uncomfortable.

"It's awfully good of you," she began. "Really it doesn't matter. If you could lend me a nightdress and a dressing gown perhaps I could have my food in my room? I don't think your mother will need me tonight."

"Oh no, she's going to the theatre. We're all going." Evelyn moved over to the bell pull. "Look here, I'll have to go down, but I'll ring for my maid and get her to look after you. You'd rather that, wouldn't you? I'm sorry I can't stay. Don't think I'm rude, but my new fiancé's coming, and I don't want to be late."

She pulled the bell while Mary attempted to express her thanks.

"You look terribly tired," Evelyn began, and stopped abruptly. Someone had tapped upon the door, and the next moment a voice which both girls recognized demanded cheerfully, "May I come in?"

"Darling!" said Evelyn, and ran towards the door.

It opened, and over her shoulder Mary stared into a startled and horrified face which she recognized instantly.

Evelyn seized his arm. "I'm coming down at once. You shouldn't have come up. Oh—er—by the way, let me introduce you. This is Mother's new companion, Miss Mary Coleridge— Sir Peter Muir-David."

There was complete silence in the big room. The man in the

doorway did not move but remained perfectly still, staring out over Evelyn's head at the bedraggled little figure who looked so pale and fragile amid the luxury of the gracious bedroom.

Mary did not speak. She felt that her capacity for surprise had been exhausted. So many extraordinary things had happened to her in the past twenty-four hours that she was conscious only of a great weariness.

That it was actually Peter himself who stood before her she had no doubt, in spite of the considerable difference in the name. She had recognized his voice, and his face was unmistakable, although it was paler and more finely drawn than it had been when she had known him at Merton House.

It was Evelyn who spoke. Her glance travelled to the girl and back again to the man, and she laughed awkwardly, a little embarrassed sound which had a hint of annoyance in it.

"Oh, I see. You—you know each other."

"No," said Peter so violently that both women stared at him. "I mean," he added awkwardly, "I thought I recognized this lady, but I don't."

It was such a lame denial, and Mary could so easily have refuted it, but the expression on his face silenced her. He was looking at her imploringly; there was no other word for it. His blue eyes sought hers and held them with an earnestness of appeal that was irresistible.

In spite of all the questions which rose to her lips, in spite of the momentary sense of relief and safety which had swept over her, only to be dashed aside a moment later, Mary was brave enough and feminine enough to rise to the occasion.

"No, I've never seen you before," she said with a little laugh, and although the lie did not sound convincing even to herself the sallow girl in the beautiful evening gown seemed satisfied.

She was not pleased with Mary, however, and her dark eyes narrowed under her heavy brows, while the sulky expression upon her mouth was intensified.

She linked her arm through the man's own possessively.

"Come, Peter, we must go downstairs. Mother's waiting for you. Has Lord Tollesbury arrived?"

The words had hardly left her mouth when an extraordinary thing happened. Peter swung round and placed his hand over her lips. It was an entirely involuntary gesture, and his eyes, which were frightened now, rested upon Mary's face.

"Come," he said hastily to Evelyn as she gasped at him. He dragged her out of the room, shutting the door firmly behind him.

It was a ridiculous departure—the essence of flight—and Mary was bewildered by it. The name that he had been so anxious to preserve stuck in her mind—Lord Tollesbury. It conveyed nothing to her except that she fancied she had heard it or read it in connection with some financial undertaking.

Meanwhile she remained where she was. The room was warm, and as her chilled body reacted to the comfort she became aware again of her sodden clothes. She caught sight of herself in the long mirror before which Evelyn had been posing when she first came in. As she saw herself a faint smile passed over her lips. She could have forgiven Peter if he had not recognized her in her present condition. She had never seen such a forlorn object in her life. Her eyes were dark smudges in a white face, and the soaked tweed clung to her slender figure, making her look positively emaciated.

But he had recognized her. She was sure of it. That first moment of mute appeal had been too obvious to be ignored. Slowly she realized what this new development meant. Peter, the person whom she had instinctively regarded as her only friend, was engaged to another woman, frightened of herself, and not prepared to recognize her.

It was one of those moments of despair at which the very depth of misery seems to have been plumbed and when mind and body feel no greater wretchedness can be endured.

Mary pulled herself together and found to her astonishment that she was able to do so. She reviewed her position calmly. She was alone with her back against the wall. There was no living soul to whom she could turn. And yet, by some mysterious trick of fortune, the man who had sent her to this house believed that she was worth getting out of the country and pensioning off. It was a chance, a life line, and she made up her mind to seize it and hang onto it.

Meanwhile the practical side of her nature asserted itself. If she remained any longer in wet clothes the chances were that she would become seriously ill.

She went over to the cupboard which Evelyn had indicated and found a thick, quilted silk dressing gown there. She changed and waited barefoot for the next development. The house seemed silent, and presently she moved quietly over to the door and, slipping out onto the landing beyond, peered over the white balustrade into the lighted hall below.

The passage in which she stood was in darkness, and she looked down with the satisfaction of knowing that she could not be seen from the ground floor.

From above the bright hall presented a picture of soft hangings, bright carpets and flowers. The low murmur of voices reached the girl, and, craning her neck, she saw Peter and the woman she knew as Mrs Mortimer deep in conversation outside the door of the room to which she had been taken on her first arrival.

She could not hear what was being said. The two were speaking in a low tone, although there was a considerable amount of urgency in the timbre of their voices.

As she looked down at the plump, businesslike little figure of the woman, Mary received once again the impression which she had formed of her before. Although friendly, she seemed loth to associate herself with the reality of the business in hand. She shrugged her shoulders, turned her head away, looked vague and noncommittal.

It was Peter who seemed so intense. Mary caught the word "must" and again "recognized me."

The doorbell brought the conversation to a close. Peter stepped back into the shadow of the curtain as the manservant hurried down the hall to answer the door. Mary felt the current of cold air from the street as the door flung wide, and the next moment she saw Peter hurry forward with an exclamation which sounded like the single word "Tollesbury."

The actual doorway was hidden from her by the angle of the stairs, but although she could not see the newcomer she heard his voice raised pleasantly.

"Hallo! Did she come safely?"

And then, at what must have been a warning gesture from Peter, the voice was lowered, and only an indistinct rumble came to her from the hidden corner.

Mary drew back. She had heard the voice and recognized it. This recognition made the whole business more incomprehensible even than before, for the man who had been addressed as Tollesbury was the mysterious Mr Jones who was so anxious to get her out of the country, and what possible danger her presence in England could be to that distinguished financial magnate was more than Mary could imagine.

She was still hanging over the rail when a hand on her shoulder startled her, and she swung round to find herself looking into the face of a quietly dressed lady's maid. The woman stared at her suspiciously.

"Your dinner's waiting for you in your room, miss," she said. "I see you've found a dressing gown. Will you come this way, please? I'll attend to your wet clothes afterwards."

Mary followed her up the staircase to a little room at the top of the house. It was quiet and comfortable, and there was a very welcome meal awaiting her, but afterwards, when she peeped out onto the upper landing, she found that although her door was unlocked there was another maid on guard at the head of the stairs. This, too, was an elderly woman, who stared at her inquisitively and asked her very pointedly if there was anything she wanted, and on being told that there was nothing suggested firmly that she should go to bed and try to sleep.

16

MONEY TALKS

Y ou're sure she recognized you?"

The man whom Mary knew as Mr Jones and who was in actual fact Lord Tollesbury, President of Cosmos Limited and many other big concerns, walked slowly up and down the library of his sister's house. He paused to put the question, swinging round upon the younger man who sat before the desk in the centre of the room, his chin resting on his hands.

Peter Muir-David looked up.

"Oh yes," he said quietly. "She recognized me. She recognized me then, and she recognized me this morning. How could she help it?"

Lord Tollesbury shrugged his shoulders.

"Oh well, it doesn't matter," he said. "I've fixed up everything most satisfactorily as far as she's concerned. She'll play her part. I think she's very satisfied, but I never met anyone so cautious in my life. I meant to get here earlier, but I relied upon Edith to warn you, and of course she didn't realize that you would go straight upstairs to see Evelyn. I went along to my club to change."

He brushed a speck of dust off the sleeve of his tail coat as he spoke.

Peter nodded absently. He did not seem to have heard. There was an introspective expression in his eyes, and his face looked more drawn than ever. The older man stood regarding him contemplatively for some little time. At last his eyes twinkled, and an amused smile flickered for an instant over his cadaverous face.

"Rather an awkward moment, I imagine," he said. "Did you have any difficulty explaining to Evelyn?"

"No," said Peter slowly. "Mary pretended she didn't know me."

"Really?" Lord Tollesbury raised his eyebrows. "That was rather odd, wasn't it? She's a much more conscientious young woman that I dreamed, unless—I say, my boy, you are sure we're not on a wild-goose chase, running away from a bogey which isn't there? She *does* recognize you?"

"Oh yes," said Peter wearily. "I told you, she knew me all right, just as I knew her. Both of us look a little the worse for wear, but we knew each other."

Lord Tollesbury, who was in the act of lighting a cigarette, paused, the match half raised to his mouth. He let it burn down, threw it away and lit another one before he spoke, and all the time his sharp, dark eyes were fixed upon the younger man's face.

"Look here, Muir-David," he said, "I know you're your father's son and I trust you, but young men do do ridiculous things where young women are concerned. Did you ever confide in that girl?"

Peter sat up stiffly, his face pale and his eyes angry.

"No," he said. "No sir, I didn't. Sometimes I wish I had. Sometimes I wish—"

He broke off and relapsed into his original position, his head resting heavily on his hands.

The older man sat down in one of the deep armchairs before

the fire and smoked for some moments in thoughtful silence. He was evidently waiting for Peter to go on, but when the young man showed no signs of doing so Tollesbury began to speak.

"Let me see," he began, and his voice was studiously casual, "you have been engaged to my niece Evelyn ever since you were twenty-one. Not actually engaged," he corrected himself as Peter looked up, "but there has been an understanding between your family and hers for the last seven years that a marriage would be advantageous. Isn't that so? I've always understood it was to take place when Evelyn was twenty-four—this spring, in fact. Is that true?"

"Yes," said Peter heavily. "My father made the arrangement before he died."

Lord Tollesbury nodded. "I often wonder whether these arrangements are a good idea," he said. "They certainly help to conserve family fortunes, and I know they're very common among moneyed people. I think on the whole," he went on judicially, "that I approve. You'd be throwing yourself away, my boy. Mary Coleridge is a nice girl, a shrewd girl—I shouldn't mind having her working for me—but she's penniless, and I really think you'd be well advised to maintain the present state of affairs. It's much less expensive in the long run."

The young man stared at him. He was slowly growing crimson.

"There's another consideration," Peter said stiffly, "and I'm afraid that's the one that's bothering me. When one's been engaged to a woman for seven years—" He broke off expressively, and the older man laughed.

"My dear Peter, quite a Galahad in your own way, aren't you!" he said. "Don't misunderstand me, my boy; I appreciate it. And I think, too," he went on, a note of sternness creeping into the smooth, half-frivolous tone, "that you would be very unwise indeed to make—er—any drastic change in your private affairs.

After all, she has a powerful family, of which I am afraid I must point out I am a part."

Peter met his eyes steadily. "Yes," he said. "I was thinking of that."

"Oh well, now we understand one another," Lord Tollesbury seemed relieved. "Let me try to cheer you up a little. Whereas Evelyn is a gentle, sheltered little girl of the type you know and understand, I think you may have made a serious mistake about the girl Coleridge. She's no tender little flower, believe me. I never had a more interesting interview with anyone in my life. She played me like an old hand, took the way that was most advantageous to her but didn't grant me an inch. She made no admissions at all. Her story to Lissen was highly coloured but quite ingenious, and might at a stretch have served as an excuse for her consenting to the interview if she wanted to get out of the arrangement afterwards."

Peter thrust his hands through his hair.

"We're all so subtle," he said helplessly. "We're all so clever. Don't you think, sir, that we may be sometimes a little too—too clever by half? I'd have staked my life on it that that girl was as straightforward as a child."

"Part of her cleverness," said Tollesbury airily. "Good heavens, my boy, d'you think she'd have agreed to the proposition if there hadn't been something in it?"

"You're sure her story wasn't true?" Peter spoke nervously, a wavering hope in his voice. "You're sure she wasn't being perfectly innocent? You're sure what you thought was subtlety wasn't ignorance?"

Lord Tollesbury's dark face took on a deeper hue.

"My dear Peter," he said stiffly, "I admit that young men often understand young women so much better than their elders, but I would like to point out that I'm not a complete fool. I've had some experience in business affairs and—"

"Oh don't!" Peter spread out his hands helplessly. "I'm sorry, sir. You must forgive me, but I got to know the girl quite well, and, as I told you when I reported her recognition of me this morning, I heard the story of her life, and the facts I told Lissen seem to have been true. She never struck me as being shrewd or subtle, that's all."

"Yes, yes, she's a very charming little thing," said the older man, as though an entirely different question had been asked him. "Quite the type who might wreck a promising young man's career, especially if she had some serious hold over him. You leave this to me, you young idiot," he went on with an entire change of tone. "You made love to her, I suppose?"

"No," said Peter. "No, never."

"Thoughtful of you. Still, I believe you. Otherwise we might have a much more difficult business on our hands."

"You've got her all wrong," said Peter. "She—"

Lord Tollesbury sprang to his feet. "Peter Muir-David," he said, "did you or you not see that girl in the De Liane house? Did Lessen follow her from the De Liane flat this afternoon or did he not? Did she see him and slip away from the De Lianes and lead him on a wild-goose chase on foot through London until he picked her up well out of their sight?"

Peter sighed. "You've told me so, and therefore I suppose it's true," he said unhappily. "I suppose what you say about the De Lianes is true."

Lord Tollesbury laughed. "I haven't begun to tell you about the De Lianes, mother and son," he said. "Life's too short. I would rather place myself at the mercy of all the blackmailers in the world combined than grant that old woman half an inch. However, we've scotched them, or we shall have done when we can get the girl out of the country. If they haven't got her as a witness they can do nothing. She's the only person, you see, who knows that young Mr Peter Muir, employee in that dangerous new concern, Holly and Holly, Limited, makers of synthetic mica, is Sir Peter Muir-David, the bright young man behind the scenes at Cosmos Mines. In other words, my dear Peter, that girl is the only person whose testimony could set the stock markets tumbling about our ears, the only person who could prove that you were a spy sent out by one great firm to facilitate its dealings with a dangerous rival. Need I be more explicit? Or must I tell you just how much we should lose, what my own position would be, or what would happen to your own and your father's fortune?"

Peter stood up resolutely. "I've done it," he said. "I'm sorry I did it, but I've done it and there's no help for it. If I'd known at the beginning, when you put up this—this fantastic scheme to me, what it was going to lead to, I never would have done it, even though Holly's had ruined us."

"Then somebody else would have done it," said Lord Tollesbury easily. "I don't understand you, Peter. I've always thought you were one of the most promising of my younger men, but it seems to me you're liable to get hysterical. What's the matter, man? You're behaving as though you're in love."

Peter did not answer. He stood looking straight in front of him, and there was tragedy and weakness and despair in his face.

Lord Tollesbury eyed him. "'... For he had great possessions,'" he quoted softly. "Don't be silly. These things do happen, I know. They upset one. One's private affairs are always butting in and trying to spoil one's chances in the great game."

He paused and, when the younger man did not speak, went over to him and spoke to him with deep sincerity, all the more startling because of the emptiness of his creed.

"Money, my boy," he said. "It's a hard master but a great master. You've got to serve it utterly with everything there is in you. You've got to make sacrifices for it, and you've got to face dangers for it, but in the end it repays you. It gives you power, the one thing of real value in the world."

Peter looked at him steadily. "I—I wonder," he said, and his voice was none too steady.

Lord Tollesbury turned his back upon him and walked over to the fire again.

"Everything else passes," he said. "I've been in love myself in my time, deliriously in love, but do you know, at the moment I have forgotten her name. Well then, this is the situation. While the De Lianes have that girl on their side they are in a position either to ruin us or to blackmail us. Knowing them, I think they would choose the latter. While we have the girl they can do nothing. We can laugh at them. They might try to get other witnesses, but she's the only dangerous one. You may have to disappear yourself for a month or two. She'll go to Canada with Edith, and we shall carry out our obligations to her implicitly. It'll be well worth our while. That's that. Now I think we'll go on to the theatre, where those two girls are waiting for us so impatiently. Are you coming?"

Peter nodded. He walked with heavy footsteps. His eyes were dull, and his face was drawn.

Lord Tollesbury glanced at him sharply. "I should avoid this house until Friday," he said, and in his mouth the words were a command.

"I thought I might just have a word with her," Peter began. "I didn't want her to think—"

"What does it matter what she thinks? Forget her. You are not to see her. Put her clean out of your mind. She's just one of those little sacrifices one has to make in the course of a great career. Understand?"

For an instant a light of rebellion crept into the younger man's eyes, and it seemed as though he were about to make a stand, a protest against the system which was crushing him, but before the expression in the other man's face his spirit weakened and his fire died.

"Understand?" repeated Lord Tollesbury.

"Yes," said Peter, and followed him miserably from the room.

17

YOU WON'T FORGET ME

I think you look very nice."

There was begrudging admiration and a hint of wistfulness in Evelyn Mortimer's voice as she looked at the girl in the plain grey tweed suit which had just come from an Oxford Street store.

"It fits perfectly," she went on, walking round Mary. "You're very lucky to be exactly stock size. You didn't mind not coming to choose, did you? Uncle—I mean Mother thought there was no point in your going out of the house until you sail tomorrow."

"Oh no, I didn't mind," said Mary absently. "I think it's very kind of you to get such pretty things."

The two girls were in the little bedroom, which had been growing more and more like a prison to the younger girl for the past three days. On the floor stood a new cabin trunk, and in it were already packed the few things which Mary needed for her voyage to the New World.

Having ascertained that the suit fitted, Mary changed into a navy-blue house frock which had come with the other things and began to pack the suit into the trunk.

Evelyn Mortimer lingered. Great pains had been taken with her own clothes, but she made a very insignificant figure beside Mary in the plain, almost school-girlish frock. In spite of her worries, the rest had done the girl good. Her red-gold hair shone, her cream skin had lost its pallor, and although her eyes were still dark and anxious their original beauty was not altogether eclipsed.

"Do you want to go to Canada?" Evelyn Mortimer sat down on the edge of the bed to watch Mary pack.

"Yes." There was no hesitation in Mary's reply. Her new-found self-reliance warned her to be very careful to whom she spoke about her affairs. She had no idea how much Evelyn knew about the business, or indeed how much of the business there was to know.

"Perhaps you're going out there to get married?"

"No," said Mary and then, anxious not to sound sullen, added in a more conversational tone, "No, I'm not."

"Are you engaged to anyone over here?"

"No."

"Are you in love?"

"No."

"You're wearing an engagement ring ..."

Mary looked down at the little round of diamonds on her finger and shivered in spite of herself. She felt suddenly very much older than this sullen, petulant child at her side and was glad that she had taken off the wedding ring which Richard had bought her and had hidden it in her pocket.

She wondered if it was still there now that her clothes had been dried and made a mental note to look.

But although she was so obviously not anxious for conversation, Evelyn Mortimer was clearly eager to talk.

"I'm going to be married to Peter in the spring. We've been engaged for seven years. Peter told me you looked like somebody he knew once, but he wouldn't tell me who she was. You thought you'd seen him before, didn't you?"

"No," said Mary. She was naturally averse to lying and wished the girl would leave the subject. All the same she was curious about Peter. "Are you—are you very fond of him?" she asked.

"Oh, as much as one ever is, you know." The young voice sounded inexpressibly bored, and Mary was shocked. "It's all been arranged for years that we should marry. He's very rich and so am I—or rather, I shall be. Money's terribly important, don't you think?"

Mary did not answer. So that's how it was then. She understood. She found herself feeling very sorry for Peter.

"It'll be fun when I get married," the other went on. "I shall go everywhere and know everybody, and I shall have a title. I'm quite looking forward to it. When Mother comes back we're going to start getting my trousseau."

"Has Mr—I mean Sir Peter, been here lately?" Mary tried to make the question sound disinterested.

"No. Sometimes I don't see him for ages. He's so busy, you see. Uncle says he's going to be one of the richest men in the world before he dies. It's terribly thrilling, don't you think?"

"Is it?" said Mary. "Yes, I suppose so."

Evidently the girl found her very dull, for presently she rose to her feet and wandered over to the doorway.

"I brought the papers up. I don't know if you're interested," she said: "I can't read 'em myself."

She went out, and Mary finished her packing.

The pile of newspapers lay upon the bed, and when she had finished folding her clothes into the trunk she turned them over idly. *The Times* lay under the rest of the bundle. It was unopened, and Mary, glancing at it casually, caught sight of something in the personal column which fastened her attention at once. The printed words stood out from the page vividly, as though they had been printed in blacker type than the rest.

"Hallo Angel," she read, and beside it, in smaller type, *"Mary, I am heartbroken. Never realized before what it was like to fall in love. At my wits' end. Have a little pity. Your husband, Richard."*

She never doubted for an instant but that the message was for her, and the appeal came startlingly, as though it had been made in words. To her astonishment she found that she was breathless and that her heart was thumping painfully in her side. She sat down, the paper in her hands, and as she looked at it the message faded and she saw instead Richard de Liane's face as vividly as if he were before her.

She saw him as she had first seen him, lying in the great bed, his skin brown against the white linen, the two deep creases in his cheeks, and his blue eyes dancing with amusement as he smiled up at her impudently.

She threw the paper down. She was trembling and suddenly terribly afraid. All her new calm deserted her. The experience had been so real, and there was his message, clear and concrete, for her to read again and again.

That was the first time it had ever dawned upon her that the thing which she had most to fear was herself.

For some little time she sat struggling with an inclination to reread the message and suddenly gave way to it.

"Never realized before what it was like to fall in love."

The sentence stood out from the others, and for a minute or two she allowed herself to bask in the warm, satisfying feeling, the strange contentment which it gave her, but immediately afterwards her brain rebuked her. Richard de Liane had probably not inserted that advertisement, or if he had it was done at the instigation of his mother.

Once again in her mind Mary heard that terrible gentle voice and saw that placid face with the gentle mouth from which such cruel words could come.

She tore the sheet of paper into small pieces and burned them in the grate, and forced herself to forget the odd experience of a minute or two before when her heart had bounded so unaccountably and she had experienced that strange feeling of content.

When Mrs Mortimer's maid came up to bring her some tea she was placidly looking over her new clothes.

The following morning it was raining when the chauffeur and the butler between them carried Mary's trunk down to the waiting Daimler and Mary climbed in beside Mrs Mortimer. It was early, and as yet the streets were empty of heavy traffic.

Throughout the journey to the station the woman was very silent. She sat huddled in the car, wrapped up in a big mink coat, and Mary, very small and young looking in her new grey travelling coat, sat quietly by her side. So far she had stuck resolutely to her purpose not to think of Richard de Liane. Peter she felt she understood, and she was sorry for him, but not for herself where he was concerned.

As they neared Euston Mrs Mortimer peered at her from among her furs.

"I hope you're a good sailor, my child," she said. "I'm not. I do dread these journeys so. Evelyn was going to see us off, but I told her not to. It's so terribly early. Lean back, dear. There's no need to look out of the window." The last words were spoken petulantly, and Mary turned away from the window obediently.

When they arrived at the station the old-fashioned courtyard was crowded with cars and an excited throng of porters. Mrs Mortimer proved to be a fussy, excitable traveller, and Mary had her mind fully occupied with the business of getting the luggage onto the train, and it occurred to her then that whatever ulterior motive the woman might have had in engaging her as a companion she certainly needed someone to look after her and her belongings.

"Mary, you have your tickets and your passport, haven't you?

I gave them to you yesterday. You did remember them?" ...
"Mary, have you seen my small brown handbag? —the crocodile
one?" ... "Mary, I believe there's another suitcase."

It seemed impossible that any woman could lose so many
things, and any emotions which Mary might have experienced
on leaving her country were temporarily forgotten in the
excitement of managing her volatile employer.

At last they climbed into their reserved seats, and their hand
luggage was duly stowed about the carriage. They had it to
themselves, and Mrs Mortimer was loudly relieved, since, as she
said, the journey to Liverpool was a long one.

They were still considerably early and, discovering that she
had at least fifteen minutes to spare, Mrs Mortimer could not be
content to stay placidly where she was.

"I'm just going down to the bookstall," she said, "and I've just
thought of something I must tell the chauffeur. He won't have
gone yet. Just stay where you are. You *have* got your passport,
haven't you?"

"Yes," said Mary wearily and leaned back in her seat, idly
watching the excited throngs of passengers and their attendant
porters bustling up and down the platform.

She sat quite still for five minutes, keeping her thoughts reli-
giously upon the journey ahead of her and the possibilities of
life in the new land. She dared not think of what had passed.
That was gone, she told herself resolutely. In a few days now she
would be free.

She was still trying to concentrate on the journey when she
heard her own name in the corridor.

"Miss Mary Coleridge in here?" said a voice a little higher up
the train. "Miss Mary Coleridge? Miss Mary Coleridge?"

She rose to her feet and went to the door of the carriage. A
man in chauffeur's uniform looked down at her.

"Miss Mary Coleridge?" he enquired.

"Yes. What is it?"

"Mrs Mortimer said, would you come along for a moment? She's been taken queer. Would you know her car if you saw it? It's nothing to worry about, lady, but she was running out across the courtyard to find her man when a taxicab—"

He broke off, seeing Mary's horrified face.

"It's all right," he said kindly. "It's shaken her up a bit, that's all. Can you come? The train doesn't go for another seven minutes."

Mary was already out of the train and hurrying down the platform. The man strode at her side, pouring reassurances into her ear.

When they came out into the courtyard the crowd of cars seemed, if anything, thicker than ever, and, taking her arm, he steered her among them.

"There she is," he said. "Is that her own chauffeur with her?"

Mary caught sight of the back of a Daimler car standing against the curb with its door open. Standing on the pavement, his legs visible, was another chauffeur.

Mary ran forward. As she came level with the car the man's grip on her arm tightened, and with a sudden movement he thrust her into the darkness within.

At the same moment, it seemed, the door slammed behind her and the car slid away from the curb.

Breathless from shock and with cold terror rising in her heart, Mary scrambled up from her knees and as she did so touched the skirt of a stiff silk gown.

In the darkness beside her she heard a little sigh. It was the ghost of a sound, but one that sent the blood drumming in her ears and forced her heart into her throat. There was only one person in the world who sighed quite like that.

"Mary, *my dear!*" said Eva de Liane.

The physical shock of her sudden capture temporarily stunned the girl. The whole thing had happened so quickly. Never for an instant had she doubted the integrity of the stolid, honest-looking chauffeur who had seemed so anxious not to alarm her about her employer's accident. He had conveyed that Mrs Mortimer had been knocked down by a taxicab without actually saying so, and his reticence had alarmed Mary much more than any bald statement of fact could have done, so that the sudden kidnapping had come completely unexpectedly.

As she crouched on the soft skin rug at the bottom of the car only one thing was real to her, one terrible, overwhelming fact: Mrs de Liane had captured her again. Not the Mrs de Liane of the last few days, a remote, half-shadowy figure, but Mrs de Liane herself, vital and terrifying.

Meanwhile the car had swung out of the station and, finding a comparatively deserted path, was speeding down the Euston Road.

After her first shock anger took possession of the girl.

"Let me go," she said passionately. "Let me go! Stop the car!"

She made an effort to scramble to her feet and reached for the curtained window, but her movement was anticipated. A strong hand came out of the darkness, catching her arm and forcing her down upon the seat.

"Don't be a darn fool," said a voice in her ear. "You've made quite enough trouble already. Keep quiet, for God's sake."

It was Edmund Beron. Even before she heard the voice she recognized the strong grip on her arm. She peered through the gloom and saw them sitting there, one on either side of her, Mrs de Liane and her eldest son.

The only light which entered the tonneau came from the front of the car, where she could just see through the windscreen the rows of rain-soaked houses rushing by. It was a different car from the Daimler the De Lianes usually used, but the chauffeur was the same. Mary recognized his square, stolid back and the short iron-grey hair showing beneath his peaked cap.

The windows were curtained with old-fashioned fringed

hangings which conveyed rather a sense of cosiness than an attempt at secrecy to any observer on the pavement.

Mary bided her time, and when the car slowed down to take the turn which would lead eventually on to the Great North Road she screamed. She did so deliberately, making as much noise as she possibly could. She had just time to see the chauffeur wince and to realize that he had trodden on the accelerator when a handkerchief was thrust over her face with a force which warned her that, struggle how she would, she was helpless.

She tried to grip the hand which was suffocating her, while she kicked and fought violently in the back of the car. The pressure was loosened for a moment, and in that instant she bit through the handkerchief into the hand that held it. There was an exclamation of pain, and the next instant something happened which she was never to forget or to forgive.

A man's fist crashed down upon her jaw with a savage brutality behind the blow and almost stunned her. The blood sang in her ears. She felt sick and above all furious. Through the mists which enveloped her she heard Mrs de Liane's quiet, reproving voice.

"My dear Edmund, you really shouldn't have done that. Poor little thing! You don't want to disfigure her." And then, turning to Mary: "Sit still, dear. You'll get hurt, you know, if you're silly."

Mary put up a hand to touch her bruised chin. Her lip was bleeding where it had been forced against her teeth, and the salty taste nauseated her.

Edmund Beron thrust one arm round her, gripping her further arm, while with the other he held the wrist nearest him.

"I hope that's taught you something," he said savagely. "You dirty, double-crossing little rat! We want a complete explanation from you, and we want the truth. Don't you forget it!"

"Edmund! Edmund!" Mrs de Liane's voice had a little tremor of laughter in its gentle depths. "My dear boy, you sound quite angry. Mary's only frightened. I'm sure she's not a fool. On the contrary she's quite a clever little girl. She simply doesn't quite realize yet where her real interest lies. Don't sit so tensely, dear," she continued, shooting the girl a little sideways glance that revealed the flash of her bright eyes in the gloom. "There's nothing to be frightened of if only you keep still."

There is something about physical violence which is more shocking to a girl of Mary's temperament than anything else in the world. It was not the actual pain, although that was considerable; but the outrage of the blow, the appalling quality of its complete viciousness, made her feel utterly helpless. She was too overcome even to cry, and sat there staring in front of her like one in a stupor, her mind blank, her emotions suffocating her.

The rain, which seemed to have been continuous ever since she had first set out on her journey to Heronhoe at the beginning of the nightmare experience, was still pouring down upon the broad London streets. She could hear the water beneath the car wheels and the vicious rattle of the heavy drops upon the roof. The windscreen was obscured save for the half-circular oasis made by the slowly moving wiper.

The silence lasted a considerable time until at last it was broken by Beron again.

"No sign of Richard," he said.

It was a curious remark in the circumstances, and it penetrated the clouds which were enveloping Mary and raised a question in her mind. Mrs de Liane laughed.

"Did you think there would be?" she said. "I told you from the very beginning, Edmund, that was quite absurd."

The man murmured something Mary could not catch, and the old lady went on placidly, smoothing the folds of her silk gown which peeped out from between the skirts of her fur coat.

"I don't think this is the time to discuss Richard," she said pointedly, and again Beron was silent.

Richard ... The name had a welcome sound to the bewildered girl in spite of everything. Richard would never have struck her. She had no reason for such a belief, but in her heart she knew it was true. Richard de Liane and Edmund Beron were half brothers, but they were two very different men.

They drove for some little time without further conversation. The rain grew very much finer as they left the city, and by the time they were on the wide highway to the north the windscreen was nearly clear.

Mrs de Liane looked down at the girl.

"Now, my dear," she said, "we have a nice long drive in front of us. Suppose you tell us where you've been? Or is your mouth too sore to speak? Poor child! Edmund was very rough. He always was as a little boy. All the same, you shouldn't have annoyed him. The great thing in life, Mary, is to be reasonable. Take the straightforward path. It always pays in the end. Now, my dear, I've got my little daughter back, and I'm not going to let her go again. Where have you been?"

"How—how did you find me?" Mary hardly recognized her own voice. It was hoarse and shaking, and the swollen state of her lower lip distorted the words.

Mrs de Liane chuckled. "I don't see why I should tell you," she said. "Still, it may as well be a warning to you. Did you know that there were such things as shipping lists, and that people who go to catch boats nearly always go by the specified boat train? Travelling under your own name, my dear ... amazingly indiscreet! Or was it the passport difficulty? I'm only thankful I was in time."

Mary said nothing. Mrs de Liane sighed.

"It's very trying for us all, my dear," she said. "Edmund's nerves are overwrought, or he would never have forgotten himself as he did just now. Don't be obstinate. Tell the truth as quietly and intelligently as you can. Where have you been? How did you get the money for your passage? Whom have you been talking to?"

The girl stared in front of her, her eyes unwontedly dark, her lips closed. Beron's grip upon her arm and wrist tightened until it hurt her.

"Talk, damn you!" he said. "Talk or I'll make you."

"Edmund, Edmund ... really!" Mrs de Liane's amusement seemed to be increasing. "That is *not* the way. Mary is a dear girl ... my dear little daughter. But she mustn't be obstinate."

She bent forward as she spoke, and Mary looked into her face. There was more light now that the weather was clearing, and she could see the gentle features plainly. It was a terible face, those bright dancing eyes, the gentle mouth, and smooth, porcelainlike contours, all controlled or inhabited, as it were, by a spirit indefinably and indescribably malicious.

"She mustn't be obstinate," she repeated. "She's not fool enough to make either of us angry with her. We've been so worried," she continued gently. "You had no money, dear. A pretty girl alone in London with no money on a wet and cold winter's night ... ! Dear child, anything could have happened to you! Didn't you realize that?"

"Yes," said Mary grimly.

"What did happen?" It was Beron who spoke. His fingers were hurting her arm, and she moved uneasily. "Who have you been talking to? What did you tell them?"

"I think you ought to tell us, dear." Mrs de Liane's placid voice contrasted oddly with the nervous tension in the man's.

Mary hesitated. It was obviously necessary to say something if she was going to protect herself from another exhibition of brutality like the last. She began to speak with difficulty.

"I—I met an old friend of my father's. I told him my troubles, and he took me to his sister's house and lent me the money to get to Canada."

"What was the name of the man?"

Beron spoke roughly, and she could feel him trembling at her side.

"I—I won't tell you. I'll never tell you."

She turned away from him, shrinking back as though she feared another blow.

To her complete astonishment, Mrs de Liane appeared to accept her explanation.

"Oh well then, no harm's done," she said. "That's all we wanted to know. Your father's friend, whoever he is, doesn't know where you are now, and it's most unlikely that he'll find you. And even if he does, we shall be very pleased to see him."

"If you think …" Edmund Beron began, but his mother's quiet voice silenced him.

"I believe implicitly what Mary tells me," she said. "I've never had any reason to think that she is a liar."

"How you can say that after—"

"That will do, Edmund. How pleasant it is now that the weather's cleared up, isn't it?"

The abrupt change in the subject silenced the man, but his grip upon the girl did not relax.

Meanwhile the car sped on down the road and presently turned off into a byway, where it splashed on through a couple of villages, following the winding road over a strip of common to a network of lanes beyond.

Beron, who had looked up sharply when the car had turned off the main road, leant forward to follow the route, and as the car turned once again he sat back with a muttered exclamation. Mrs de Liane answered his unspoken question.

"I thought it best to go the back way," she said. "After all, dear Mary has already proved to us that she is a little hysterical. I think I was justified."

"All the same I don't see why we should go *this* way." There was a peculiar emphasis on the word which Mary noted without being actually aware of it. Mrs de Liane's next remark caught her attention.

"You're so squeamish, Edmund. After all, there's no reason why we should meet."

"All right—all right." He silenced her roughly, and the old lady answered him with some asperity.

"Your nerves are in a shocking state, Edmund," she said. "You don't get enough sleep."

"Can *you* sleep?" The question seemed to be dragged out of him, and Mary caught an inkling of the strain under which he was labouring.

"I always sleep," said Mrs de Liane, and leant back among the leather cushions as though she intended to do so at that particular moment.

The car swept on, carrying them through a deserted strip of country until Mary realized with a shudder that they had not passed a dwelling for nearly twenty minutes.

The man's appearance on the road, therefore, came as a little surprise to her. She saw him slouching along the grass verge fifty yards up the deserted lane.

Beron caught sight of him at the same moment. The girl felt him stiffen at her side and saw him lean forward.

"It's—Whybrow!" he said. "I'll tell the man to drive on, shall I?"

There was no immediate reply from Mrs de Liane. She too was bending forward, peering through the double thickness of glass at the slouching figure in the ragged coat and dilapidated cap who was approaching them so rapidly.

As they watched, the man in the road recognized either the approaching car or its driver, for he stepped out into the fairway and held up his hand.

"Drive on—drive on!" said Beron excitedly.

Mrs de Liane waved him silent. Taking the speaking tube from its holder at her side, she spoke into it:

176

"I think you had better stop, Walker. Be ready to drive on immediately."

"With the girl here?" Beron's question was partly a reproach.

His mother sighed. "Always so impetuous, Edmund," she said. "Why shouldn't the poor man speak to us if he wants to?"

As the car slowed down to a stop she let down the window at her side and, pushing back the curtain, peered out. Over her shoulder Mary caught a glimpse of a grim red face peering up at the woman. The man was a little over forty, with a raw skin, narrow, red-rimmed eyes, and a ragged mouth which at the moment was twisted into a leer of recognition.

"You've come at last, have you?" he said, and there was a knowing familiarity in his tone which was surprising.

"I'm passing this way," said Mrs de Liane quietly. "I can't go up and see your wife now, but tell her she will receive full instructions from me any day this week."

"Aren't we high and mighty!" said the man contemptuously. "I tell you things aren't going to be so easy. We've had enquiries from the school. We shall be having inspectors round any day now. The kid's over age, you know, and he ought to go to school. He's strong enough ... just."

There was a dreadful inference in the pause before the last word. Mary heard it and shuddered.

"Jean's not my child—anybody can see that," the man continued, "and if I'm to say he is there'll be a lot of nosy-parkers asking questions. We don't want that, do we? Eh, lady?"

"You keep a civil tongue in your head," said Beron from the darkness of the car. "You've heard what Mrs de Liane says. You'll get instructions."

"Oh, you're there, are you, sir?" The bully's tone was markedly more respectful. "I didn't see you."

"So I observed," said Beron drily.

The stranger was trying to peer into the car, and Mrs de Liane deliberately obscured his view.

"Your wife will hear from me," she said in her sweet, precise voice. "And if it's a question of another shilling or two ..."

"Shilling or two?" The man's voice rose in a whine. "Think of the risk, lady. Besides, he's getting bigger. He eats more. He's naughty, too. We keep 'im in his place, but it's not easy."

"I rely upon you to be strict." Mrs de Liane's voice was gentle, but Mary had a vision of the little boy who was just old enough to go to school and who was so naughty that this brute with the red face and ragged mouth had to be told to be strict.

"Your wife shall have extra money, but I rely upon you to manage the boy."

A project which had been lurking in the back of Mary's mind ever since the car pulled up suddenly presented itself to her, and, at the risk of another blow from Beron she put it into execution. With a sudden thrust she threw herself against the old woman, pushing her out of the way.

"I am Mary Coleridge, being taken by Mrs de Liane to Baron's Tye, Heronhoe," she shouted. "You'll be rewarded if you tell Lord Tollesbury."

Beron had dragged her back, and the chauffeur had let in the clutch practically before the last word was out of her mouth. The car leapt forward, and she crouched back, waiting for the attack which did not come. Instead there was a soft laugh at her side, and Mrs de Liane, in a voice in which satisfaction and triumph were blended, said quietly, "Lord Tollesbury, is it, Mary? That's very interesting. Very interesting indeed. Just exactly what I wanted to know."

18

CONFERENCE

Y es, yes, very unfortunate. Very unfortunate indeed. But not your fault, Edith. Don't get hysterical."

The brusqueness of Lord Tollesbury's tone belied his words, and Mrs Mortimer, sitting in one of the leather armchairs in the office in which Mary had had her interview with him only a few days before, wiped her eyes.

"It happened in a flash," she said. "I saw her going through the booking hall with a man in chauffeur's uniform. When I shouted she didn't hear me, and I reached the pavement in time to see him push her into a car, which drove off at great speed. Before I could catch up with him through the crush he had disappeared. There were so many men in chauffeur's uniform," she added lamely.

Lord Tollesbury passed his hand over his sparse grey hair and glanced across the room to where Peter, pale and expressionless, stood with his hands in his pockets looking helplessly at the woman.

With his chief's eyes upon him the young man appeared to make a violent effort to grasp the details of the situation.

"When you say 'thrust' ..." he said. "Did she go unwillingly?"

"Oh yes. I'm sure of it." Mrs Mortimer blinked at him. "It was most extraordinary. When I saw her in the booking hall she was talking earnestly to the man. She looked worried and sort of excited, and he was grave too. But when they reached the car he seemed to gather up his strength and push her in, if you see what I mean. There was no pause for conversation or anything like that, but the door slammed behind her and the car moved off at once. It looked almost like a kidnapping."

There was a long silence after she had spoken, and after a pause she tried to amplify her story.

"I didn't like to go to the police. I didn't know what to do. So I came straight to you."

"Yes yes, quite right, Edith, quite right." Lord Tollesbury spoke absently, but his cadaverous face wore an expression of acute anxiety. "Did you get the number of the car?"

The woman looked at him pathetically. "No, it was wet, and I couldn't really see. There was mud all over it. It was GG something, I think."

"That's Scotland. That doesn't help us much. Oh well, all right, Edith. You go along home and wait. I'm sorry your trip has been postponed like this but—"

"Oh, Miles, I'm so sorry!" Her voice broke, and he went over to her, putting his arm round her and leading her gently towards the door.

"There there, my dear," he said. "There there. It can't he helped." He patted her hand, allowed her to peck his cheek and dismissed her.

When she had gone he closed the door and sighed heavily.

"Well, Muir-David," he said, "any ideas?"

Peter seemed to force himself to speak.

"If she was kidnapped," he said, "and by the De Lianes, it would look—"

"If! If! There're too many ifs." The words broke from the older man.

180

"I never thought she was a liar," said Peter doggedly, "and if—"

Lord Tollesbury met his eyes. "There's something in that," he said. "You mean her story may be true?"

He touched a bell under his desk and spoke abruptly to the secretary who answered it.

"Send Lissen."

George Lissen, stolid as ever, came into the room and stood looking at his master woodenly.

"Can you remember that girl's story? You know what I'm talking about."

Mr Lissen bowed his head in courteous acquiescence.

"I can remember some of it, my lord."

"What was it?"

The two men pieced together the fragments of Mary's confession that Lissen could remember. Peter listened to the revelations, his round eyes hard and startled.

"Married to a dying man ... Impersonation of absent cousin ... Forced to become a crook ..."

Lord Tollesbury threw up his hands. "It sounds like the ravings of a lunatic. We're doing no good, Peter. We're doing no good at all."

The young man was silent. There were beads of sweat upon his forehead.

"If it were true," he said half under his breath, "if it were true ..."

Lord Tollesbury looked at him sharply. "A case against them, you mean? That's almost too much to hope for. That De Liane woman has always managed to keep just on the right side of the law. She'd hardly fall down in her old age unless—"

He broke off.

"Unless—?" repeated Peter enquiringly.

"Unless the price was a very great one indeed," said the older man slowly. "Think, Lissen, think! Did Miss Coleridge tell you the name of the girl she's supposed to be impersonating?"

George Lissen made an effort to cast his mind back over the interview he had had with the girl in the tea shop.

"I didn't pay much attention to it," he murmured apologetically. "It seemed such a wild story. I think she did mention a name. Would it be Mason? Marie-Elizabeth Mason?"

"It's hardly a name you'd invent," said his employer, and, pressing the bell again, he summoned a sallow young man in horn-rimmed spectacles. "Denver," he said, "I want you to check up on something for me. Is there an heiress, a woman of considerable fortune, called Mason?"

Leslie Denver, who was one of those invaluable human encyclopedias who are often employed in big City offices solely because of their remarkable powers of assimilating facts, blinked behind his spectacles.

"Yes, I think there is, sir," he said. "I read something about her in the unofficial financial sheet only the other day. I fancy I made a note of it—in fact I'm certain of it. I'll just go and look it up, sir."

He hurried out of the room, and Tollesbury looked after him, a faint smile upon his thin lips.

"Denver has a nose for money," he said. "It's a peculiar gift. Ought to get him somewhere."

The young man was back again within a minute or two. Lord Tollesbury answered his discreet knock irritably.

"Well?" he demanded.

"Miss Marie-Elizabeth Mason inherits three hundred thousand pounds, mostly invested in—"

"You can skip that. Who is she?"

Mr Denver looked hurt. "The money was her mother's, and the girl remained in Australia until her majority. She has now come over here and is staying with her guardian, who until now has had full control of the interest from the fortune."

"Who is that? What's the name, man? Don't beat about the bush. ..."

"Her aunt, a certain Mrs Eva de Liane, living at Heronhoe in Bedfordshire. Latcher is the solicitor."

There was a long silence. Lord Tollesbury took a deep breath.

"Thank you. You may go, Denver. And you too, Lissen. I want to talk to Sir Peter."

As the door closed behind the two men Peter came forward shakily.

"Then it's true," he said huskily. "It's true. My God, what that kid must have suffered!"

He stopped abruptly before the cold expression in the other man's eyes.

"Many mistakes have been made, my dear Peter, by people jumping to conclusions," Lord Tollesbury remarked coldly. "This story needs very careful verification. But if it's true ..."

He did not finish the sentence. Instead he strode down the room, his hands clasping and unclasping behind him.

"If it's true?" said Peter hoarsely.

"If it's true we'll get the whole lot of them in jail. Safest place for them, from our point of view. This may be the biggest stroke of luck we've ever had in our lives. Eva de Liane and her son in jail! There's a husband too. I believe he'll be in it."

"And the girl?" Peter demanded.

"Oh, the girl as well. Her most of all. She's the person we have to fear."

"But if she's innocent?" Peter's voice had an agonized appeal in it which he could not hide.

Lord Tollesbury looked at him steadily, his fine brows arching over his sunken eyes.

"My dear Peter," he said, "no young woman who impersonates an heiress worth three hundred thousand pounds can hope to be considered innocent."

19
BLACKMAIL

S till no sign of Richard?"
      Edmund Beron stood by the fireplace in his mother's magnificent Chinese bedroom at Baron's Tye.

Old Mrs de Liane was sitting up in bed, a pile of reference books and a portfolio of papers spread out on the counterpane in front of her. She looked very charming in her lace shawl, a lace bonnet over her soft white hair.

"No, not yet."

"But how amazing to walk out of the house like that on the very night the girl disappeared, and then not to return!"

Mrs de Liane's blue eyes clouded. "Yes, it is a little unusual," she said. "But then Richard was always impulsive. I don't think any harm has come to him. And," she went on, looking at her elder son sharply, "I don't think he has done anything rash."

Edmund Beron was silent for some moments, his heavy, handsome face dark and thoughtful.

"You don't think he'd double-cross us for this girl?" he said with sudden frankness.

Mrs de Liane considered. "Men are strange about women," she said. "But I don't think you understand Richard. Richard is not the sort of man to fall in love with any woman, unless there was some definite material gain to himself."

"I wonder ..." said Beron.

"I think so," said Mrs de Liane. "He might forget himself in a moment of passion, but in the end, in the long run, his thought would be entirely for himself. I imagine he's amusing himself quietly somewhere until he sees which way the cat is going to jump. Richard wouldn't even risk my anger for that girl. You won't see him back until things are going smoothly again."

"Young skunk," said Beron bitterly. "I never liked him."

"No, you didn't," said Mrs de Liane complacently, and the telephone bell began to ring.

She took the white receiver from its place by the side of her bed, and as she recognized the voice on the other end of the wire a certain hardness crept into her expression.

"Oh, hallo Ted," she said, more for Beron's benefit than her communicant's. "I hope you're ringing from a call box. You are? It's very late. Oh, I see—from a hotel. Yes, we have our little daughter back. No, my dear, you can't come home. Not yet. I particularly want you to stay on at Merton House for a day or two. Make all the enquiries you can about a young man called Peter Muir. He left there about the same time that Mary did. Find out what he was, where he worked and how long he stayed there. No, don't bother about where he's gone. We know that. Good night. Good-bye."

She rang off.

Beron stared at her. "What are you playing at?"

Mrs de Liane leant back among her cushions and switched off the reading lamp by her bed.

"A very interesting little game," she said. "Very interesting indeed. I am enjoying it. And now, my dear, I should go to bed."

"All right. What about the girl? You're sure she's safe in her room?"

"Oh, perfectly. I showed her the dogs from the window. I'll

afraid they caught sight of her. They're very ferocious. She seemed quite alarmed. She won't try to get out of the house by the window, and her door is locked. Do go to bed and get some sleep, Edmund. Your nerves are beginning to worry me."

The man moved towards the doorway and looked back at her enviously.

"I wish I had your secret," he said. "I wish I knew how to sleep."

"It's your conscience," said Mrs de Liane, yawning.

He laughed bitterly. "You haven't any, I suppose?"

Mrs de Liane turned over. "None at all," she said contentedly.

Meanwhile, in the room which had been assigned to her on her first arrival at Baron's Tye, Mary sat up in the great bed and shivered. The little lamp in the canopy above cast an oasis of light on the blue coverlet amid the surrounding shadows.

Outside she could hear the rain falling steadily, drenchingly, upon the dead leaves. She was back again, back in this terrible old house whose very mellowness had now a sinister quality which sank into her bones and made her heart turn painfully in her side at every untoward sound.

This time there was no escape. She knew it instinctively. As soon as she had seen from the window the four great mastiffs picking their way over the rough grass at the back of the house she had known she would never attempt to step out on the balcony and climb down into the grounds. Even if the dogs had not been there she did not think she would have gone. When she had escaped in London Mrs de Liane had recaptured her, so what possible chance would she have here in the open country, with every passer-by willing to give information about the presence of a stranger?

If Baron's Tye had been terrible before, now there was a new horror about it. The whole household was her enemy, all openly against her: Louise, Beron and old Mrs de Liane. The two who had shown her at least verbal kindness had gone. There was no sign of the woman in grey, and Richard had disappeared.

She sat up in bed shivering, although the night was not cold. She was afraid, so frightened that she could not even bring herself to turn off the light and lie down. The swelling on her lip had gone down, but it still hurt considerably, and there was an ugly bruise on the point of her chin. Her hand hurt her too. She looked down at it, and a little thrill ran through her. The narrow circle of diamonds on her finger had bitten into the flesh, and, as the little stones winked up at her, she realized all over again what they meant. She was married, bound by law to a man she did not know and whom all outside evidence proved to be a criminal and a weakling dominated by a woman whose very personality seemed to be wholly evil.

The other thing she might escape. Lord Tollesbury, for his own mysterious reasons, might save her from a great many of the dangers. But one thing neither he nor any man could ever alter—she was married.

While her thoughts were running on she had been listening half unconsciously to the steady beat of the rain. Now there was another sound. She sat forward, crouching in the bed, her eyes wide, her heart thumping so loudly that its beat seemed to fill the room.

The sound came again, nearer this time. A scream rose in her throat and was stifled there. She was sure of it now: someone was coming softly along the balcony, someone who had braved the presence of the great dogs loose in the grounds.

There was a moment of silence, and then, as every separate and particular hair seemed to rise up on her head, the window was thrown up from the outside. The long blue curtains billowed out into the room, and a gust of rain-soaked air swept over her as she sat petrified in the bed.

Once again there was a pause, and then, when it seemed that

her heart must burst and her scream choked her, a tall, rain-coated figure stepped lightly into the room.

She saw his face smiling at her in the faint light, a lean brown face flecked with raindrops, two dancing blue eyes peering impudently at her.

It was the man she had secretly longed and secretly dreaded to see, the man to whom the law gave almost every right over her, the man of whom she was afraid.

"Hallo, Angel," said Richard de Liane. "See my advertisement?"

Mary did not answer. She sat very still, the light hidden in the canopy over the great bed shining down upon the bronze-gold of her hair, and her big, grave eyes wide with apprehension and something which was not altogether alarm.

The man stood looking at her silently for a moment or two. His smile had vanished, and he hesitated, as though uncertain of his welcome.

Outside the window the rain still pattered down upon the leaves and the stone of the balcony. There were sounds in the great house too, strange creakings and rustlings in the old corridors and in the curtained fastnesses of other bedrooms. But there was no definite commotion; the effect was rather one of pregnant silence.

Richard closed the window, and, when the blue curtains hung once again motionless in their place, he came quietly across the room.

Mary shrunk back from him involuntarily, and at the movement he stopped dead and remained where he was, standing at the foot of the bed, his hands thrust deep into the pockets of his raincoat and the faint gleam from the canopy light catching the folds of the wet garment.

"Well?" he said.

She was straining back against the pillows, her shoulders tense, her eyes more frightened now.

"Well?" she echoed uncertainly and raised her chin on the word.

The light caught the ugly bruise across her mouth as she moved out of the shadow. Richard de Liane caught his breath.

"My God!" he said explosively. "Who did that?"

She put up her hand instinctively to hide the mark, and he strode round the bed and wrenched her wrist away.

"Let me see," he commanded. "Who did it?"

She turned away from him, hiding her face in the pillows, her other elbow raised as though to ward off a blow. The instinctive movement brought an exclamation to his lips. He dropped her arm and stood back, looking down at her, an indefinable expression on his lean brown face.

"Who did it, Mary?" he said unsteadily. "Who did it?"

"No one. Nothing. It doesn't matter." Her voice was muffled by the pillows, and he stretched out his hand to her as though he would have laid it upon her cheek. She did not see the movement, however, and evidently he thought better of it, for he drew back again and strode down the room with a jauntiness which was not altogether natural.

"You're not answering questions, are you, Angel?" he said. "What about my first one? Did you see my advertisement?"

"In *The Times?*" Her tone rather than the words made him swing round on his heel with unfeigned eagerness.

"You did? Well, what about it? Indignant, angry or merely amused?"

There was a wistfulness in his tone which Mary had not heard before and which held a new appeal for her. She held her breath. He was still waiting for her answer, standing in the middle of the room, his eyes fixed not upon her but upon the carpet at his feet.

She moved slowly into a sitting position, holding the coverlet so that it hid the bruise upon her chin and the discoloured mark upon her lower lip. She could see him distinctly, although the light was not strong. She saw the droop of his shoulders and the angle of his bent head.

She remembered the advertisement, remembered every word of it with a clarity which astounded her. She was afraid of herself. Her heart was beating wildly, and there was something which was not hope of rescue, not relief at finding a friend, but rather a complete recklessness, which bewildered her. It would have been so easy to hold out her hand to him.

Suddenly, when the desire to do so was quite overwhelming, he swung round and she saw some of the old amusement dancing in his eyes.

"I'm not doing this very well, am I?" he said. "I could do it so much better if it wasn't genuine. D'you know that? I'm afraid I'm a hopeless person, Mary. Good God, what a time to come barging in like this, covered with rain! It's enough to frighten you out of your wits."

He moved over to the bed again and sat down on the end of it, where she was just out of reach of his hand.

"You've been frightened rather a lot, haven't you? How did they get you back, my mother and Edmund?"

The question was obviously genuine. Mary's heart bounded as she realized it. He did not know what had happened. He was not associated with his mother and half brother—or at least not now.

She told him in jerky little sentences, her voice muffled by the coverlet.

"I was on a railway carriage—someone came to tell me that the woman I was travelling with had been run down by a cab—I went out with him—there was a car waiting—they pushed me in and—and—and it drove off."

"I see." His eyes were holding her own. They were darker than she had imagined, and there was something in their depths which she had not seen there before, something which made her heart contract painfully. "Did you scream?"

190

Her eyes widened, and there was terror in them.

"Yes."

"I see." The man leant forward and, jerking down the coverlet, looked steadily at the discolouration on the white moulding of her chin. "And Edmund did that?"

"Yes."

She half expected him to be angry. She expected the colour to go out of his face, expected his eyes to narrow, but she was not prepared for the sound which escaped his lips. It was very soft and like nothing she had ever heard before. The next moment he was on his knees by her side, one arm thrust beneath her head, while with the other hand he held her face gently and peered down into her eyes.

"I love you, Mary," he said. "What's going to happen to me? What's going to happen to you? This is the thing that ought never to have happened. This is the thing that makes us both utterly helpless. I love you, my dear, I love you so."

Mary's hands moved slowly until her fingers touched the hard, shorn curls at the back of his neck, and she pulled his head down gently towards her.

The great room was very silent. To its two occupants the world seemed to have paused. Then, from the other side of the apartment, there came a strange sound. It was a little ghostly, fluttering sigh.

A moment later the velvet curtain over the door rustled on its slender brass rings, and Eva de Liane, a filmy bundle of Shetland lace, moved quietly into the room.

"You did that very nicely, Richard," she said. "But I ought to have told you, my dear, we've rather changed our plans. You ought to have seen me first. When you went away this was the line of campaign on which we had decided, but since then Mary had become quite reconciled to her position, and there is now no longer any need for this type of play-acting."

Her voice was clear, pleasant and inclined to be amused.

There was not the vestige of irritation in its bell-like tone. She sat down on the end of the bed and smiled at them both.

Richard had risen slowly to his feet, and now he stared at the old woman, his face white, his lips quivering. Once again Mary was aware of that strange gift of silent communication which these two possessed. She had seen it before on that dreadful occasion which now seemed so long ago, when he had convinced the old woman that Mary had told the truth and was not indeed Marie-Elizabeth Mason. Then they had been allies, but now she was aware of a silent quarrel going on between them.

Had she kept her head and permitted herself to watch that eerie contest things might have been different, but she was a very human little girl and the old woman was far too clever for her.

The quiet, matter-of-fact words sank into her mind and poisoned it just as they were intended. She had been on the point of admitting the love which she had been fighting against so desperately for so long. All her doubts of Richard, all the haunting questions which had clamoured to be answered whenever she thought of him and which had been shelved by her during that brief moment of passion, now came crowding back.

Mrs de Liane laughed. "I'm afraid I haven't been very tactful," she said. "I've made you look rather silly, haven't I? You poor boy, I've spoilt your beautiful scene..."

She turned to the girl.

"He was always so good at acting, even as a little boy. I thought it wasn't very fair on you, my dear: that's why I interrupted. After all, there have been so many complications in this little business, and I didn't want to make any where none existed."

She paused and looked from one to the other of the two young people. A quiet, rather mischievous smile appeared at the corners of her mouth.

"Of course," she said, picking her words with quiet deliberation not at all unmixed with humour, "as long as you both understand each other perfectly, as long as Mary realizes that Richard and I have discussed this—shall we say line of conduct—it's all perfectly all right. I mean, my dears, you *are* married and—"

Richard caught the woman by the shoulders.

"Stop!" he said. "Stop!"

Mary felt as though she was going to faint. She saw the strange scene enacted at the end of her bed as though it had no reality. Richard and the old woman seemed to have no substance. It was as though they were both phantoms, shadows on a screen, or marionettes in a puppet show. She saw the old woman put up her hands and flick her son's grasp from her shoulders as though it had barely existed, and she saw her rise and stand looking at him for a moment.

Richard turned to the girl.

"I suppose it's no good asking you to believe?" he began passionately.

"No ... no!" Horror and a sense of physical disgust which she could not understand had swept over the girl. She covered her face with her hands. "Please go—please!"

"Mary ..." The man's voice was shaking, and the girl, looking up, saw him standing pale and haggard, his eyes dark with wretchedness, his hands outstretched; and behind him the old woman, quiet, self-possessed and very much amused.

The memory of her own inclination to hide herself in his arms, burying her face in his neck, and to forget the misery of the past days, coupled with the discovery that she had been deceived, was too much for the girl.

"Go away," she said, the tears streaming down her face. "Go away. I can't tell you how I loathe and despise you. I never want to see you again. I—I'd like to see you dead."

MAXWELL MARCH

She was unconscious of the intensity of hatred infused into the last words.

The man drew back. "I believe you mean that, God help me," he said slowly.

Mary met his eyes. "I do."

He turned on his heel and without another word strode out of the room. The curtain over the door billowed, and the rings rattled, and then there was silence.

Mrs de Liane walked over to the girl.

"You may be angry with me now, my dear, but you'll be grateful later on," she said gently. "Richard's a dear boy but not very scrupulous. Good night."

Mary could not answer her. Her heart felt like a dead weight in her breast, and there was a pain in her throat much worse than tears.

"Good night," said Mrs de Liane again, and, moving quietly across the room, she too went out.

After the curtain had fallen in place Mary heard the soft click of the key in the lock.

20

INTERESTS INVOLVED

I told you everything I could remember when I first came back from that damned uncomfortable boarding-house three days ago. You've got all the facts, Eva: what are you worrying for now?"

Ted de Liane paused before the large desk in the library at Baron's Tye and looked down at his wife, who sat before it, a sheaf of papers under her hand. The old man was querulous and truculent.

"I told you this business would bring trouble," he said. "I never liked it. You're getting old, my girl, that's what it is. You've got megalomania or something."

A frown appeared on Mrs de Liane's white forehead.

"You may go back to your own room now, Ted," she said. "You fidget me."

"Fidget you!" said Ted de Liane with some violence. "I want to know what you're doing. When I first came back and gave you the information you were pleased enough with me. Now, because I can't remember anything else, I fidget you. And what's the matter with that girl? What's she cowering in her room like some little dark-eyed ghost for? And Richard too? He goes out of the house the first thing in the morning with a gun and doesn't come back until the last thing at night. They never see each other, never speak to each other. What are you playing at?"

The telephone bell prevented Mrs de Liane from having to reply. She picked up the instrument and had a brief conversation with someone who was presumably a broker in London. Her husband listened to her decisive orders, his eyebrows raised.

"You're using that girl's fortune to fight Cosmos," he said. "What's the idea? D'you know anything, or have you gone mad?"

Mrs de Liane smiled complacently. "I'm not using very much of her fortune, not yet," she said. "Latcher is very cautious. However, he's parted with enough to make our friends excited."

"Excited!" echoed Ted de Liane. "Be careful you don't get too excited yourself." He looked at the woman shrewdly as he spoke. There were two bright spots of colour in her cheeks, and her eyes were dancing. Eva de Liane had been a gambler all her life, and now she was enjoying some of the strange thrill which only gamblers in big money know.

The man stood looking at her curiously. "You're happy now because you're winning," he said, sneering at her, "but wait till you lose."

An amused little laugh escaped the woman. "I'm going to win, Ted," she said. "I'm going to win, and nothing in the world is going to stand in my way."

Ted de Liane went out of the room. For some little time Mrs de Liane continued to work at the big desk. The afternoon sun shone waterily through the tall windows and glinted upon her soft white hair and upon the diamonds on her finger.

An outsider might have thought her some gentle old lady absorbed during the evening of her life by some charitable organization and might have marvelled at the diligence with which she totted up rows of figures and made little notes in a small black book.

Once again the telephone bell rang, and this time the excitement was even more apparent in her bright blue eyes and the smile on her soft lips even more jubilant

She was resting for a moment, her hands folded on the fine Italian blotter and a faraway expression on her calm, still lovely face, when the door burst open and a man hardly recognizable as the Edmund Beron of a week before rushed into the room.

He was pale. The blood had drained out of his heavy face, leaving it grey and unhealthy and covered by a network of little red veins. He looked dishevelled, and when he spoke his voice was high and uncontrolled.

Mrs de Liane glanced up at him, and the panic-stricken words he had been about to utter were frozen on his lips.

"Well, what is it, Edmund?" The old woman's voice, clear and sharp as a lash, provided just the corrective the man needed to hold him together. He straightened himself and came slowly towards her.

"We've got to get out," he said.

She frowned. Edmund had been showing signs of strain of late, and he was not the panic-stricken, hysterical type that she had come to recognize in her husband. Edmund's fears were usually well grounded.

"What is it?" she demanded. "What's happened?"

There was no fear in her voice, simply command.

The man glanced about him nervously, as though he dreaded that even in that great room he might be overheard.

"There's been a man in the village," he said. "He's enquiring about us. He interviewed the parson, and one of those clodhoppers who carried Richard downstairs for the wedding had a talk with him too. He's finding out about us. We must get away. The game's up."

To his astonishment the old lady leaned back in her chair and laughed. It was a spontaneous ripple of pure amusement, and he gaped at her.

"Mother," he said sharply, "are you mad?"

The sudden alarm in his eyes seemed to amuse her still more, and she leant forward across the desk and patted his hand.

"No, my dear, no," she said. "It's nothing to get alarmed about. This man wasn't a policeman, was he?"

"Why no." There was a puzzled expression on the man's face. "I don't think he was, as far as I could find out. 'A lawyerlike sort of chap' was the only description I could get from the village, but if that means Latcher we shall soon have the police. I tell you, Mother, I think we ought to go. After all, we've laid our hands on a great deal of money and—"

"Edmund!" Mrs de Liane's tone was gently reproving. "I don't think it is Latcher. I don't think your friend is anything to do with Latcher. I think the people who are so interested in us are quite a different firm altogether. Dear me, this is very amusing!"

"I am glad you find it so," said Beron, his fears somewhat allayed but his temper nettled. "Personally I think it's terrifying. We're in considerable danger."

"Edmund, you're getting old." Mrs de Liane seemed quite concerned at the discovery. "Everything's going splendidly. My dear boy, you can trust me. You know that, don't you?"

"Yes, I think so." Beron turned away. "I only hope you're not being foolhardy," he said over his shoulder. His eyes had wandered to the scene outside the tall window, and an exclamation left his lips.

"Look!" he said huskily. "Look!"

As Mrs de Liane left her seat and came to his side he pointed towards the black saloon car which was making its way slowly down the drive. It was a magnificent vehicle, sleek and purring like a well-fed cat, glistening discreetly with metalwork, its paint winking in the sunlight.

Mrs de Liane caught her breath.

"Visitors …" she said. "At any rate, my dear boy, it's not the police. I never heard of a policeman yet who arrived in a Rolls-Royce. Dear me, I rather thought this would happen."

She walked over to the mirror in the door of one of the bookcases and surveyed herself with satisfaction.

"You will wait here, Edmund," she said. "I shall see my visitor in the drawing room. I look so well in the drawing room, I always think."

Beron was still staring at her in astonishment when a maid came in to announce a visitor. Before the girl had opened her mouth, however, Mrs de Liane had spoken.

"I will see Lord Tollesbury in the drawing room. Oh, you've put him there, have you? Very well, I'll come at once."

The girl went out, but before his mother could follow Edmund Beron had caught the old woman gently by the wrist and swung her round.

"Lord Tollesbury?" he said. "What on earth are you doing? What are you after?"

Mrs de Liane smiled up at him for a moment and then, lifting a small hand, pinched his cheek.

"Money, my son," she said softly, "and still more money."

Lord Tollesbury, his tall, elegantly clad figure looking strangely in keeping with the quiet magnificence of the Baron's Tye drawing room, was standing on the hearthrug, his hands clasped behind his back, when the door opened and Eva de Liane came in.

They were old enemies, but until this moment they had never met, and now the man felt a sense of astonishment creep over him as his eyes rested upon the graceful silk-clad figure with the soft white hair and the priceless lace at her throat and wrists.

The words he had prepared as an opening died upon his lips. Lord Tollesbury belonged to a race of men who do not easily blackguard a lady in her own drawing room. He returned her bow but not her smile.

"Mrs de Liane," he said, "my name is Tollesbury. We haven't met."

Mrs de Liane shot him one of her charming smiles.

"No, but we've corresponded, haven't we?" she said, and laughed.

The woman and her attitude were both so very different from anything he had expected that Lord Tollesbury was taken completely off his guard. His cadaverous face grew blank, and for a moment his piercing dark eyes wavered.

In that moment Mrs de Liane took command of the situation.

"Do sit down," she said, settling herself gracefully in one of the high-backed easy chairs. "It's very kind of you to call upon an old woman as soon as you come into the district. Or is this a business visit?"

Lord Tollesbury, who had not taken the offered chair, regarded her calmly from his position by the fire.

"You're unexpectedly courageous, if I may say so," he observed.

"Courageous?" Mrs de Liane looked delightfully puzzled. "I don't think so. I live a very quiet life, you know. It's easy to be courageous if one has nothing to fear."

Lord Tollesbury rearranged his programme. Clearly he had expected a different sort of interview, but since it was to be a delicate affair he made it apparent that he did not object.

"Mrs de Liane," he said, "you are an astute businesswoman, and I think you will understand me if I put the situation to you in the following way. You have private information which you do not hesitate to use to send the shares of a company in which I am interested slowly further and further down. Now I think— correct me if I am wrong—that the very very discreet letter which I received from you two days ago could be interpreted to mean that your memory is not reliable in these matters and that you could be trusted to forget this interesting piece of information which you have if your mind was—shall we say—diverted by the knowledge that a very large sum of money had been transferred from my banking account into yours. There's a rather ugly word for that, you know."

Eva de Liane rose to her feet, walked across the room, opened the door, peered out of the windows and satisfied herself that both she and her visitor were not overheard. Then she resumed her seat and smiled at the man disarmingly.

"One has to be so careful in business," she said, adding impudently, "I dare say you find that too."

Lord Tollesbury checked an exclamation.

"Can you answer my question now?" he enquired.

Mrs de Liane hesitated. "Well ... shall I say that you seem to be quite as intelligent as I thought you were?" she said.

"You admit it?"

"What a very ugly word! I think you are intelligent. Let's leave it like that."

The man bowed ironically. "Very well then. This is my answer to that letter. I too have private information about another affair, and one which intimately concerns you and your family. I am able to prove that the girl who has married your son and who is reputed to be an heiress to a considerable fortune is nothing more or less than an impostor, a creature used by you to take the place of the real girl, who is dead. If this information should get into the right hands your position would be very precarious, Mrs de Liane. You are an old woman, and a term of imprisonment would rest very heavily upon your shoulders. Well, how do we stand now?"

He had been watching the woman narrowly as he spoke and was disappointed. She showed no sign of faltering. Her colour was unchanged, and her eyes were still dancing. When he finished she laughed.

"It's a very interesting story," she said, "and one that will amuse my family."

He shook his head at her. "I'm not a fool, Mrs de Liane. I should not come to you with a story like this if I did not know it was true. Certain enquiries have been made in Australia, and it may interest you to know that the girl who is masquerading as Marie-Elizabeth Mason does not resemble in any way the real Marie-Elizabeth Mason, your niece and your ward."

Mrs de Liane shrugged her shoulders.

"That would be very extraordinary if it were true," she said, "and naturally no one would be more interested in such a discovery than I—or more astonished."

The emphasis on the last word made him look up.

"Oh, I see, that's your game, is it? You're going to blame it all on the girl—the innocent little girl who tricked you. Oh, very clever, Mrs de Liane! Very clever indeed! But you won't get away with it, you know. Suppose I go straight to Latcher? What then?"

Mrs de Liane yawned. "Lawyers move so terribly slowly," she said. "Have you noticed it? It's so different on the stock market, isn't it? Such a lot of damage can be done in a few hours in money matters while lawyers are still writing letters and debating whether they can ring up the police with safety. I was talking to my broker on the telephone just before you came," she added, apparently as an afterthought.

Lord Tollesbury's face grew dark.

"Is that your final answer?"

Mrs de Liane smiled. "You're dying to get to a telephone, aren't you?" she said. "I'm so sorry I can't lend you mine. There's one in the village, only of course they often take such a time to get through. Still, I mustn't keep you if you want to go. It must be nearly closing time on Change."

The man towered above her.

"You're playing with fire," he said. "I'm a very rich man, and I'll smash you. I'll smash you whatever it costs me."

"I wonder ..." said the little old lady.

He had reached the door when her quiet voice arrested him, and now, with his hand on the knob, he turned and looked at her.

"What do you wonder?"

Mrs de Liane smiled. "I wonder if you are so very rich," she said deliberately. "You put practically all you had in Cosmos, didn't you? Thank you for telling me this amazing story about the bona fides of my daughter-in-law. I must ask my lawyer to go into them."

The man was very pale, and the bones stood out on his thin face, making it very like a skull.

"Suppose I paid you?" he said contemptuously. "I should have to go on paying. Look here, Mrs de Liane, this is the brutal truth. Perhaps you haven't been so very far out in your guessing. Do you know what happens when a man who has been blackmailed is bled white? The blackmailer goes to jail. Perhaps you've demanded what isn't there, Mrs de Liane."

"Perhaps," said the old woman judiciously. "But I don't think so. After all," she added, surveying the tips of her tiny buckled shoes, "one always has to take risks, doesn't one?"

Tollesbury grinned mirthlessly. "Does your daughter-in-law know the risk she's taking?"

Mrs de Liane shrugged her shoulders. "Dear Mary," she said. "She's such a nice girl. I really couldn't believe she would do anything dishonest—unless, of course, I had absolute proof."

Lord Tollesbury strode out of the house. His car was speeding down the drive at a considerably faster pace than it had entered when Mrs de Liane walked slowly into the library, where her elder son awaited her. At the sight of her face he rose to his feet from the armchair by the fire.

"What is it? What's happened?"

"Nothing," said Mrs de Liane. "He was not quite frightened enough to be reasonable, that's all."

She spoke brightly, but there was a thoughtful expression in her eyes, and when the telephone bell rang she went over to take up the instrument mechanically, a preoccupied expression on her face.

At the first sound of the voice on the other end of the wire, however, she was alert and interested. Her eyes had narrowed, and Edmund, watching her, saw with sick apprehension the colour slowly ebb out of her cheeks.

"My dear Mr Latcher, how very extraordinary!" she said, her voice retaining by a superhuman effort much of its old spontaneity. "Really? Are you sure? How terrible! Yes, she's here—in the house. What shall I do? No no no, we don't want a scandal. Oh, but how awful! This is dreadful—dreadful!"

Her voice quivered, and there were actual tears in her eyes.

"You must advise me. What shall I do? ... Yes, I know it's very awkward—awkward for all of us, you too ... Keep her here until you come in the morning? All right ... Don't alarm her? No, of course not. Of course not ... What? For my own sake? My dear Mr Latcher, for all our sakes! I can't believe it ... Goodbye."

She had hardly put down the receiver before Beron had caught her by the shoulders. His face was pasty, and beads of sweat had appeared upon his forehead. He shook her in his terror, hardly realizing what he did.

"He knows!" he said, his voice cracking horribly. "He knows! What are we going to do? How can we get away? Oh my God!"

"Edmund, pull yourself together." Mrs de Liane was as white as he, but her lips were firm and her voice studiously controlled. "Tollesbury hasn't told him—someone else knows. We must work very quickly."

"But what can we do?" The man's face was ludicrous with terror.

"Lie," said the old woman calmly. "The girl deceived us. That's the only way."

"But they'll find out. There's so much proof. We're done. They're going to get us."

"Wait—wait." The little voice cut through his hysteria. "Latcher won't be here until the morning. No one but an old-fashioned lawyer would be such a fool as to have phoned. There's still time. The girl must take the blame. She can stand for everything."

"But the police'll make her talk." There were tears of pure fear in the man's eyes. "And when she talks they're bound to prove some of her story. She'll talk—she'll talk!"

Mrs de Liane raised her hand and laid it over his mouth. She looked very small and very gentle standing there in her grey silk gown, the white curls framing her sweet pink-and-white face, but there was a strange power in her blue eyes.

"Yes," she said, and there was something in her voice which sent a thrill of fear through even the man who knew her better than anyone else in the world. "Yes, my dear. Mary must take the blame. That means the police must take her. But does it occur to you, Edmund, that when they take her she may not be *able* to talk?"

He gaped at her, but she silenced his unspoken question.

"We must hurry, my dear boy," she said. "We haven't very much time."

The two stood looking at one another, the woman so frail and yet so oddly dominant, and the man so weak in his fear for all his physical heaviness.

"What are you going to do?"

The words came slurred together from between the thick lips, and Edmund Beron's small eyes were contracted into little pin points of terror.

"Edmund, Edmund—" there was strength in the old voice, and the small white hand which Mrs de Liane laid upon her son's arm gripped his flesh with solid pressure— "pull yourself together. There's nothing to be afraid of—yet. Go home. Tell Jane that Richard will sleep at your house tonight."

"Richard? What are you going to do?"

A faint smile appeared upon the small, soft mouth.

"All in good time, my dear," she said. "All in good time."

There was something terrible about the smile, and the man put up his hands in a little involuntary gesture, as though he would hide it from his view.

"Sometimes you frighten me," he said.

Mrs de Liane laughed. "What a sweet boy you are!" she said.

2 1

RED TAPE

My dear Sir Peter, while I appreciate your obvious efforts to help me in every way, really I must protest! I am a professional man, and it is not at all proper for me to discuss a client's business with a—a stranger."

Little Mr Latcher strode about the hearthrug in his slightly old-maidish office like a very small tiger in a large cage. His sparse hair was rumpled into unusual disarray, and he blinked nervously every time he peered at his excited visitor.

Peter Muir-David rose to his feet. A remarkable change had taken place in his appearance during the last few days. He looked pale and exhausted, and his cheekbones stood out prominently in his haggard face.

"I know, sir," he said in a tone which was meant to be conciliatory but in which exasperation was very thinly veiled. "I appreciate your attitude, believe me. It's quite right, quite understandable, and perfectly proper in ninety-nine cases out of a hundred. But you must believe me when I tell you that this is the exception. A girl is in danger, serious danger, and when I ask you to throw discretion to the winds and come with me immediately to Heronhoe I know what I'm asking you. This is no time to hang about, Mr Latcher. Something's got to be done at once."

Mr Latcher bristled, and the faint colour burned in his sallow cheeks.

"This is outrageous," he said. "If I didn't know you for a man of intelligence, Sir Peter, I'm afraid I really should have to ask you to leave my office and—and—er—take your hands off my affairs. I've done all I can possibly do at the moment. Acting on the unofficial information I received from you I have—ah— instigated certain enquiries, and I do intend to travel down to Bedfordshire tomorrow morning. Indeed, I think I may tell you without breach of good faith that I have already notified a—er— certain lady who shall be nameless that I intend to visit her in the course of tomorrow morning."

"You what—?" The words burst from Peter's lips, inter- rupting Mr Latcher's nervous flow. "You've told Mrs de Liane that you're going down there tomorrow morning? You've warned her? Good heavens, d'you know what you've done?"

The horror-stricken words coupled with the young man's expression impressed Mr Latcher in spite of himself. Neverthe- less he stood his ground.

"I am a very much older man than you are, Sir Peter," he said, "and perhaps you will forgive me if I tell you that in the course of a very long and I hope not undistinguished career I have never lost my head. In legal affairs one must move circum- spectly and with deliberation."

"In legal affairs, yes. But this is a matter of life and death." Peter was trembling. His face was pallid, and his hands, thrust deep into his pockets, were clenched. "Look here," he went on with a sudden burst of confidence, "you believe that Mrs de Liane is a very honest, straightforward woman who may have been the dupe of an intelligent swindler. I know you are wrong, but I cannot prove it to you in the little time that is left to us. All I ask you is to give me the benefit of the doubt. Come down with me at once and start your enquiries. If you are right no harm will have been done, but if I am right—and I know I am—then a great wrong may be averted, possibly a great crime."

"This is most melodramatic," said Mr Latcher, calmed in spite of himself. "I'm willing to help you in every way, Sir Peter, but I really don't see how you come into this affair at all. Am I to understand that you have a personal interest in—ah—Mrs de Liane junior?"

Peter winced at the name. "She is—actually married to him?"

"Oh, without a doubt." The little solicitor seemed to derive a certain amount of satisfaction from the announcement. "I have seen the marriage certificate—unless you wish me to believe that that too is a forgery."

Peter ignored the thrust. "Mr Latcher," he said, "do you find the new Mrs de Liane is amazingly extravagant with her new fortune?"

"That's an unpardonable question, Sir Peter." Mr Latcher coloured and bridled at the enormity of the indiscretion. All the same, Peter could see by the anxiety which had crept into his little grey eyes that he had not been far out with his guess.

"It might be very awkward for everybody," he went on, pressing his point home, "if any great inroad was made upon the fortune before it was realized that a mistake had been made. The question of good faith might come up and all sorts of things."

"My dear sir!" Mr Latcher, now thoroughly roused, positively bounced with rage. "To come into my office, insult me to my face! I tell you I was grateful for your first hint and I'm having investigations made, and when I receive the results of those investigations I shall act, but not before."

Peter looked at him helplessly. "I implore you," he said. "I shall go down there myself, of course, but without your authority I shall be very useless. What can I do, an outsider? It's in your interests to make use of every assistance I can give you.

You know who I am, you know I'm a person of repute most unlikely to lead you on a wild-goose chase. Why won't you trust me? Since you've actually warned that woman absolutely anything may happen."

"If you're suggesting anything in the way of physical violence," murmured Mr Latcher primly, "I think I may say that even if the utterly unthinkable had occurred and—ah—a certain lady had considered taking such a ridiculous course, my warning must have scotched any such attempt. After all, imagine her position, my dear sir—her legal position—if anything should occur to the girl in the meantime."

Peter laughed bitterly. "Mr Latcher," he said, "your innocence terrifies me. Very well, if you won't come with me I'll go alone, but I think you'll be very sorry."

Mr Latcher's acid reply was cut short by the ringing of the telephone bell on his desk. He picked up the instrument, and Peter, looking at him carefully, saw a flicker of interest in his pale eyes as he recognized the voice on the other end of the wire.

"Yes," he said guardedly, "yes. I—ah—I'm not alone at the moment, but if it's very important ... Oh, I see. Yes, well, I'm waiting."

Peter could not hear the indistinct murmur of the instrument, but he could and did see Mr Latcher's changing expression. The little man's guard was completely broken down. His pale eyes widened, his eyebrows rose until they seemed in danger of disappearing altogether, and the colour came and went in his sallow cheeks.

"Really!" he said at last. "You—you have proof, you say? ... What? ... But this is incredible! ... Oh yes, I know, I know. Go on ... What hotel? ... Oh, I see ... Yes, I'll come along at once. I—ah—have a very valuable witness here. I'll bring him along if I can."

He hung up the receiver at last and stood for a moment

wiping his forehead with a trembling hand. At last, and with considerable deliberation, he turned to Peter.

"I hardly know what to say," he said in a strangely quiet voice. "It may be that I owe you a sincere apology, Sir Peter. Dear me!" He sat down at his desk. "I think I must take a glass of water, if you don't mind."

Peter waited with impatience while the little man poured himself a drink from a cut-glass carafe on the desk. When he had drained his glass Mr Latcher dabbed his lips with a large white pocket handkerchief.

"That was a message from my confidential clerk, Lane," he said. "A remarkable fellow, wonderfully efficient and more tenacious than any detective. He has just made a very extraordinary discovery. I want you to come with me at once to the Hotel Splendide."

Peter stood his ground. "No. I'm going straight to Heronhoe."

Mr Latcher put out a hand appealingly. "Come to the Hotel Splendide first. If the discovery Lane thinks he has made proves to be correct not only you and I but half Scotland Yard will go to Heronhoe within the next three hours."

Peter leant forward. "What is it? What have you found?"

Mr Latcher shook his head. "No," he said. "You're a valuable witness. I dare not put any suggestions into your mind. Come with me at once, and then, if it is true and the utterly miraculous has occurred, we will go to Heronhoe."

Peter thrust his hand wearily over his fair hair.

"All right," he said. "All right. Only for God's sake let's hurry."

2 2

THE MOVING FINGER

I t's too cold for you to sit up here, miss. You'll be ill."

Louise had entered the room silently. Her squat black figure moved so quietly that the girl standing by the window in the big blue bedroom swung round, a little nervous cry on her lips.

There was nothing very terrifying about Louise, however. In one hand she carried a small portable oil stove which she set down in the middle of the room.

"This won't give out much heat for some time," she said. "This is a big room. You'd better go down into the breakfast room."

"But I'm quite all right, Louise. I'm quite all right here."

There was appeal in the girl's voice as well as protestation, but the woman ignored it.

"The mistress wishes you to sit in the breakfast room while this room is made warm."

There was nothing human in the flat, expressionless voice, and Mary, looking at that broad sallow face, found herself wondering if the woman could ever have had any emotional life at all. She looked like an automaton, moved and spoke like one.

"You'll go down to the breakfast room."

It was a command, and Mary, who had grown used to being ordered about, nodded meekly.

"Very well," she said.

The woman watched her go, and it was not until the door had closed quietly behind her and the gentle click of her heels had died away down the parquet corridor that the French-woman allowed her features to relax. Her eyes were still dull, but a curious expression had appeared on the broad, unlovely features. It was part repugnance, part cunning.

She dropped down upon her knees by the oilstove and lowered the wick. Then she lifted the contraption onto a long-haired rug so that the air space beneath the stove was almost entirely blocked. Then with infinite caution she raised the wick again.

After a moment or two the stove not unnaturally began to smoke, but the woman made no effort to check the stream of black, greasy vapour which curled its way up to the white ceiling and laid inky fingers upon the delicate hangings of the lovely room.

Instead she stood back and emitted a little sound of satisfaction, and after a while, as the noisome fumes became unpleas-ant, she tiptoed gently from the room, closing the door behind her.

At the far end of the corridor she caught sight of her mistress, who glanced at her enquiringly. Louise nodded, and Mrs de Liane passed on to her own room, a faint smile upon her lips.

Meanwhile, downstairs in the little breakfast room, which was so lovely in summer and so inexpressibly cheerless when the view from its wide east window was leafless and forlorn, Mary sat hunched up over the small fireplace and tried not to think of the nightmare of which she found herself a part. She was aware that something was happening. There was unusual activity in the house and a strange sense of foreboding utterly unlike anything she had known before. She had been frightened in the past, moved to unfathomed depths of terror, but this was different. Now she was not merely afraid: she was oppressed, weighed down with a sense of brooding evil. She felt as though the very air she breathed were solid. It was the hour before the storm.

An instinct made her turn and glance over her shoulder at the bleak landscape, and as she did so her heart contracted painfully. Striding across the lawn towards the french windows of the room in which she sat was the person she had been avoiding so carefully for the past three days.

Richard de Liane paused with his hand on the doorknob and peered in. The girl rose to her feet and stood looking at him uncompromisingly, warning him by her expression that she was in no mood to talk.

He hesitated, and it seemed at first that he would turn away, but a moment later he had changed his mind again and let himself quietly into the room.

Mary met his eyes. She had steeled herself to withstand his laughter and the light, charming way of his which always fascinated her, but she was completely unprepared for the change in him. All his swagger had disappeared. He looked forlorn, almost a little untidy, and he stood looking at her for some time, his eyes dark, his expression heavy and morose.

"You've been hiding from me," he said.

The colour came into the girl's face. "I've been avoiding you. That's rather different."

He shrugged his shoulders, and the old bitter smile twisted his mouth.

"Why?"

"Because I did not want to be subjected to the same sort of ignominious experience that I had the other night."

To her surprise he nodded gravely. "It was ignominious,

wasn't it?" he said. "I felt that. All the same I think you might speak to me. We have to live in the same house, you know."

Mary looked at him contemptuously. "I'm not quite as hard as you are. I haven't had the training. But I'm getting it. The tanning process is taking place. Within a week or two I shall probably have a skin like the rest of you."

He did not laugh. To her astonishment something very like alarm came into his eyes.

"Oh no," he said, "no!"

There was passionate protest in the word, and he came forward and looked down into her face. Mary felt herself becoming breathless and was aware that her heart was racing in her side. All the same she was terribly angry with herself. He had made a fool of her again. He would always make a fool of her.

Because she was so angry she let her bitterness overflow.

"I shouldn't worry yourself," she said. "After all, you've rather lost any power you might ever have had to influence me one way or the other, haven't you?"

She was looking at him, forcing herself to smile as she spoke, and as her words sank in she saw his face change, saw the old smiling mask slip over it.

"You're getting a new spirit, aren't you, Angel," he said. "It's very becoming. I'm old-fashioned enough to like it."

Mary did not trouble to repress a little shiver of distaste.

"I've told you I loathe you," she said. "Must you force me to make it clear every time I meet you?"

He stepped back from her.

"You put things very brutally, don't you, Angel?" he said. "But perhaps that's my fault."

He turned and went swiftly out of the room by the same door through which he had come. Mary stood looking after him. Her thoughts were in turmoil, and she found that she was pressing her clenched knuckles against her mouth, while her eyes were bright with unshed tears.

She had barely regained her composure when Mrs de Liane hurried into the room.

"Mary, my dear," she said, "such a tragedy! That stupid, stupid girl Louise! All over your pretty hangings, all over your clothes, the whole room covered with carbon. I've always said I wouldn't have oilstoves, but of course they're so useful—or they seem to be until something like this happens. We shall have to change your room at once, my dear."

It took Mary some little time to discover exactly what had happened, and she was surprised to find Mrs de Liane almost human in the face of this minor domestic catastrophe.

They went up together to see the damage.

As Mary followed the little figure in the grey silk dress up the wide staircase at Baron's Tye the sense of foreboding, of breathlessness, of silent waiting, which had assailed her earlier in the afternoon came back with overwhelming force. It startled her. Mrs de Liane's manner had been more nearly ordinary than she had ever seen it before, and yet there was something about the house growing dark in the evening which caught at her throat and filled her with heavy apprehension.

"Look," said Mrs de Liane, throwing open the bedroom door. "Isn't it terrible? Your pretty, pretty room!"

The oilstove had certainly done its worst. Carpet, bed cover, curtains were covered with greasy black carbon, while all over the walls and ceiling unsuspected gossamer spider threads had sprung suddenly into inky prominence.

"I'm afraid you'll have to have the little suite at the top of the house for the time being, my dear," said Mrs de Liane, breaking into the girl's exclamation of dismay. "I'll tell Louise to find you some clean toilet things and to rescue your clothes from the cupboard. You do realize we couldn't possibly get all this clean today?"

"Oh, of course not," said Mary hastily and stopped abruptly, a thrill of fear touching her heart. There had been some unusual meaning behind Mrs de Liane's last words, she was sure of it, and the old woman was looking at her sharply with an inquisitive, birdlike glance which seemed to be searching for some suspicion or objection in her face.

Mary's reaction appeared to satisfy her, however, for she laughed, a little regretful sound tinged with an attempt at philosophy.

"Oh well, it can't be helped," she said. "It's a nuisance, and I'm furious with Louise, absolutely furious, the silly girl! I shall make her clean every inch of this room with her own hands tomorrow. If it wasn't so late in the evening I should insist on its being done tonight, but that might annoy the other servants. They go home early this evening, you know."

Mary nodded absently. She knew that the other maids at Baron's Tye slept in one of the lodge cottages, while the chauffeur occupied the other. Louise was the only servant who slept in.

Why this recollection should have added to her feeling of oppression she did not know, and she strove angrily to cast it off. In her heart she realized that her interview with Richard had shaken her much more than she would ever dare to admit. As the days passed it was becoming increasingly difficult for her to get him out of her mind. She was in love with him, and he amused himself with her. It was an ignominious, unbearable situation.

She dragged her thoughts away from him and followed Mrs de Liane obediently to the little suite at the top of the house which she had occupied on her wedding night. It was cold and deserted, and she stood by the barred window peering out over the dark garden.

The rain had cleared but it was very cold, and there was a

small moon rising. She could see the trees, black and spidery against the sky, and far away in the valley the gleam of water.

Louise came in and built a fire in the grate. She was more taciturn even than usual, and when Mary attempted to condole with her over the affair of the oilstove she maintained a sullen silence.

"Dinner will be a little earlier tonight, miss," she said at last, when the fire had been coaxed into a promising blaze. "The other girls are going to a concert in the village. I think you'll hear the gong up here."

Suddenly the thought of going down through the dark house to sit at a table with Richard and Mr and Mrs de Liane became unbearably distasteful to the girl. She turned involuntarily to Louise.

"I—I have a headache," she said. "Do you think Mrs de Liane would excuse me? I'd like to go to bed if I might. I shan't want any food. Could you—could you put it to her, Louise?"

Something very like a smile appeared on the woman's broad face, and she turned her head away sharply to hide it.

"I'll ask her, miss," she said, and went out of the room.

Mary pushed up the window and peered out into the night. Escape was unthinkable. She had given up hope of that long ago. She moved restlessly. There was something strange about the house tonight, something quite different from all the other nights. There was frost in the air, and the smell of the wet leaves was not so apparent.

She shivered. Even the garden seemed to be breathless. Even there the unnatural hush seemed to have penetrated. She saw a car turn into the drive and sweep round to the front door. That was Edmund, she supposed, coming down from his little cottage above the village where he lived with his wife.

She heard the squeak of the brakes as the car pulled up and the sound of the door slamming, and it seemed to her that there was a nervous, irritable force about these things which she had not heard before.

She left the window and went over to the fire, where she sat for a long time crouching over its warmth and peering into the flames.

23
THE LITTLE SOUND

M y dear Richard, I am sure I am right. Mary is a dear girl but oversensitive. Accept Edmund's invitation for a day or two, and the chances are she'll come round."

Mrs de Liane, placid and charming as ever, with the candle-light shining down upon her white hair, studied the toe of her satin-shod foot on the fender as she spoke. They were all in the drawing room, Ted de Liane, Edmund and Richard. Ted was hovering in the background, and the two younger men stood side by side on the hearthrug in front of their mother.

"She wouldn't come down to dinner this evening. That was your fault, Richard. Now don't be unreasonable. I can quite understand the girl doesn't want to face you after marrying you under false pretenses."

"How can you talk like that? You make me sick!"

The words escaped the young man before he could control them, and the old woman, raising her eyebrows, looked at him coldly.

"So that's how it is, is it?" she said. "In that case, my dear, I think you'd better go at once, because the girl evidently doesn't like you, and if you stay you'll make a fool of yourself, if nothing worse."

Richard de Liane's lean figure drooped.

"I'm afraid you're right, Mother. You usually are," he said quietly. "All right, Edmund. I'll get a pair of pajamas and meet you at the car. Good night, Mother."

He went out of the room, and Edmund Beron took a step forward. His face was livid, and his whole body trembled.

"What are you going to do?" he said, bending down so that his face was within an inch or two of the old woman's own. "What are you going to do?"

She patted his cheek. "Nothing, my dear, nothing. Take Richard up to your house and keep him there. Understand? Keep him there."

The man drew back from her. "All right," he said unsteadily. "All right. I'm in your hands."

Mrs de Liane did not answer, and he marvelled at her calm in the face of the disaster which overshadowed her.

Richard's voice called him from the hall, and he pulled himself together with a start and went out of the room without speaking.

Mrs de Liane waited until the sound of the car had died away and the house was silent. Ted de Liane sat watching her from the other side of the room, and she became aware of his little frightened eyes fixed upon her. She stirred herself like a small grey cat and stretched her toes out to the blaze.

"There is something very lovely about this fire," she said. "It's very peaceful here, isn't it, with the two dear boys out of the way, and the servants home, and only Louise and you and I in the house."

"And the girl," said Ted de Liane. "And the damned girl. She's going to be the end of us, Eva. I've known it ever since I set eyes on her."

Even to the man who had known her so long Mrs de Liane's reply was surprising.

"Well, it's either her or us, isn't it?" she said. "It's very late, Ted. I think I shall go up to bed. That's a very nice room of yours, with the steps going down to the garden. It's a very nice house altogether. I should be sorry if—if anything happened to it."

"If we lost it, you mean?"

"Yes," said Mrs de Liane thoughtfully. "If we lost it. However, it's our comfort and safety that counts, and one sometimes has to make sacrifices for that. But I'm tired tonight, Ted, and I don't want to talk. Go to bed."

Because he was used to obeying his wife in every particular, Ted de Liane went off grumbling. Mrs de Liane followed him, apparently with the intention of going into her own room, which was on the same floor, but as soon as his door had closed behind him she retraced her steps and, looking like some little grey ghost in the gloom, crept down into the service quarters.

She was down there alone in the great kitchens for some time. She moved with remarkable agility for so old a woman, and time and again her little figure passed by the patch of moonlight coming through the big kitchen window, unwieldy bundles in her arms.

Nearly an hour later Ted de Liane, hearing a sound in the bathroom which connected his room with his wife's, pushed the door open cautiously, to see her closing the door of the medicine chest. On the table by her side was a cup of cocoa.

She turned round sharply, and for a moment there was something akin to apprehension in her eyes. The next moment, however, she was smiling.

"I've just remembered that poor child didn't have any dinner. Louise reminded me and went down and made a cup of cocoa for her in the housemaid's pantry. She can't sleep very well either, poor child, so I put an aspirin or so in it. Louise is going to take it up to her now. Go back to bed, dear. It's terribly late, and so cold and frosty."

Ted de Liane returned to his own room without a word, but as soon as the light in the bathroom went out he crept back again and went over to the medicine chest. For a long time he studied the contents thoughtfully, and the expression on his weak face might have been ludicrous in any other situation.

"Veronal ..." he said. "Now I wonder what that's for? What's she up to now?"

It was typical of Ted de Liane, however, that he did not attempt to find out. He shrugged his shoulders, decided that whatever it was it was none of his business, and went back to bed.

Louise, still in her prim black dress, met her mistress in the corridor. She took the cup without question and made her way up the little winding staircase which led to the tiny suite, so inaccessible from any other part of the house.

Mrs de Liane hesitated. Then she glanced at her watch, which dangled on a gold chain round her slender neck.

"Three quarters of an hour," she said under her breath. "Yes ... yes, I really think so."

Meanwhile Mary had been awakened out of a fitful sleep by the entrance of the Frenchwoman, who had turned on the light and now came quietly towards her.

"The mistress remembered that you'd had no dinner, miss," she said. "She's most anxious that you should drink this."

Mary blinked at the cup. "Thank you very much, Louise, but I don't really think I want it. I was asleep, you know."

The woman did not move. "The mistress said you were to drink it. I went downstairs and made it myself."

A pang of conscience stirred Mary as she thought of the enormous number of stairs that this hard-working woman had scaled on her behalf.

"It's very kind of you, Louise," she said, and stretched out her hand.

But Louise did not go. Evidently she had no intention of leaving until her offering had been consumed.

Mary shivered. "I've been dreaming," she said. "The house is very quiet and ghostly tonight; don't you think so?"

"I wouldn't notice it, miss." The woman turned her back upon the girl in the bed and went over to the fire, which she stirred into flame.

Mary tasted the cocoa. It was very sweet and sickish, but she forced herself to take it.

"It's very late, isn't it?" she said.

"Just past midnight, miss."

"Really? Well, this is extremely kind of you, Louise." Mary took another gulp of the unpalatable stuff.

Louise straightened her back. "It was the mistress's orders," she said without turning round.

Rebuffed, Mary finished the draught and set the cup and saucer down on the bedside table. As she lay back among the pillows she was aware of a soothing, restful, sleepy feeling. The house did not seem so quiet, the sense of apprehension not so strong. The room looked warm and comfortable, and the fire danced pleasantly.

A thousand thoughts began to chase each other through her mind with the smooth bewilderment of a pleasant dream. Her adventures of the past few weeks rushed back to her, but now they had lost their terror and had become merely interesting unrealities.

She looked at Louise. She was a Frenchwoman. The fact struck a chord of memory. She had heard another French name quite recently, and it came back to her.

"Louise," she said, "who is Jean ... little Jean?"

Nothing she could possibly have said could have had a more astonishing effect upon the square, ugly woman who stood by the fireplace. Every vestige of colour drained out of her face, and the next moment she was at the bedside, her strong hands cutting the girl's shoulders, while a stream of French poured from her lips.

Mary looked at her with dazed, bewildered eyes. Louise looked very funny standing there shouting, she thought in the new impersonal way in which her mind was travelling. There were tears in her eyes, actual tears, tears rolling down her broad, livid cheeks.

"What are you saying?" she said in English. "What do you know? Where is he? Where is he? Do you know?"

The urgency of the demand cut through the vapours of the drug which was fast overpowering the girl.

"On the road … the back way from London to here … where you turn off down a long straight strip, a lane with high hedges. Do you know it? … a lane with high hedges …"

Her voice trailed away, and the woman shook her.

"Go on!"

Mary struggled. She was very sleepy. Louise seemed very far away.

"We met a man. He was looking after Jean for Mrs de Liane. He thought Jean was old enough to go to school."

The last word was distorted on her lips. Her eyes closed, and she began to breathe heavily. Louise shook her.

"Wake up! Wake up! Did you see him?"

Mary did not answer. Her breath was coming rhythmically and heavily.

"Mon Dieu, le pauvre petit! Mademoiselle … mademoiselle! Dites moi!"

But Mary did not stir.

The woman took a deep breath and stepped back from the girl. She picked up the cup and smelt the dregs, and her small black eyes were bright with intelligence.

"Jean!" she said huskily. "Jean!"

For a moment she stood irresolute, and then hatred, terrible in its intensity, appeared upon her face, and she stood repeating the muttered words which the girl had told her.

"Immédiatement," she said suddenly. "At once … now!"

Turning, she sped silently out of the room, switching out the light as she passed.

She fled through the great silent house with swift, noiseless footsteps, down the corridors, down the wide staircase to the library.

For some time she worked there feverishly, and then the little reading lamp over the big desk went out. There was a step in the hall. The front door opened, and a blast of icy air burst into the house.

Then the door closed, and there was silence again, save for the quick patter of footsteps on the gravel of the drive.

Meanwhile, in the darkness of the little suite at the very top of the old oak-and-plaster house, Mary slept heavily. The powerful drug had done its work. She did not move but lay as one dead, one arm flung out on the pillows, her cheek resting on her bright hair. No sound would have awakened her. An alarm could have been rung in the room below, and she would not have heard it.

For a long time there was no sound at all in the big room, but after a time a keen ear might have detected a little terrifying sound. It was not loud and was far away in the very depths of the old wooden house—a little crackle, a scurry of mice in the wainscots and then a crackle again, and finally a roar which was not the roar of water but an angrier, fiercer sound which must have struck terror into the heart of anyone who heard it.

Baron's Tye was ablaze.

Entirely unaware of the carefully built bonfire in the kitchen of the house which she had just left, Louise sped on down the gravel drive. The frosty night was still clear in spite of occasional drifts of cloud passing over the moon.

It was very late. Down in the valley the clock in the tower of the village church struck the half-hour, and there was something ghostly about the far-off collection of huddled roofs, dark and silent in the faint light.

Louise hurried on. In the last half-hour she had made a discovery which had revolutionized her life. Even now a few half-sheets of ill-spelt writing nestled in the pocket of her coat, and her thoughts were on something that had happened long ago.

The moonlight shining down upon her face showed that a change had taken place in it. Her closely set black eyes were bright and hard, and there was grim determination in the line of her mouth which ennobled her whole appearance. Now she was a woman with a purpose, a woman keyed up to do braver things than could ever have been expected of her.

She passed under the thick belt of trees at the end of the drive and turned abruptly down the little path which led to the lodge cottage in which the chauffeur lived.

Only once, when she paused outside the little dark door almost hidden by an overhanging shelf of ivy, did she hesitate or the determination upon her face waver. She recovered herself, however.

Stepping onto the grass, she moved over to a darkened window and tapped peremptorily upon the glass.

It took her some time to wake the man within, but he came at last to the front door, pulling on his coat over his pajamas and trousers.

"Hello!" he said in astonishment. "What's up? Anything wrong up at the house?"

"Plenty." The woman spoke grimly and pushed past him into the little kitchen-sitting-room, which, with the bedroom, composed the entire accommodation of the bungalow.

There was such authority in her manner, such determination in her voice, that he admitted her without protest and, after lighting an oil lamp, raked together the white embers in the little stove.

"Don't worry about that. It's not cold." The woman spoke sharply, and when he turned to peer at her in amazement she stepped close to him and looked up into his face.

"Jack Walker," she said, "you've known me for five years, haven't you? And during that time I've done you a few good turns."

He stepped back from her; her passionate intensity was alarming.

"Yes," he admitted cautiously. "Yes, you've helped me several times. I admit that."

"Helped you!" she said contemptuously. "I've shielded you. I've known we were both in the same boat. Mrs de Liane has some hold over you, hasn't she? I don't want to know what it is, but I can guess. They never caught the man who escaped from Pentonville just before you got this job, did they?"

The man had whitened at the beginning of her remarks, and now an exclamation escaped him. Louise waved him silent.

"I haven't come to talk about you," she said. "The time has come when you can help me. This is where we can get even with this woman if we work together. Oh, it's no good pretending any loyalty to her: you know as well as I do that neither of us would stay in her employment if we could get out of it with safety. You've got to help me now, Jack Walker. You've got to get out the car and take me to a cottage just off the London road because in that cottage there's a child."

Her voice quivered, and he glanced at her sharply.

"I don't know anything about it," he said. "The mistress never let me go up to the house. I know where it is, though."

"You know!" she gasped at him.

"I know that there's a cottage off the London road where there's a child in which Mrs de Liane takes an interest. That's what you're talking about, isn't it?"

"You never told me? Le pauvre petit Jean!"

The man's surliness reasserted itself.

"There's a good deal I don't tell," he said grimly. "Anyway, why should I?"

Fearing she was antagonizing him, the woman laid a hand on his arm.

"Listen to me," she said. "Long ago I was the nurse to Madame Lebonheur. I don't suppose you recognize that name...."

The man looked at her curiously.

"There was a big French financier called Lebonheur who went smash and was sentenced to seven years imprisonment. D'you mean his wife?"

She nodded, her lips white and her small black eyes strangely near tears.

"He knew the crash was coming. So did Madame. She was beside herself with worry, and when the baby came she died. Just before they came to arrest him, André—that is to say Monsieur Lebonheur—gave me all Madame's jewels. 'Take the child, Louise,' he said. 'Take Jean and look after him. You'll have enough money from the sale of the jewelry to keep him until I come out. Take care of him. I trust you, Louise, I trust you.' Then they took him away."

The man was looking at her steadily, and she went on quietly with her story.

"I came to England. It seemed the safest place. But I was very frightened. I was an ignorant country girl, you see, and it was a great responsibility. On board ship I met what seemed to be a very kind little old lady. She took pity on me, and I told her my story."

A grim smile spread over the man's face.

"I know the missus in that mood," he said. "That's how she took me in."

Louise's passionate voice continued:

"We all stayed at the same hotel in Folkestone. I slept very heavily during the night, so heavily that I know now I must have been drugged, although at the time it never dawned upon me that the coffee which the kind old lady had given me just before I slept contained anything other than it was supposed to do. In the morning both Jean and the jewels had disappeared.

"I was beside myself. I was a stranger in a strange land. I could not speak the language. I wanted to go to the police, to the French consul, but Mrs de Liane dissuaded me. She seemed to me to be so kind, and she took me into her service and promised to do her best to help me find the child again. In these last five years I have found out what she really is, and deep in my heart I have known that it was she who was responsible for my whole tragedy, but I have not been able to get proof until tonight. Now I have the proof, and I must find the child.

"André comes out in the early part of next year. He will find me, and what shall I be able to tell him if I have not got the child?"

Her voice died away, and the man stood looking at her curiously.

"You're in love with him?" he enquired brusquely.

The woman met his eyes squarely. "There are some men who are made to be loved," she said quietly. "You take me to find Jean. You must get the car out and take me at once."

The man hesitated, but at last, after what seemed an unbearable interval, he shrugged his shoulders.

"Well, I've done enough dirty work in the last five years," he said. "I may as well do something on the level for a change. It's stealing the car—I suppose you know that?"

"What does it matter?" the woman said wildly. "I have proof, I tell you! I can get her arrested. I can get her imprisoned."

The man took down his heavy greatcoat from its place behind the door.

"All right," he said quietly. "Come on."

Together they pushed the car out of the garage behind the chauffeur's cottage and onto the main road before starting the engine. The night was still fine, and the white road stretched out in front of them like a ribbon among the ploughed fields.

As they passed the brow of the hill Walker looked over his shoulder and pulled up.

"I thought I saw something like a light down there in the house," he said. "It's gone again now. If she was to telephone to the police to stop us ..."

The woman tugged at his sleeve.

"Come on. Hurry. She will not telephone the police. Once she knows I am gone she will be afraid of the police."

The man sighed and let in the clutch.

"I don't know why I'm taking this risk for you," he said. "But there's some things one doesn't forgive. It was dirty to take the child. That's how she kept you with her, I suppose ... always promising?"

Louise nodded. "Always promising," she echoed. "Come. Hurry. Drive faster."

They pulled up at last in a narrow lane. The man climbed out.

"There's the house," he said, pointing to a ramshackle building silhouetted against the brightening sky. "There's a light. I've never been up there myself. She used to leave the car here."

But Louise had not heard him. Already she was halfway up the narrow overgrown path which led through the dilapidated garden. He could see her square figure moving silently through the dawn.

He came up with her just as she reached the window, and together they peered in through the dirty panes at the scene within.

It was a poor room lit by a single oil lamp. From the furniture and the remnants of a meal still on the table it was evident that it was the family sitting room. Lying on a bed made of a couple of chairs pulled up in front of the fire was a child, a slatternly woman bending over it, weary exasperation upon her face.

Louise had no eyes for the woman. Her gaze was fixed upon the little boy with dark hair and bright, feverish cheeks who tossed and turned upon his uncomfortable bed.

She caught her breath. "He has grown up so like Monsieur André!" she whispered.

"Are you sure it is him? You haven't seen him since he was a baby."

Louise looked at him contemptuously in the dusk.

"I would know him anywhere," she said. "Le petit Jean ... le pauvre petit Jean."

She turned on her heel, and he caught her arm.

"Here, what are you going to do?"

"Go to him," said Louise simply. "But naturally."

Crossing the garden, she raised her hand and beat loudly upon the wooden door.

24
THE FIRE

S tanding on the lawn, his white hair dishevelled and his dressing gown huddled round his shapeless form, Ted de Liane made an unforgettable picture. He had lost his head completely and was shouting meaningless words at the excited villagers who were fast crowding upon the scene.

Baron's Tye was blazing like a funeral pyre. In the window of her beautiful Chinese room Mrs de Liane stood silhouetted against the glare within. She was wonderfully calm, and her tiny figure, clad in its silk shawls, seemed to sway in unison with the dancing flames around her.

The dark garden was already alive with people. Ted, awakened by the smell of smoke, had come down, forced his way through the long windows in the library and given the alarm by phone.

At the moment the fire was confined to the back of the house, but the light lath-and-plaster construction of the building left very little hope that the local fire brigade might get the blaze under control before the whole place was destroyed.

At the very top of the house a barred window stood open. It was the window of the bridal suite. Within the room Mary slept heavily, completely oblivious of the roar beneath her or of the fumes pouring up into the room.

It was just before the dawn. The moon had slipped out of sight behind the heavy banks of cloud on the horizon, and a light wind had sprung up which fanned the flames into a furious tarantella.

All the lower half of the back of the building was a seething mass of fire. Long flames curled out of the windows, casting an unsteady light over the scene as far even as the river at the foot of the valley.

Every minute more and more people from the village crowded into the grounds, and a chain of buckets had been formed from the stream to the kitchen windows. But in spite of the feverish activity of the workers the feeble splashes of water did very little to discourage the flames.

Ted de Liane was shouting for Walker, but the man did not appear, and it was one of the farm hands who fetched a ladder from the coach house and carried Mrs de Liane down to safety amid the cheers of the crowd.

She lay, a little limp bundle, in her husband's arms, and as the village women bent over her murmured something incoherent and then appeared to lose consciousness.

Some considerable time elapsed before she revived, and it was while Ted de Liane was still bending over her that the village policeman, a rugged individual considerably flustered by his position of authority, came hurrying up.

"I see all the maids are out, sir. They sleep out, don't they? There's no one else in the house, is there? I haven't seen Mr Richard."

"Richard's staying with his brother this evening," said Ted de Liane, and would have continued had not a little moan from the woman lying on the blankets at his feet distracted his attention.

Meanwhile the flames were creeping higher and higher up the house. All the lower windows had been forced open, and rescue work was going on. Furniture and pictures were being carried out into the garden.

The arrival of a car driven at reckless speed scattered the crowd, and Edmund Beron sprang out, his face pallid in the crimson light from the blazing house. He pushed his way through the group round his mother and dropped upon his knees by her side. Those in attendance recognized him and stepped back.

For some time Mrs de Liane remained impassive, but when with a crash the kitchen ceiling fell in and the crowd's attention was once more diverted towards the fire itself she opened her eyes and looked up at her son.

"Edmund," she whispered, "get into the library. You know where the safe is? Let into the floor under the knee hole of the desk. There're some papers in there. And find Louise. I haven't seen her. Get the papers. They're important."

"Where's the girl?" he whispered. "I never dreamed you'd do anything so horrible as this—"

"Hush!" The command cut through his words. "Get the papers. The girl's all right. Have you left Richard at home?"

"Yes. I slipped out without calling him. How do you mean, she's all right?"

One small white hand was pressed to his lips.

"Get the papers," the woman insisted. "They went out of my mind until now. They concern the child."

He left her side obediently, and she saw him threading his way through the crowd towards the library windows, which were still dark although smoke was pouring out of them.

Eva de Liane looked up at the house. It was doomed. Anyone could see that a rescue from that inferno must be an impossibility.

She dragged herself to her feet and allowed a thin scream of pure horror to escape her.

"Mary!" she cried. "Where's Mary? Oh my God!"

Instantly she was the centre of a crowd again, and the policeman came hurrying up. With tears streaming down her face and her lips quivering Mrs de Liane poured out her story.

"Hasn't she been roused? Hasn't she been called? I thought she was safe. I made certain you'd get her out first thing. Oh, where is she? Where is the poor child?"

It took some time for the excited onlookers to get the actual facts out of her, she seemed so distraught.

"She's up in the tower, in the bridal suite. Oh, how terrible! How dreadful! What shall I do? She can't be *in* there ... she *can't!*"

The soft voice was quivering with terror, and there were many in the crowd gathered round the old woman who were moved by the pathetic picture she made. She looked so small, so helpless, so inexpressibly tragic in her grief.

She turned to her husband.

"Ted," she implored, "she was saved, wasn't she? She's out here somewhere, surely ... surely?"

The old man gaped at her. Even now she could shock him; even now, after all these years, she could still send a chill of horror trickling down his spine.

"I—I forgot," he mumbled. "I thought she was in her usual room. I made certain that she would have escaped at the same time that I did. My God, Eva, this is terrible!"

"Well, do something! Do something, my dear! Get her out! Find somebody to get her out. Walker's a brave man. Where is he?"

As Ted de Liane stumbled off, the constable who had been standing in the little group came over to the woman.

"The young lady was sleeping in her usual room, wasn't she?" he said.

Mrs de Liane seized his arm. "No, no. The oil heater smoked, you see, and we had to move her to the suite at the top of the house because there wasn't time to get her room clean. She must be up there. Oh look, look! Isn't it terrible?"

She flung out her hand, and the white-faced onlookers followed the direction of that slender arm to the little tower at the top of Baron's Tye, the topmost story of all which looked out over the rolling countryside. It was still dark against the sky, but beneath it and all round it the dancing flames pressed still farther and farther on.

One of the farmers in the crowd took command of the situation.

"I don't reckon it's possible to get her out of there," he said. "It's a terrible thing. I can't understand why she hasn't come to the window. Probably overcome by the fumes by this time. Still, we must try if we can reach her. Get me a ladder, boys. We'll see what we can do."

The local fire engine, a primitive affair mounted on a hand-cart, had reached the scene by this time, but since all the water had to be pumped or brought from the brook its efforts were severely handicapped, and Baron's Tye burned vigorously against the gradually lightening sky.

Mrs de Liane watched it. To all outward appearances she was a figure of tragedy, a gallant little creature bowed down by overwhelming grief. But there was a new light in her dancing blue eyes, a strange grimness in the lines of her soft mouth.

She was standing quite alone on the far side of the crowd which surged and milled round the blazing building, a crowd which grew every moment as new arrivals from outlying farms arrived in their cars and traps.

All the back of the building had been demolished and now rose up, a charred skeleton, over a red inferno within, while the flames were fast forcing their way to the library wing, two stories over which was the tower. Ted de Liane materialized out of the darkness and caught his wife's elbow in an urgent grasp.

"It's come," he whispered. "It's come. I knew it would. They're here. I've seen them. They're looking for us."

She turned slowly and looked up into his face. He could see her eyes in the unnatural glare from the burning house.

"Who?"

"Latcher and the police. He's got Peter Muir-David, and there was someone else there too, someone I couldn't see. But I caught the gleam of uniforms. What shall we do?"

He felt her stiffen for a moment, and then she laughed.

"Keep your head. For God's sake keep your head! They'll get us. Don't you see, they've come for the girl." Ted's voice was shaking. Mrs de Liane silenced him with a single expressive whisper.

"Well," she said, "they'll find her."

Ted de Liane gaped, and the woman went on.

"Look," she said, nodding at the tower. "When it falls—and it will fall—she will go with it. Oh, they'll find something of her in the end, and we shall be brokenhearted over the loss of our little daughter-in-law. Afterwards, if we find out, if it is proved to us, that she was a wretched little swindler who deceived us, we shall be very sorry. But nobody can blame us."

The man stepped away from her. There was fear in his eyes, fear and repulsion.

"You're a devil," he said huskily. "You're … horrible."

Mrs de Liane ignored the outburst.

"Where's Edmund? Edmund should be here. And where's Walker? I may want the car soon. He ought to be here at once."

Ted de Liane had turned away. His was a weak nature, one which shrank naturally from any sort of violence. The scene before him and the discovery of where the responsibility lay was too much for him. He felt physically ill. The world reeled about him.

Eva de Liane remained perfectly calm, huddled in her heavy silk Chinese shawls. She was quite ready for Latcher and his policemen whenever they should find her. She was quite prepared to put on an exhibition of grief and despair that would have convinced the most sceptical policeman alive. She knew she was safe. In Mary alone lay proof of her guilt, and Mary was in the tower, the tower that must crash at any moment into the mass of flames below.

But it was Edmund Beron who found her first, Beron forcing his way through the crowd, his eyes wild and his mouth distorted. He found the woman and, passing his arm round her shoulders, led her a little apart into the shadow of some bushes on the edge of the lawn.

"Well," she said eagerly, her hand outstretched, "you've got the papers? And where's Louise?"

"They're gone," he said dully. "They're all gone."

He heard her catch her breath in the darkness.

"What do you mean?"

Her small hand gripped his coat sleeve and shook him in her excitement.

"What do you mean?"

"They're gone," he repeated dully. "Someone had opened the safe before the fire. It was lying open. And the woman's gone too. I've been making enquiries. She and Walker seem to have disappeared in the car."

"My God!" The words were whispered, but there was something in their quality which frightened the man more thoroughly than anything he had ever heard before.

He bent down to look into her face and saw for the first time that she too was afraid. For a moment stark, undisguised terror was in her eyes.

"Louise—the car—the papers—gone! Edmund, do you know what this means? Oh, why should it happen now! What shall I do? What shall I do?"

He shook her. Now that she knew fear some of his lost spirit returned, and he was stronger than she.

"Were those the papers relating to the child?"

"Yes," she whispered. "Yes. There's a case against me there—a criminal case. They've gone to the cottage. Walker knew the way. Quick, Edmund! We've got your car. We must get there first. We must stop her somehow. The others must fend for themselves."

Beron hesitated. "No," he said. "They'll lose their heads, I know them. We daren't risk it. Ted must come too, and we must warn Richard."

"All right. Anything you like, only hurry."

He had never known the woman in this mood. She was almost docile in her anxiety.

They found the car without much difficulty. Latcher and Peter were on the inside of the crowd nearest the house and did not see them go.

By the time Beron had found Ted de Liane and dragged him towards the car the old woman was already seated beside the driving wheel, a dark rug pulled over her white shawl.

They crept slowly off down the drive. The noise and excitement round the burning house was so great that their unobtrusive departure was not noticed.

Just as they reached the gates at the far end of the drive, however, a figure on horseback swung into the headlights and Mrs de Liane touched her son's arm.

"It's Richard," she said. "Quick. ..."

Beron pulled the car across the road, and the rider came to a stop within a foot of them. It was Richard, only partially clad, astride a hunter from the village. The horse was barebacked and flecked with foam.

As Richard caught sight of Edmund his face cleared.

"Oh, it's you, is it?" he said. "Have they got her? Is she safe?"

A laugh escaped the woman.

"I'm here, Richard," she said. "Or were you enquiring about your little impostor?"

"I'm talking about Mary—I'm talking about my wife. Where is she?"

Edmund sighed with impatience. "I'm sorry," he said. "We couldn't do anything. She's trapped in the bridal suite. You can't do anything. Nobody can do anything. We've got to make a run for it. Something's gone wrong. There's not time to tell you. Turn the horse loose and come with us. It's your one chance."

Ted de Liane pushed open the back door of the car.

"Get in," he said. "Get in, my boy. The place is alive with police. It's no good worrying about the girl now. That's madness."

Richard did not seem to have heard the invitation. Instead his eyes were raised to the blazing roof of the house, the flames shooting up over the trees.

"In there?" he said huskily. "In there?"

And then, before they realized what had happened, he had swung the horse round, digging his heels into its sides. The animal leapt forward, and they got a final glimpse of him, a wild, fantastic figure silhouetted against the glare of what once had been Baron's Tye.

Mrs de Liane's face was very grim.

"Hurry, Edmund," she said. "Hurry. If the boy's determined to be a fool he deserves all he gets. We've got to save ourselves."

There was urgency in her tone, and the old note of command had crept back into it. Beron let in the clutch and trod hard on the accelerator.

25

"I'LL FOLLOW YOU ..."

B ut this is terrible, absolutely terrible! It's a nightmare.
Whoever the girl is, whatever she's done, she can't have a
death like this. It's ghastly—unbearable!"

Little Mr Latcher was twittering in his anxiety, and at his
side Peter Muir-David covered his face with his hands.

"I daren't," he said. "I tell you, Latcher, I love that girl. I
believe in her innocence. But I'm a coward. I never realized it
before tonight. I couldn't go into that inferno ... I couldn't!"

"But of course not, sir. Nobody could."

The farmer who had taken charge of the rescue attempts
spoke roughly but with conviction.

"It's suicide, that's what it is," he continued. "I've been up as
far as the ladder will take me myself, but I couldn't go any
further. Nobody could. It's throwing your life away. Besides, the
girl's dead. The fumes must have killed her. Pull yourself
together, sir. What you want's a drink."

Peter turned away shuddering.

"I can't look at it," he said. "I can't. I tell you I'd give anything
I possess. I'd pay anything in the world to get her out of there,

but I daren't attempt it myself. I daren't! God help me, I'm afraid. ..."

The farmer laid a heavy hand on his shoulder.

"You're not the only one, sir," he said. "We'd all go, any of us, if there was a chance, but there isn't. It means death, that's what it means. Look at it now."

Peter forced himself to stare at the blaze. Practically all the roof was alight. Only the little tower with its single window was dark against the early morning sky.

A great hush had fallen upon the crowd. The news that a woman was lying in the little dark room at the top of the house had spread through it, and now it seemed to each man who watched that he was going to see death himself in perhaps his most terrible form.

Peter turned away. Every line of his body drooped, and his chin had fallen forward on his breast.

Suddenly there was a strangled cry from Mr Latcher, and at the same moment a great sigh passed through the whole crowd. High up on the roof, silhouetted against the pale stars, a tall, thin figure had appeared.

"It's Mr Richard!" "It's her husband!" "It's Mr Richard!"

The whisper ran round the huddled group, but there was no cheering. The moment was too tense for that.

"He'll kill himself—he'll kill himself." Mr Latcher did not realize that it was he who had spoken.

Slowly, inch by inch over the red-hot tiles, the tall figure edged its way. Now and again a sheet of flame or a shower of sparks hid him from view, and there was one moment when he was entirely enveloped in a great billowing cloud of smoke which seemed as though it must suffocate him and send him pitching down into the blazing cavern below. But when it had passed he was still there, still moving furtively towards the tower.

Now he had reached it and had begun to scale the ornamental half-timbering. He reached the window at last, and in the crowd a woman screamed.

They saw him fighting with the slender iron bars, and all the time the flames roared below him as another and yet another beam crashed in the old house, and the whole structure shook and sagged.

Now he had disappeared. There was a long breathless moment. Peter had sunk to his knees on the grass, covering his face, and Mr Latcher heard himself swearing softly in a strange voice he did not recognize as his own.

It was an unbearable moment.

Then, just when it seemed that the whole crowd must lose its head, there was a movement at the window again. Richard reappeared, and across his shoulder lay the slender, drooping form of a girl.

The crowd did not cheer. It screamed. A hoarse sound, hardly human, rose above the roar of the flames.

Instantly there was violent activity. A sheet blanket was held out, and from below came hoarse injunctions commanding him to jump.

Richard struggled for a foothold. The flames were almost upon him now. At any moment the king beam of the house might give way and precipitate the two into eternity.

"Now!"

They heard his voice, clear and oddly calm, in the uproar.

"Coming!"

He threw the girl from him, and they saw her slender figure silhouetted for a moment against the sky. Then, as the crowd roared, she dropped into the centre of the blanket.

Eager hands carried her to the lawn, and again all eyes were fixed on the roof. They saw that the man was reeling. The fumes were rapidly overpowering him. He staggered and regained control of himself.

"Jump!" they shouted, and again he answered them:

"Coming!"

As he hit the blanket there was a roar and a crash behind him. The house seemed to writhe like a live thing, and the tower, its supports eaten away, crashed downward into the blaze.

"Very well, sir. But I've had my orders."

The plain-clothes man spoke roughly but not without a certain respect. He had been present at the rescue and knew a brave man when he saw one.

He was standing in the doorway of the maids' lodge, which remained one of the few standing buildings at Baron's Tye, looking in at the man, still dishevelled and black from his adventure, who stood in the centre of the room.

Mary lay on a couch, where the women who had attended her had left her at her husband's request.

Both Richard's arms were in bandages, and there was a livid scar across his cheek where a falling beam had glanced it.

"I've had my orders," the man repeated. "As soon as she recovers consciousness you've both got to come down to the station. I've got another officer in the car outside."

Richard nodded. "All right ... all right. We'll come. I promise you."

The door closed behind the man, and Richard turned back and threw himself on his knees beside the girl. She opened her eyes and looked at him.

"Oh Richard—" her voice was very weak—"I dreamed ... I dreamed, oh, terrible things!"

He did not speak but knelt looking at her, and there occurred one of those extraordinary understandings which do sometimes happen and are afterwards inexplicable.

Quite suddenly and without any word the girl slipped her arm round his neck and drew his head down towards her, and he kissed her lips.

For a long time there was silence in the little room, and at last he rose heavily to his feet.

"We've got to go," he said. "They're waiting for us. I'll get you out of this, my darling. God knows you've never done anything that anyone in the world could blame you for. I'll get you out of this somehow."

Very unsteadily she climbed off the couch and came towards him.

"I want to be with you," she said. "I know it now. I love you. I want to be with you."

They were in a strange mood as they sat together in the back of the police car and were driven down to the little station in the village street. A crowd had gathered to see them, and there were whispers and some cheering as they appeared.

The two plain-clothes men helped them out of the back of the car and took them into the square, ugly building. Mary's mind was reeling. She was only vaguely aware of what had happened. She only knew that she had been in great danger and that Richard had saved her and that she loved him. And that now the worst had happened and he was going to be arrested, and she with him.

In the little anteroom she saw Mr Latcher talking to a man in police-inspector's uniform. The little solicitor glanced up as they appeared, and an odd expression came into his eyes.

He began a conventional speech of congratulation on their safety but broke off abruptly as he saw that both young people were on the verge of collapse. He turned to the inspector.

"I hardly know if it's wise," he began. "I fancy—ah—it—ah—may be a great shock."

"We'll risk it," said the inspector grimly. "Come on, you two."

He flung open the door of the inner room, and Mary stepped into a brightly lit apartment whose pale-green walls were bare and inhospitable. Slowly her heavy eyes travelled round the room and came to rest at last upon the three people who sat at the table under the window.

One was a policeman, one was Peter Muir-David, and the third was the one woman in the world she had thought never to see again. Mary stood there swaying, her eyes riveted on the stranger. The world seemed to be crashing about her ears, and darkness descended over her.

"Say, look out! The kid's fainting. ..."

The big red-haired girl in the mink coat was on her feet and across the room to catch the other woman before she fell.

"Poor little kid," said Marie-Elizabeth Mason. "I may have returned from the dead, but it looks as though you've killed this young woman. Clumsy just isn't the word for it!"

Some minutes later she was still talking.

"Now look here, my dear good people," she said, thrusting her expensive hat a little farther on to the back of her head. "I—I don't want to push myself forward in any way, but it seems to me that this is my show. I mean if anybody's been aggrieved it's me, anyway from the legal point of view. That's so, isn't it, Judge?"

Little Mr Latcher coughed and grew pink.

"Not—ah—*Judge*, my dear young lady," he said hastily. "But as your legal adviser I think I can safely say that the onus of prosecution lies with you."

"Let's leave prosecution out of it for a bit," said Marie-Elizabeth, drily. She was standing by the doorway of the big, cheerless room, still supporting the fainting Mary with one strong fur-clad arm. "This is a friend of mine. You've heard me speak of her lots of times, haven't you, Elmer?"

The small fat man with the bald head and the outrageously luxurious motoring coat who had wandered in from the outer office said, "Sure!" without batting an eyelid, and Marie-Elizabeth beamed on him.

"There you are," she said. "The mighty word spoken by the

little millionaire himself. I'd like you all to know that Elmer Tench backs his wife up in every particular. What I say goes, doesn't it, Elmer?"

"Sure," nodded the plump man again, and his small black eyes danced at her appreciatively.

Marie-Elizabeth turned to the inspector.

"Well, that being so, I'd like to have a few words with my friend in private, Captain. We've been out of touch with each other for a week or two while I've been honeymooning, and things sort of seem to have got out of hand."

The inspector hesitated, and the Australian girl waved her hand towards Richard.

"You can have the boy friend," she said, "and if you're not busy with him he could do with a bath and some breakfast, couldn't you, buddy?"

Richard did not speak, but a faint smile appeared upon his tired face.

Mr Latcher and the inspector had a hasty conference. The effect of Marie-Elizabeth's sensational personality was considerable. The inspector was definitely flustered by her. The only person who did not seem to realize what was happening in the room was Peter. He sat at the table, his head in his hands, and stared at the rough deal boards, his eyes heavy and his thoughts far away.

In the end Marie-Elizabeth got her own way, as she was destined to do from the first moment she opened her mouth, and she and Mary found themselves in a little warm cubbyhole called "the matron's room." A police constable sat in the passage outside, but he was out of earshot, and the two girls were alone.

Mr Latcher had strongly opposed the interview and had taken it upon himself to warn his client that Mary was a dangerous criminal and that any conversation would be best conducted in front of him. But Marie-Elizabeth had merely replied, "You're telling me, Judge!" and had gone her own way.

As soon as the two girls were alone, Marie-Elizabeth set her companion down in the one comfortable chair the room contained and made up the fire with a fine disregard for government coal.

"Well now," she said at last, wiping her hands on a big chiffon handkerchief, "you've been having quite a time gadding around as me, haven't you?"

Mary caught her breath. "I can't believe it *is* you," she said. "They told me you were dead. I—I saw you buried. ..."

"I know." The big redheaded girl looked momentarily serious. "That was just terrible. My old auntie seems to have been quite energetic in her own quiet way. I tell you, kid, I had no idea what I was letting you in for. Auntie appears to have been several varieties of crook. I'd like to meet her."

"But the funeral ..." Mary persisted. "I saw you buried."

"No, kid. Not guilty. It wasn't me. That was a girl called Ruby." Marie-Elizabeth made the astonishing statement without turning a hair. "I guess I'd better explain. When I left Granny's little dugout in Merton House I went to the Imperial Palace and booked myself a suite for a fortnight. I was going to do the thing well, you see. I took all your things there, as we arranged, and I booked the room in your name. And then I walked out, and I met Elmer."

"Elmer?"

"Yes. You were fainting, or you'd have seen him. He's among all the cops in the waiting room. Mary, he's not much to look at—" Marie-Elizabeth's voice had become very earnest and her big grey eyes were steady— "but he's got a heart of gold and he's a millionaire—a multimillionaire. It's not only his money," she continued. "I thought it was at first, but it's not. I'd have married Elmer if he was broke."

She paused and glanced at Mary reflectively.

"You may think it was a bit sudden," she said, "but I'm like that, and it was all fixed up within forty-eight hours. He said,

'Come on, let's get married and nip off for a cruise,' and I said, 'Right.' And that was all, or it might have been all if I hadn't met Ruby and she hadn't been down on her luck. She was a little actress, a red-haired kid who was a bit wild. I met her at one of the agents' who I'd been to see before I realized that Elmer was on the level. She had no money and no place to go, and I said, 'Well, come round and have some grub with me one night.' She turned up immediately, and I was going off with Elmer by that time, so I said, 'You can caretake my room for me at the hotel.' And she did. I told the management that I'd taken the place for her and that she was the real Mary Coleridge—that was just in case they got mean and wouldn't stand for a transfer—and that's how the trouble started. She went joy riding, got herself killed, and I guess you can understand the rest of the story."

She paused and stood looking at Mary, a contrite expression on her fine, clear-cut face.

Mary passed her hand over her eyes. "It seems incredible," she said. "I suppose it's no good me telling you that I didn't intentionally assist Mrs de Liane in her attempt to get hold of your fortune?"

"Oh, that. ..." Marie-Elizabeth shrugged her shoulders. "My dear child, you don't have to tell me you're honest. That's the first thing I told the solicitor's clerk when he found me and what I've been telling that little dried-up hen, Latcher, ever since I met him. I know you're honest, Mary. I'm not crazy, and I'm not blind, dumb or half-witted. Some people are so honest it's embarrassing. You're one of those. Auntie seems to have been a different proposition altogether."

She laid her hand upon the other girl's shoulder as she spoke, and Mary found the grip of those steady fingers very comforting in a world of chaos.

"But the money," she said at last. "I don't know what's happened to it. I don't know how much she's had. I couldn't do anything to stop her ... I couldn't."

"Oh, don't worry about that." Marie-Elizabeth spoke magnificently. "Latcher says she may have gone through ten thousand at the most since she pulled the swindle, although she's had the interest on the three hundred thousand for years, the old haybag. And anyway, what's ten thousand? Elmer's got three million. It's extraordinary, you know, because he's just like a kid. He and I understand each other, and we get along fine.

"However, I don't want to bore you with rhapsodies about my husband. I want to know about your position."

Mary shuddered. She felt dizzy and frightened. The amazing truth was only forcing itself upon her very slowly.

"I don't understand," she said at last. "D'you mean that you're not going to prosecute me? D'you mean they're not going to arrest me? D'you mean that you really believe that I'm not a crook?"

"Bless the girl!" said Marie-Elizabeth hastily. "You're off your nut, my pretty. What d'you think I've been telling you all this time? —how to make flapjacks? I'm very sorry I let you in for all this. I blame myself. If I'd gone down to Auntie I'd have handled the situation in my own way, and, although we might have killed each other, she'd have had her work cut out to manage me. But instead of that, I sent you, an innocent little schoolkid, and played right into her hands. I'm so glad you haven't died. I'd never have forgiven myself. I'm going to make it up to you somehow—don't you worry about that."

Mary looked at her wonderingly. She looked so strong, so amazingly smart in her long mink coat and elegantly cut tweeds. All the same she wondered. If Eva de Liane had met the real Marie-Elizabeth on that night at Baron's Tye, would she have found her match? Mary was inclined to doubt it.

Marie-Elizabeth had perched herself on the edge of the table.

"There's one little thing we've got to settle right away," she said. "It's a delicate matter, and I hardly know how to approach it. When I heard from Latcher and that fellow Sir Peter what-ever-his-name-is that you'd actually married Auntie's son, well, then I did wonder whether you'd gone out of your mind. A girl can do a lot for pity, but marriage—well, I ask you! However, now I've seen the boy friend I'm beginning to get a hold of the situation. I don't blame you, kid. I don't blame you at all."

Mary grew crimson. "Oh, but you don't understand," she said. "I wasn't in love with Richard. I'd never seen him before. I thought he was going to die. I wasn't in love with him—not then."

Marie-Elizabeth raised an eyebrow. "Not *then?*" she said. "That's what I wanted to know. All the same, don't you run away with any illusions, young woman. If Auntie had taken you upstairs and shown you a little measly cross-eyed under-sized sniveller and said, 'Look, it's going to die. Marry it,' you'd have been awfully sorry for her but you wouldn't have married. No, my pet, it's the man himself who got you into that little scrape.

"Now look here, do you want the marriage annulled and the lad stuffed in jail with the rest of the gang? Or d'you want me and Elmer to exert our influence? Just say the word."

Mary rose to her feet. "I love him," she said quietly. "I want to be with him always."

"Atta girl!" said Marie-Elizabeth Mason with approval. "Well, hold your hat on, sweetie, and leave it all to me. Let's go and talk to Elmer."

Mary held out her hands. "I never met anyone like you in all my life," she said unsteadily. "You're wonderful."

"Don't you believe it," said Marie-Elizabeth Mason. "I'm not a darned fool, that's all. When something sticks out under my nose I see it. Don't cry, kid. The fun's just beginning."

Blindly Mary followed her.

26

THE SHOWDOWN

"Mother, are you afraid?"

Edmund Beron put the question as they pulled up in the dawn in a deserted lane some little distance from the cottage which Louise had visited earlier in the night. He caught a glimpse of Eva de Liane's reflection in the windscreen, and something new in her face had made him turn to her.

She did not reply immediately, and it was Ted's blustering voice from the back of the car which answered him.

"Afraid? No, she's not afraid. Why should she be?"

There was a forced heartiness in his tone, and in spite of himself the last words were a question. Eva de Liane drew her shawls a little more closely about her. Although she was fully dressed, she shivered as though with cold, and there was an expression in her dancing blue eyes which Beron had never seen there before. It was a weariness. She looked strained, exhausted.

However, her voice had its old indomitable quality as she spoke.

"Oh no," she said. "These people must be taught to be reasonable, that's all. Louise may be a little difficult, dear girl, but I think the Whybrows are far too sensible to listen to her. What are you waiting for, Edmund? There's no time to lose. Hurry."

Beron started the car again unwillingly. "I was thinking," he said slowly, "that if we drove straight on to the coast it might be the safest thing to do. I've got a little money. I've been carrying it about with me for some time lately, and if I know you you've done the same thing, and so has Ted."

"Yes, I've got a little money. Not much, but enough to keep me going for a week or two."

There was a shamefaced quality in Ted de Liane's mumble from behind them. Mrs de Liane laughed.

"I have nothing," she said. "Nothing here or anywhere. I converted everything I had and everything I could get out of Latcher in my attempt to smash Cosmos."

Beron let the car swerve, and he righted it again before he spoke.

"Were you mad?"

The words broke from him. Again the old woman laughed a little.

"No," she said. "It was a gamble, and it was worth it. Everything depends upon these people here. The girl is safely dead. With her out of the way we can meet any charges that are brought against us. There is no proof. No one has any proof—"

"Except Louise," said Beron.

Eva de Liane caught her breath. "Except Louise. And if you think a woman like that is going to confound me you're wrong."

Beron said nothing. They had turned into the lane now, and the black Daimler was still standing in the road. Beron pulled up behind it.

"They're still here, then," he said, his face pale and his lips working. "We're wasting time, I tell you. There's only one thing for us to do, and we'd better do it quickly. Let's get away. After all, we don't know what's happened back at Heronhoe. Even now the police may be on our track. Even now they may be warning the ports. Let's make a dash for it."

"No." The voice of authority was still there, and as the old woman climbed out of the car and stood in the dawn she was the commanding figure she had always been. "We won't lose our heads. Edmund, you stay here. Ted, come with me."

The older man obeyed her grudgingly, and Beron remained crouching over the wheel.

"Be as quick as you can," he said. "I'm not happy about this delay."

Mrs de Liane's laugh drowned the rest of his sentence.

"You were always nervous, Edmund," she said, "even as a little boy. There was a time when I had great hopes of you, but now I'm not so sure. Wait here until we come back."

Edmund Beron did not answer. He remained bent over the wheel of the car, his eyes fixed gloomily on the back of the Daimler in front.

Together Mr and Mrs de Liane toiled up the narrow, over-grown path through the straggling little garden of the Whybrows' cottage. It was a desolate scene. White frost lay on the brown earth and yellow grasses, and the cottage itself looked lonely and deserted.

It was typical of Eva de Liane that she did not hesitate, did not reconnoitre, but walked straight up to the low doorway and, pressing down the iron latch, stepped swiftly into the stuffy room within.

Ted de Liane hung back, but when she turned and glanced at him he shambled after her, and together they burst upon the scene within.

The oil lamp was still burning, although daylight was creeping in through the windows. The place was in the same disorder, but instead of the weary Mrs Whybrow it was Louise, her dark eyes alight with eagerness, who bent over the sleeping child. Walker sat in a corner of the room, dozing in a chair.

They both rose as Mrs de Liane appeared, and for a moment there was complete silence as the two women faced one another, Mrs de Liane calm, dominant and smiling, and Louise fierce and vigorous with a new determination which the other had not seen in her before.

"Well?" It was the old woman who spoke, her voice soft and gentle, her lips smiling. "So you've found my little surprise, Louise?"

The Frenchwoman did not answer, and just for a moment Eva de Liane was nonplussed. She had expected an outburst, but not this silent, stolid waiting. She turned her attention to Walker.

"I don't mind you taking the car on occasions," she said, "but you really must ask my permission first or it's stealing, you know, and with your record—"

"That'll do from you." The man spoke quietly and without excitement, a quality which lent his words a strange authority.

Ted de Liane backed instinctively towards the door, but the old woman stood her ground.

"I think it's time we understood one another," she said. "Louise, wrap that child in a blanket and take him down to the car. Walker will drive you back to Heronhoe."

"No." The Frenchwoman stepped forward, placing her body between Mrs de Liane and the child, who had wakened and was beginning to whimper. "Go away. Oh, you need not be afraid of me. I shall not hurt you," she added as the old woman retreated a pace or two. "The police will do that."

"Really? You've communicated with the police? That was very foolhardy of you, Louise." Mrs de Liane's ivory skin had taken on a deeper pallor, but otherwise she showed no sign of discomfort. "Don't be ridiculous, my dear child. After all, we've understood each other very well these last five years. Surely we can come to some arrangement?"

THE DEVIL AND HER SON

The rage which had been smouldering in the black eyes suddenly boiled over.

"Arrangement!" she said. "How dare you speak to me of arrangement? Will arrangement give Jean back his health? Will arrangement compensate him for his years of misery? Will arrangement makeup to me the hours of fear that I have spent? You are unspeakable! I tell you, madame, I know you for what you are, and I will see to it that the world knows it. There is no pity, there is no kindness left in my soul. I will make you suffer as I have suffered. The police shall know everything."

The intensity of her attack was enhanced by the unnatural quietness which had preceded it, and involuntarily the old woman stepped back before that blazing fury. She was not beaten, however.

"You're a fool, Louise," she said, her voice rising out of control. "A fool! Where are you going to get help if not from me? If you think these people are going to assist you you're wrong. They'll do anything for money. They're only interested in money. They're not going to do anything to help a miserable little waif, the child of a convict. How are you going to pay them for it? Come with me. You're wasting your time here."

"That's where you make your big mistake."

The speaker emerged from the doorway which led into the only other room on the ground floor. Dick Whybrow was not a pleasing person to look at in the ordinary way, but he made a very different picture now from the whining brute who stopped the car when Mary had journeyed back to Heronhoe from London. There was a spark of decency left in him, and it had come out.

His wife stood behind him in the doorway, moistening her dry lips with the tip of her tongue. Eva de Liane could see her sharp eyes fixed upon the Frenchwoman.

"You get out of here. We've been talking, and I think we all understand one another. We know what we've got to do and don't you be afraid, we're going to do it."

Whybrow's slow voice was menacing.

"We didn't know what we were up to when we took the child in. We believed your story, Mother and me, and it seemed a fair way of earning a shilling or two. But we didn't dream that you were turning us into criminals. We didn't dream that you were making us kidnappers."

Mrs de Liane was beaten, but she would not admit the fact. She came forward, her silk shawl glistening against the drabness of the room.

"Let us all be sensible," she said. "I take it you're all interested in money. You used to be, Mr Whybrow. Now if you're wise you will stick to those who can help you. What can you get out of these people—a penniless lady's maid and a chauffeur with a prison record? Be sensible."

There was a moment's silence, and, thinking she had won her point and that the man was wavering, she let her smile broaden.

"We are all people of the world, aren't we?" she said.

"Some of us are human," said the man in the doorway, "and some of us are not. That's the great difference, lady. All of us, all of us in this room, except perhaps the kid, have done one or two things that they wouldn't like talked about, but we're not all monsters. Some of us have got a bit of good stuff left. Some of us don't want to steal from children, and there's two here that want justice. There's two here that want to see you in a prison overall, my lady, and one of 'em's me and one of 'em's that woman over there with the child."

The effect of this outburst was electrifying. Mrs de Liane swung round, and the man's rough laugh followed her.

"Oh, you needn't be afraid. We're not going to arrest you ourselves. We're only going to give information. The police'll get you—don't worry! This is a tight little island, and it's not so simple to hide in it. And now get out of my house."

Mrs de Liane stiffened. Her face was waxen and her lips livid. She turned to Walker.

"You can drive me back to Heronhoe," she said.

Walker shook his head. "Not me. I'm not going to hitch my painter to a sinking ship. Tell the police what you like about me: they won't believe you as long as I'm not with you. The car's outside. There it is and there it's staying, as far as I'm concerned."

"Louise—" Mrs de Liane held out her hand to the woman— "Louise, I've been kind to you ..."

The narrow black eyes grew blank as the Frenchwoman looked at her former mistress.

"Go," she said huskily. "Go before I drive my nails into your face."

From the doorway behind her Whybrow issued a shrill peal of laughter. Mrs Whybrow was amused. The derisive sound, horrible in its cruelty, echoed down the garden path as Mrs de Liane, followed by Ted, sped out to the waiting cars.

Beron was in the road when they appeared, and he came hurrying up.

"What's happened?" he demanded. "Where are they?"

Mrs de Liane threw off his supporting hand.

"Imbeciles!" she said. "There's no time to manage them. They're mad. They're not open to reason. We shall have to make for the coast as you said."

Her hand was already on the door of the car when he came up with her. The bones in her face were standing out, and her little mouth widened into a ragged wound.

It was the first time he had ever seen her without her mask of charm, and he drew back from her. She was very terrible.

"Drive!" she commanded. "Drive! Don't stand there like a fool. Edmund, what's the matter with you? Get in—hurry!"

"Wait...." Beron seized her shoulder. There was a strange expression on his face. His blustering excitement had given way to something much more alarming. There was a new slyness about him, a shamefaced sneakishness. "I remembered that there was a phone booth in the village down the road here, and while you were in the cottage I rang up Jane. The girl did not die. Richard saved her. They've both been arrested."

"You're lying!" The words were uttered in a scream. All pretensions of grace and dignity had fallen from the woman. She looked like some little maniac crone. "You're lying, Edmund! You're lying!"

"I'm not—it's true. Jane was at her wits' end. I didn't tell her where I was."

"Richard saved the girl! ... What a fool, what a fool I was to leave him! Oh, why couldn't they have died? Why couldn't they both have been burned until they were unrecognizable? It's not true, I tell you! It's not true!"

The man pushed her away from him.

"You've gone to pieces," he said contemptuously. "You're a fool. You won't face the truth. You've got us into this mess and you can't get us out of it, and so you're screaming. Look here, I've been thinking. The police will be after us. They'll have sent the call out to the ports by this time, and it's not going to be so easy to get away. There's only one thing to do."

He hesitated, and she saw what was coming.

"You're not going to leave me?" She was hysterical. "You're not going to leave me, Edmund?"

There was a long silence.

"Well, you got us into this, didn't you? It'd be safer if we split up. They'll be looking for two men and an old woman. Two men might get by. We've got a little money; you haven't any. I'll give you a fiver—it's all I've got to spare. You take your car, and Ted and I will take mine."

The woman had begun to sob, great tearless gulps that were horrible to hear.

"You're cruel," she said. "You're only thinking of yourself. Ted, make him see reason! Make him think of me!"

The old man shook his head. "The time's come, Eva," he said quietly. "You've had it coming to you for a long time now, a very long time. You can't get away from it. We've got to think of ourselves. You've never thought of anyone else in your life. Now no one dare think of you."

He got into Edmund's car. Beron took five pound notes from his wallet and put them into the old woman's hand.

"They'll let you down lightly," he said brutally, "because you're old and because you're a woman. It would go more hardly with us."

She put out her hand, but he was in the car before she could seize him. The engine started with a flurry, and with a crash of gears the car swerved round the Daimler and off down the muddy road.

The old woman screamed after them:

"Edmund! Ted! Edmund!"

But the vehicle did not slow down. Rather it gathered pace. In a moment it had reached the end of the lane and had swung out of sight round the corner.

Eva de Liane looked at the money and suddenly laughed.

"Five pounds!" she said. *"Five!* I was after a million. ..."

She threw the money from her, letting it fall in the mud at the side of the road. Then, picking her way with a return of her old grace, she went down to the great black car and climbed in.

The engine started at a touch, and the car glided off down the road at a sedate and dignified pace.

2 7

THE END OF THE DAY

I really think it's in my client's interest that I should accompany you, Inspector, don't you?"

Little Mr Latcher, pacing up and down in the deserted commercial room of the Blue Boar at Evewick, spoke anxiously, and the inspector, who was dozing in a chair before the fire, awoke with a start.

He nodded drowsily at his companion and would have passed into slumber again, for his day had been a heavy one, had not the little solicitor persisted in questioning him.

"I am most anxious for an arrest. I don't want them to get away. It's a disgraceful swindle, you see. It isn't often a firm of our standing is imposed upon in this way. And the other young lady, Miss Coleridge, seems to have been treated in a most extraordinary manner. I think that rapscallion husband of hers should come in for a lot of trouble, but my client doesn't want to prosecute there, nor does the young wife, so I suppose he'll get off scot free."

He paused and coughed.

"Not very satisfactory. ... Still, we must get the others. We really must get the others, Inspector."

The policeman yawned. "We'll get them, sir. Don't worry. We've thrown out a net that would catch a sardine. They'll stick together, I think. I can't understand why they haven't been brought in now."

A police constable put his head round the door and murmured the magic word "telephone."

Instantly all trace of slumber left the inspector, and he was out of the room in a moment. Mr Latcher waited impatiently, nobly resisting the temptation to go out into the hall and listen.

He was rewarded by the police officer's return. Inspector Evers was excited.

"We've got the two men," he said. "Picked up trying to get a passage on a sailing boat at Yarmouth."

"Splendid. But what about the woman? She's the ringleader."

"No sign of her yet. But don't worry. We'll get her." The inspector was confident. "These two had the Buick, so she must be in the Daimler. We know from that report from Deadman's End that she was in that part of the country this morning. That was a damnable business, that child abduction. She deserves all that's coming to her for that alone. We'll get her, sir. Don't worry."

The words were scarcely out of his mouth before the door again opened and a police scout hurried into the room.

"There wasn't a phone in the village, sir, so I thought it was quicker to come here. We've got word of the wanted car. A black Daimler bearing the advertised number was seen by an A. A. scout on the main road outside Fairleigh five miles away— less than twenty minutes ago. The scout in the village here hasn't seen it. So that means it's probably on the main road. It was going very slowly, the first scout reported, a woman driving."

"Got her!" The inspector was jubilant. "Come, Mr Latcher. If you want to be in at the—er—death now's your opportunity. My car's outside. We'll go down ourselves."

Five minutes later Mr Latcher was enjoying the unusual and exciting experience of taking part in a police hunt. He sat beside the inspector at the back of a car which was driven by a uniformed member of the Mobile Police, with a plain-clothes officer at his side. Two scouts on motorcycles served as outriders.

It was four o'clock in the afternoon and nearly dark, and the headlights streamed out like searchlights over the dark countryside.

They stopped just outside the village to receive news from an A. A. man that the wanted car had been seen less than two miles away. It was gathering speed, the report said. The driver seemed to be aware that she was observed.

"Fine." The inspector leant back as the car shot on. "I don't think there's a single turn between here and Black-bridge. She'll run right into us."

The car sped on through the dusk, and Mr Latcher caught his breath. In his mind's eye he could see the old woman whom he had known for so many years sitting at the wheel of her great car. It seemed incredible that she should have done the things of which he now knew her to be guilty.

He was still lost in his thoughts when an exclamation from the man at his side brought him back to the present with a jerk.

"There! There she is. Must be half a mile away. We'll pull up across the bridge, Jenkinson. Keep right across it and stop any car that comes."

The man at the wheel saluted, and a few minutes later the heavy police car was drawn up across the top of a little hump-backed bridge which gave the village half a mile farther on its name. It was a high bridge over a swiftly moving stream, and Mr Latcher shivered as he caught a glimpse of the oily water which looked so cold and dark in the glare of the headlights.

Now the beam of the other headlights, which had been just a

glow in the sky, took shape, and he saw the Daimler winding through the trees towards them.

The police car was a blaze of light: no one could miss such a barrier. Mr Latcher was conscious that he and the police must be vivid and recognizable to that other driver.

On came the Daimler, keeping a straight course, gathering speed all the time.

The police driver sounded his horn, and the tremendous racket seemed to wake the whole countryside to life.

The other car came nearer and nearer. Now it was almost upon them. Latcher caught a glimpse of a little white figure behind the steering wheel.

"My God, she's going to ram us! Jump, sir! Jump!"

Mr Latcher heard the startled words but was too fascinated to move, and it was only the inspector's grip on his arm which galvanized him to action.

"Stop! Stop! For God's sake stop!" he heard his own voice screaming in the darkness.

The car was upon them, at the very foot of the bridge. The screech of brakes did not come. Instead there was a breathless, sickening moment, an instant, paralyzingly clear, in which the whole world seemed to have gone into slow motion.

Then there was a crash and an explosion. The lights on the police car went out, and a piece of flying wing swept off the little solicitor's hat and sent him staggering back into the inspector's arms.

He saw the great nose of the Daimler silhouetted against the sky as the enormous car surmounted the parapet. For a moment it seemed to hang there and then, with a roar, toppled over into the oily waters of the river.

There was a scream. Mr Latcher did not realize that the sound had come from his own throat. A little later he was standing by the inspector, peering over the bridge, while a swarm of men with torches bore down upon the horrible, twisted thing in the fast-moving stream.

The inspector pulled out his own torch, and its thin beam pierced down through the wreckage to something white which lay back across the cushions of the mangled car. Mr Latcher caught sight of a face. The eyes were closed, the lips drawn down. Then the darkness covered it.

The inspector whistled under his breath.

"My God, what a woman!" he said in a shaken voice. "She meant to kill us all—every man jack of us!"

Mr Latcher, deeply moved, did not reply.

28

TOGETHER

If I'm a hit—and I expect I shall be, because with all Elmer's money and my talent I ought to be a riot—you'll both have to come over and see me act."

Marie-Elizabeth stood on the quay at Folkestone and took Mary's hands in her own.

"I think Paris is the place to make a hit in. They know how to dress in Paris. I've never seen such clothes in all my life as Elmer and I found when we stopped in on our honeymoon. I'm going to be a sensation, aren't I, Elmer?"

The little fat man in the magnificent coat beamed affectionately upon his wife.

"Sure," he said, and Mary smiled. If the millionaire had any other word in his vocabulary she had never heard him use it. Not that it mattered. As Marie-Elizabeth said herself, she did enough talking for them both.

It was a different Mary from the terrified girl who had been brought fainting to the police station at Heronhoe less than a month before. The colour had returned to her cheeks and the sparkle to her eyes. She was almost as full of vitality as the

Australian girl, and there was a happiness in her face which had never been there before.

Richard stood by her side. He was very quiet. There were still deep lines on his face, but much of his jauntiness had returned, and there was a new maturity which had brought him dignity as well as calm. It had been a month of change. Ted de Liane had come up for trial and received a comparatively light sentence, but Beron had not fared so well. His conviction on several charges had brought him seven years penal servitude, which sentence he had already begun to serve.

Marie-Elizabeth was still talking.

"Get the place in good order for us and ring me up if you want anything. It's much easier to get a number in Paris than to call up your next-door neighbour at home. It's a funny little way the telephone service has over there."

Mary looked up at her, and her eyes were dangerously shiny.

"I can't tell you how incredibly grateful I am," she began awkwardly. "I want to thank you for everything you've done for us, but I can't begin."

"I should hope not," said Marie-Elizabeth hastily. "I've got a boat to catch and so has Elmer. You don't seem to realize the miracle has happened. We're rich. Oh, by the way, while I think of it, I've told Latcher he must look after Louise and that kid. He's a dear old boy and very just, but frightfully mean. I'm afraid all lawyers are. I want you to keep an eye on him. Louise got a little cottage at Snaresbrook and an old woman to give her a hand with the child while he's still ill. Go down and see her sometimes and see that everything's okay."

"I will," Mary promised. "Marie-Elizabeth, you're the right person to have money."

The big red-haired girl laughed. "Of course I am! That's what I keep telling Elmer, don't I, sweetheart?"

Her husband opened his mouth, but it was his wife who took the word out of it.

"Sure," she said, and dropped a kiss upon his cheek. "Come on, my pet. You may be a millionaire, but the British navy doesn't wait for anyone—or don't the Channel steamers belong to the navy? … I never know. Perhaps it's the post office. Come on. Good-bye and good luck."

Mary and Richard stood together and waved until the boat slipped away from her moorings and ploughed through the dancing blue waters.

Neither of them spoke for a long time. Then Mary took a deep breath.

"She's wonderful," she said. "She's the sort of person who makes things happen. She was like that from the very beginning. Do you know, I'm sure she's only bought this place down in Somerset because she wanted to give us the job of looking after it. Do you think you'll like managing an estate, my darling?"

The man closed his eyes.

"I can't believe it," he said. "It's the life I love, the life I've always loved. And there's our own home there, too. I'm going to make it up to you, Mary. I'm going to make it all up to you somehow."

"Make it up to me?" She looked at him in surprise. "Make what up? I found you, didn't I?"

He laughed. "You're unreasonable, Angel. In a few years time you'll believe that you married me when I was helpless and couldn't defend myself."

Mary slipped her hand into his. "Anyway, you didn't struggle much," she said.

The man's grip tightened over hers.

"I'm going to kiss you," he said. "Do you mind if I kiss you here?"

Mary looked about her. The place was thronged with people. She laughed and dimpled.

"I don't see why not," she said.

"Angel," said Richard de Lisle.

ABOUT THE AUTHOR

Margery Allingham, born in 1904 to Emily and Herbert Allingham, was an esteemed English novelist, author, and editor of *Christian Globe* and the *New London Journal*. Considered one of the four "Queens of Crime" from the golden age of detective fiction, Allingham began writing stories and plays at a young age and published her first novel, *Blackkerchief Dick*, at nineteen. She later studied drama and speech training at Regent Street Polytechnic in London. Allingham is best known for her character Albert Campion, a sleuth first introduced in *The Crime of Black Dudley*. Campion was featured in seventeen subsequent novels, and even more short stories. Allingham continued to write until her death on June 30, 1966.

MARGERY ALLINGHAM

FROM OPEN ROAD MEDIA

OPEN ROAD
INTEGRATED MEDIA

Find a full list of our authors and
titles at www.openroadmedia.com

FOLLOW US
@OpenRoadMedia